HEMINGWAY'S NOTEBOOK

HEMINGWAY'S NOTEBOOK

BILL GRANGER

CROWN PUBLISHERS, INC.
NEW YORK

For the other women of November—

Maureen Baron, Carole Baron,

Meredith Bernstein, and Barbara Grossman.

Grateful acknowledgment is made for the use of the following:
Excerpts from *A Moveable Feast*. Copyright © 1964 Mary Hemingway.
Reprinted with the permission of Charles Scribner's Sons.

*This is a work of fiction. The characters, incidents, places and dialogues
are products of the author's imagination and are not to be construed as
real. Where the names of actual persons, living or dead, are used, the
situations, occurrences, statements and dialogues concerning those persons
are entirely fictional and the author does not purport that such situations,
occurrences or dialogues occurred.*

Published by Crown Publishers, Inc.,
225 Park Avenue South, New York, New York 10003
and simultaneously in Canada
by General Publishing Company Limited
Manufactured in the United States of America
CROWN is a trademark of Crown Publishers, Inc.
Library of Congress Cataloging in Publication Data
Granger, Bill.
Hemingway's notebook.
I. Title
PS3557.R256H46 1986   813'.54   85-13265
ISBN 0-517-55937-4
Book design by Jane Treuhaft
10 9 8 7 6 5 4 3 2 1
First Edition

NOTE

Ernest Hemingway, tired of life at Key West where friends of his second wife kept him from his work, retreated to Cuba in 1939. In April that year, at the insistence of a friend named Martha Gellhorn, he rented a house at Finca Vigia, which is in the hills of San Francisco de Paula south of Havana. He eventually bought the property and it was his principal residence until he killed himself in Idaho in July 1961. His house is preserved today as a museum by the government of Fidel Castro.

Castro apologists insist that Ernest Hemingway was a longtime "friend of the revolution." This is based on his affinity for the down-and-out waterfront characters he wrote about, drank with, and sailed with. However, Hemingway was a closet patrician and his associations with gangsters and revolutionaries, simple fishermen and smugglers, however genuine at the time, was a form of "slumming" for the doctor's son from Oak Park, Illinois. A number of the late writer's friends have said Hemingway's obvious distate for Batista in the days before the Cuban revolution was matched only by his later distaste for Castro's people.

Despite his sympathy for the Loyalist cause in the Spanish civil war, Hemingway was a ferocious anticommunist.

Hemingway killed himself three months after the Bay of

Pigs fiasco, in which Cuban troops, financed and directed by the Central Intelligence Agency, attempted an armed counterrevolt against the fledgling Castro government. It was proven later that Castro's intelligence service was superior to the Americans' in that time and place.

After the Bay of Pigs, American intelligence used members of organized crime to attempt the assassination of Castro. One scheme involved poisoning his cigars. The motives of the crime syndicate were obvious: they had flourished in Batista's Cuba with its prostitution, casinos, and drug trade. To this day, the American crime syndicate is deeply involved in gambling operations in the Caribbean, as well as in the drug trade.

Posterity shall know as little of me as I shall know of posterity.

WILLIAM S. GILBERT

Do not worry. You have always written before and you will write now. All you have to do is write one true sentence. Write the truest sentence you know.

ERNEST HEMINGWAY,
A Moveable Feast

A MAN UNDER CONTRACT

The president of the United States, his face shining under the television lights, gripped the lectern and turned in a characteristic way toward the reporter on the panel, as though he had not heard the question. After a pause and a duck of his head, he began a long and rambling discourse.

Frank Collier was watching the president's image on the screen in the corner of his darkened office in Langley, Virginia. "Jesus." He exhaled the word. "Jesus," he said again as though trying to form a prayer. "What the hell is he doing, talking about that? Does he know what he's doing?"

The darkness did not answer. The television carried the condensed sound of the president as he explained in a rambling unpunctuated way about the Central Intelligence Agency in Latin America, in the Caribbean, about the existence of a manual for guerrilla fighters, about freedom fighters, and about the fact that the CIA had hired a writer for the guerrilla manual who may have overstepped his authority. . . .

"Does he know what he's saying? He should listen to what he's saying!" Frank Collier again addressed the darkness. His voice was rising.

The president was speaking of a manual whose existence had become the talk of the Washington press corps in the long, tedious week before the second presidential debate of the campaign. There had been little else to attract attention because the campaign, despite the presence of a woman in the second position on the Democratic ticket, was not remarkable.

The manual was a simplistic guide with cartoon illustrations distributed among anti-Sandinista guerrilla rebels in Nicaragua. It had allegedly been written by the CIA—and now the president was dropping the *allegedly*. The manual urged the "elimination" of people in the Sandinista government in the troubled country on the western rim of the Caribbean Sea.

The president rambled on, explaining that the word *elimination* did not necessarily mean *killing*.

Frank Collier squirmed in the heavy oak chair and picked up the green telephone receiver in the darkness. It triggered a ring at the other end of the line. "Why the hell is he explaining this—why is he doing this?" Frank Collier shouted into the telephone.

"Damage control," the voice at the end of the line said with a measure of calm. "We'll call D.C., get some PIO on this—"

"This is network television, this is the fucking presidential debate—"

"Take it easy, Frank," said the voice.

Outside Collier's second floor corner office in CIA headquarters, the summer night crackled with the sounds of insects and the cries of owls hunting in the moonlight. Beyond the leafy suburbs, beyond the Beltway, the lights of Washington winked orange and villainous.

"I meant to say—" corrected the president suddenly, backing away from the wreckage of words spilled in the past forty-five seconds, while the Democratic candidate blinked at him, while the panel of journalists pretended to listen, while Frank Collier tapped his fingers nervously on the green blotter on his desk, and suddenly pushed his swivel chair away from the desk and away from the television screen in the corner.

2

"He 'meant to say,'" Frank Collier shouted into the green telephone receiver.

"The Old Man can take care of him," said the voice at the end of the line.

"He's thirty points up in the polls, he'd be reelected if he was embalmed, what the hell is he telling them all this for?" said Frank Collier.

"We have ordered an investigation," the president said again.

"Oh, God," said Frank Collier. "Listen to him."

"Frank, I want you to relax, try to take it easy—"

"I put that goddamned rummy on the manual in the first place. You know what he knows? I mean, you know how much he knows about everything? Not just Nicaragua, not just Cuba, but everything?"

"Frank, I don't want to know all that—"

"Son-of-a-bitch has been sitting in the Caribe since Batista, now the president is going to investigate him? Son-of-a-bitch, I only used him on the little job because he could write, and you can't find writers anymore—"

"He's vetted, Frank, he's very clear, he's all right—"

"Nobody," said Frank Collier, his voice rising, "nobody is all right when they get their back to the wall and their tit caught in the wringer." The unexpected metaphors made a momentary silence in the room. Even the television president paused, as though puzzling out the words.

"So take care of him. He's been free-lance for a while, hasn't he?"

"I can't." Pause. "Not right away. Two weeks ago, R Section sent a man down to talk to him. Try to get a line on him. Fucking R Section fucking in our business."

"I didn't know that, Frank," said the voice at the other end of the line, putting distance between them.

"Agent named Cohn. Our free lancer is playing both of us, it seems. I don't have to tell you—"

"Don't tell me, Frank," said the voice with meaning.

3

"And we're going to find those responsible," said the president.

Frank Collier felt physically sick then. "Put a gag in his mouth, please, somebody."

"Take it easy, Frank," said the voice on the line. "Nothing will happen. The Old Man will talk to him. Wait and see. Nothing is going to happen."

"You're not in the line of fire on this," Frank Collier said. He felt very alone in the dark office on the second floor of the Central Intelligence Agency complex in a Virginia suburb of Washington, D.C. He held the receiver tightly.

"No," agreed the voice.

"Things are going to happen. On St. Michel. Very soon. The writer is on St. Michel."

"I don't want to know—"

"On fucking St. Michel. I use a guy once three years ago and he disappears and surfaces on St. Michel and I got an agent from R Section down there just when we are supposed to make things pop. You got to believe in Fate after a while, you know that?"

"It'll look better in the morning, Frank." A soothing voice. "I've been there before, babysitting an operation. But this is the Caribbean we're talking about, the whole basin from Venezuela up to Key West. Nobody cares, Frank. Take my word for it. We are not talking about nuclear with the Big Red Machine, we are talking about the Caribbean, Frank. Niggers and spics and white sand beaches. Believe me, nobody thinks a thing about the Caribe until it's cold in New York in January."

"An operation. My operation," Frank said, saying too much again. He stared at the screen. The president was finished. The camera was pointed at the Democrat. Frank Collier felt drawn and cold.

"Wait and see," said the soothing voice. "Nothing is going to happen."

4

COLONEL READY

Lausanne was caught in a bright September stillness on the edge of autumn, lingering a moment with the last of summer. The city sprawled on the hillside like a tired whore. It was cool in the shade, warm in the sun. The waters of Lac Leman below the city were still and glistening and there were boats sailing on childlike puffs of breeze.

Devereaux saw the other man from the corner of his eye. He noticed him because the other man moved too quickly. The other man stepped out of the McDonald's across from the train station just as Devereaux passed the entrance.

The other man bumped him, grabbed him.

Devereaux, acting on instinct, bent his knees in that moment and reached up with both hands to grab the other man, expecting a second, heavy blow or the nearly painless slash of a razor-edged knife.

He grasped the sleeve of the other man's dark jacket and pulled his weight back, tripping him in one movement and letting the other man's weight fall on him as he knelt and shifted. In a fraction of a second, Devereaux would lift suddenly and throw the other man over his shoulder.

Except the other man stepped back at the last moment and the weight shifted back and Devereaux was pulled upright. They faced each other, flushed, breathing hard, their hands on each other's sleeves.

Colonel Ready grinned.

Devereaux did not move. He had no expression in his gray eyes. He stared like a cat at an empty window.

"Nearly as fast as you used to be," Colonel Ready said. He smiled. Neither man let go of the other.

"And you're slower," Devereaux said, because Ready expected something to be said.

"We all get old. Besides, this wasn't an ambush in Nam, was it? Just a joke between friends."

"We're not friends," Devereaux said.

Colonel Ready stood still and let the smile fade. He dropped his hands first. His classic red-head's face was freckled which might have made him look absurdly young, even as Devereaux's prematurely gray hair and wintry face made him look older than he was. But Ready's youthful looks were mitigated by the cold cast to his eyes, cold blue to Devereaux's arctic gray. And there was a broad, white scar that ran from the right corner of his mouth to the disfigured remains of his right ear.

"Not friends then," Ready said in a metallic voice. "Old comrades in arms."

Devereaux dropped his hands.

The two men stood apart from each other in front of the McDonald's. It was noon and shoppers were crowding into the metro funicular. The trains ran down the long hill to Ouchy at the foot of Lausanne and the shore of Lac Leman. Other trains rose several hundred feet to the shopping district above. A woman in a black dress and orange sweater brushed between the two men, muttering in annoyed French, and pushed her way into the line at the ticket booth for the metro.

"Are you lost?" Devereaux said.

Ready grinned. "Never lost within eyeshot of the Golden Arches. A little bit of home, makes you nostalgic, doesn't it?" He paused, still grinning. "I just had me a burger now, waiting for you. I know it sounds odd. But I miss burgers. Where I am now, I mean."

"Where you are now is here," Devereaux said, waiting.

"Not the same as home, is it?"

Devereaux said nothing.

"I had a hard time finding you."

"Why did you look for me?"

"I need you, Devereaux. That's obvious isn't it?"

Devereaux said nothing.

"Thought I'd lost you for good. I mean, everyone thinks you're dead, did you know that? At Langley, even."

Devereaux waited with gray calm.

"*I* knew you had survived," Ready said, grinning again.

Devereaux knew the smile. It was never sincere. It worked very well for Colonel Ready.

Once, in the jungle, a file of Cong had surprised Ready while he squatted in the bushes, defecating. Ready had simply grinned at them. The Cong were surprised. For a moment, they had stared at the grinning red monkey of an American with his trousers bunched around his boots, his white behind hanging out of the fatigues. It was a moment of comic surprise in a farce. The hesitation lasted as long as a double take. It was one beat too long for the Cong. Ready rose in that moment and began to spray the six guerrillas with exploding rounds from his contraband Uzi submachine gun. As someone at G2 noted later, the fantastic part of the encounter was that after the shooting, Colonel Ready squatted down again in the blood-splattered bushes and finished his business.

"If everyone thinks I'm dead, perhaps you shouldn't have come looking to find me alive," Devereaux said.

"I have faith, Devereaux. I can move mountains. I knew you survived the business in Zurich when I heard the details. 'Killed in a hotel room.' Except your body was carelessly identified, don't you think? The only people who'd believe that crap are the kind of chumps you find at Langley. Or maybe on Dzhersinski Square."

"And you shared your faith?"

"No, Devereaux. Faith is a selfish thing with me. I like to be alone, you know that. I thought it was as simple as *cherchez la femme*—'look for the woman.' It's not your girl's fault, Devereaux, I wouldn't want you to be angry with her. But I'm very good at what I do, you know that."

7

"You went to so much trouble," Devereaux said. His voice was cold and somber.

"Yes. It was a lot of trouble. A year ago, right after you died in Zurich, she went to live in Spiez. Why did she do that? She had a job in Washington. I bet she wasn't ranging too far from someone. Switzerland is a nice little place to be dead in."

"I'm not in the old game," Devereaux said, in order to end the conversation that showed no sign of ending.

"Hell, man." Smile. "I know that." Pause. "You're dead, after all." Ready smiled with the sincerity of a dentist.

Devereaux had studied him in those moments. His clothes were too light, even for the wispy warmth of early September in the Swiss Alps. His shirt and trousers were tropical weight khakis with a military cut and Ready had attempted to disguise them with a dark civilian sports coat that left too much room in the gut. Colonel Ready was cut lean, as he had been in the long ago days when he shifted between the Defense Intelligence Agency and Langley in Vietnam. He had been liaison to R Section and Devereaux there. Devereaux had never trusted him. He had been a spy on the Section and on Devereaux. It had been a game between them. They had been good players because both had survived—the game and the war around them.

"Aren't you curious?" Ready said.

"No."

Devereaux turned then and started again for the zebra crossing at the corner. He had been heading for the red stone train station when Ready grabbed him. The train from Geneva was due in twenty minutes. He had told her he would meet her.

"Damn it," said Ready after him. "I'd be curious at least."

"I told you," Devereaux said. He stopped and turned. "I'm not in the old game." His voice was just above a whisper.

"You owe me, Devereaux. You have owed me for a long time." And this time, there was no smile and the voice was so

8

quiet that it cut through the din of traffic along the Avenue.

"Both of you are in it now. I mean, I know you're not dead, don't I?"

"She's not part of this, Ready."

"I'm afraid that can't be avoided. I wouldn't wait for the train from Geneva. She might not be on it."

And then the cold filled Devereaux the way it did in the old days, in the Section. The cold found every empty place in him and settled into him until it became a comfort to him. Rita Macklin would not be on the train from Geneva.

Ready shrugged as though he might apologize. "I need leverage on you, Devereaux. It's nothing to do with her but it has to be her, you understand that. You know how it is."

"Where is she?"

"Let's just say she's not on the train from Geneva. Let's leave it at that for the moment and then we can talk about her and about other things," Ready said.

"Where is she?"

"In a little while, Devereaux," Ready said. "You know how it is. Everything in time."

And Devereaux did not speak. He could not answer that. He knew how it was. How it always had been in the old game.

3

THE OUCHY FERRY

Devereaux and Colonel Ready walked down a narrow cul de sac off the Rue St. Martin. They were in the old quarter of Lausanne, in a nest of streets that straggled down the hill from the cathedral and from the university building. They came to a five-story building of gray stucco with small balconies and tall, mournful windows, shuttered against September though the day was still calm and warm. In the summer there were concerts under the trees in the courtyard of the cathedral and the students from the university sold bratwurst and thick bread and plastic cups of beer. Children had played under the trees. Rita Macklin and Devereaux would listen to the music from their balcony window in the gray building all during that beautiful, lingering summer.

Devereaux turned the key in the lock of his apartment door and opened it. Ready said Rita would not be there and he knew she would not be there but still he expected her when he opened the door. He had bought her flowers and they stood in a bowl on the table near the French windows.

Ready had it all figured out. He'd given Devereaux orders:

"We're going to catch the two o'clock ferry to the French side. You'll need your passport."

Devereaux passed through the rooms of the small apartment. He opened the dresser drawer and took out his blue American passport. She was everywhere. He could hear her voice in the silent rooms.

He went into the bathroom, closed the door, and flushed the toilet. While the water ran out of the bowl, he lifted the lid from the water tank and removed a pistol from a holster that was glued to the underside of the lid. The pistol was black with a brown grip and was six inches long from front sight to firing chamber. It was a version of the Colt Python .357 Magnum which Devereaux had acquired years ago in R Section. He had not carried it all summer. But he had decided to keep the gun when he had been reported killed.

Devereaux spun the barrel slowly. The bullets were seated in their cylinders. He carried a revolver instead of an automatic because an automatic could always jam. Once a week, when she was not there, Devereaux would break down the parts of the pistol and rub the dark metal with oil and the oil would leave a sweet smell in the room. Rita never saw him clean the pistol or reseat the bullets in the revolving chamber because he did not want to remind her of the old life or what he had been. There was only the smell of oil that lingered after he had put the pistol away. She never mentioned it.

10

Devereaux put the pistol on a clip in his belt. They were going to take the ferry across Lac Leman to the town of Evian on the French shore. It was a quiet old spa town where old people came to cure themselves of age.

Devereaux would kill Colonel Ready in Evian after he found out about Rita Macklin and where she was. It was possible that Ready had already killed her. But then she would not be "leverage" for him anymore.

Devereaux would see that Rita was safe and then he would agree to whatever Colonel Ready wanted him to do. Then he would kill Ready near the Evian train station. It was not used much because summer was over and because most of the tourists who went to Evian drove cars or took the ferry across the lake from Lausanne.

There were two hotels on the square across from the train station but they were always empty at this time of year. There was a bar in one hotel but the owner was deaf. Besides, Devereaux would get very close to Ready and Ready would know what it meant. Ready would reach for his pistol and Devereaux would shoot him. It didn't matter very much where the bullets hit because they had exploding caps and the bullets blew apart when they hit their target.

Devereaux came out of the bathroom, turned off the light, and checked the street through the window. "I wasn't followed down here," Ready said.

Devereaux said nothing.

"They followed me as far as the airport at Zurich. I think they were from Langley. They're always watching me."

"You don't work for Langley anymore."

"In a sense, that's true," Ready said.

"Where is she?"

"We'll go down the metro to Ouchy and catch the two o'clock ferry. Don't worry, Devereaux."

■ ■ ■

The ferry had begun service on Lac Leman in 1915. It was wooden and the sidewheels churned the cold waters as the ship pulled away from the dock at Ouchy beneath the sprawl

11

of Lausanne. The paddles bit into the smooth water and the steam engine amidships chugged and vibrated as the boat struck for open water.

Devereaux and Ready stood on the empty open deck on the first-class level: no one bought first-class tickets for the thirty-minute crossing. Devereaux's face was chapped by the cold wind formed as the boat plowed into the long lake that threaded through the mountains. The French side was seven miles across from Lausanne.

"She's over there. Waiting. She's safe enough. I don't mean her any harm. Or you."

Devereaux stared at the sea and at the fog trailing down at the surface of the water. Fourteen months ago he had died in service in Zurich. He had been awarded a posthumous medal for valor. His 201 file in R Section had been consigned to the "Inactive Library." Three people inside R Section knew he was not dead. And now Colonel Ready knew it as well and Devereaux could not understand why he wanted to open the secret. Except for once, he had not crossed Ready's path since Vietnam, seventeen years ago.

Except for the favor he had asked six years ago. For Rita.

Devereaux winced. He had made himself vulnerable to Ready then.

"I remembered the girl, you know," Ready said at that moment, as though all of Devereaux's thoughts were naked to him. "From when I was still at DIA, when I still had access clearance. You wanted to know about Rita Macklin's brother, the missionary, whether he had been clean in Laos. And I told you. A little favor must have meant a lot to you."

Devereaux stared at Ready. "You shouldn't have looked for me."

"Sleeping dogs and dead agents, then? Maybe. But I cleared up the matter for you six years ago and for your girl, and I think I can ask you for a little favor."

"Ask me. You can't blackmail me with her. You know me better than that."

"I knew you. But you've changed, Devereaux." The blue

12

eyes were hard. "You'd have cut your grandmother if she was in the way, but you've changed. It's made you softer, Devereaux, not that I blame you. She's a good-looking girl. A lot younger than you are."

Devereaux would shoot Ready at the train station in Evian. He would shoot him only once, in the belly, and back away from him while Ready fell, his belly spilled open like a broken pumpkin.

"You counted on your own survival and now I'm betting that isn't as important as *her* survival. That's what I'm betting on."

"Nobody changes as much as you make out," Devereaux said.

"Your girl was in Paris and she was coming home on the TGV train to Geneva, changing to the local up to Lausanne. Instead, she got re-routed at Geneva. We waited there for her and I had my aide take to her to Evian. I wanted to get you used to the idea before you saw her. Used to the idea that I had something to talk to you about."

"Who do you work for, Ready?"

"Myself, you might say. Like you. Do you know why I knew it had to be the girl? I mean, when I went looking for you?" He smiled. "You let yourself open to me six years ago when you wanted to find out if her missionary brother was an agent. You never leave yourself open. It had to be the woman, I thought at the time. I put that away in my little file." He tapped his head with his forefinger. "Your Achilles heel, you might say."

Six years ago, he had met Rita Macklin. She had been a journalist. They both wanted the secret of an old priest who had come out of Laos after twenty years. She had wanted to clear her dead brother's name. She was closer to the secret than he, so Devereaux had used her, made love to her, conspired against her, all to get the secret from the old priest. But then he had fallen in love with Rita.

And because of that love he had exposed himself to

13

Ready. Had he left other clues on his trail for others who might want to find him alive?

Devereaux frowned. The ferry was closing on the French shore and the sleepy buildings of Evian shining in the afternoon light. It was chilly on the deck. He shivered and felt the weight of the pistol at his belt. And he saw Ready shivered as well.

"You must work in a warm place," Devereaux said softly.

"My khakis? Had regular clothes I picked up in New York, but I wore the khakis on the plane and the fucking airline lost the bag. Those two from Langley, or maybe DIA, were on my tail so I said to hell with it. Gave them the slip at Zurich. Probably a couple of stiffs from surveillance division. They've been following me around ever since I resigned from Langley six years ago. Went on my own. They think I'm a soldier of fortune."

"Are you?"

"Maybe," said Ready.

"In a warm climate," Devereaux said.

"Hell is warm," Ready said.

"Is it hell, Ready?"

"Yes. But that's not to say it doesn't have its attractions. Like this."

"What is it?"

"A gift for you, for listening to me so patiently. A bankbook. Two hundred thousand Swiss francs on deposit now to you at Credit Suisse. Is that your bank?"

"Don't you know all about me?"

"No. Not all. I told you I was in a hurry. I just remembered the girl and she wasn't so hard to find. Take the account."

Devereaux slipped the book into the pocket of his coat and felt the slight bulge of the pistol.

He could kill Ready now except how would he get off the boat? And what if Rita were not on the Evian side waiting for them?

"I've got your attention? Nothing like the ring of shekels to improve a person's hearing."

"I'll always take the money."

"A good attitude. Never let conscience interfere with good judgment. We're the same, you and I."

"Who else knows about me?"

Ready paused. He smiled. He said, "A nigger named Celezon. My aide, you might say."

The ferry sounded its horn then and began a slow turn into the water, creating a white arc of wake as it slid toward the dock of Evian. The Swiss and French flags on the white ferry snapped in the unexpected breeze.

"See her? She's okay," Ready said.

Devereaux saw Rita staring at the ferry, unable to see him on the deck. Her red hair was loose on her shoulders. She hunched against the wind inside her navy-blue coat.

Behind her was a black man in a dark raincoat.

"Celezon knows," Devereaux said in a leaden voice. "And Ready knows. And the two men who followed you to Zurich."

"No. Don't worry about them. I've been to Zurich before. They always follow me. They always send someone. I'm a soldier of fortune. That's what they think. And I put my fortune in accounts in Zurich, like all good tax evaders."

So the secret was contained. Two of them. He would have to get rid of two of them now.

The ferry churned in the shallow waters as it edged toward the concrete dock of the Compagnie Generale de Navigation. Two dockhands in blue uniforms shoved across a wooden gangplank and tied the lines. The ferry ceased shuddering in the water. The passengers crowded around the plank and started down to the dock. Devereaux and Ready followed them from the deck.

A long time ago, during World War I, spies had used this familiar crossing from neutral Switzerland to wartime France to pass secrets and create lies. It was very different now. A thin French customs inspector in a blue uniform glanced at Devereaux's passport and nodded him through. Colonel Ready followed.

Rita Macklin stood apart from Celezon but Devereaux saw that the black man held her right arm. She looked tired and pale. Her eyes were burning green. Then she saw Devereaux and she tried to shrug herself out of Celezon's grip but the grinning black man held her tightly with one hand.

"She is delivered, *mon colonel*," said Celezon to Ready, who came up from behind Devereaux to stand next to him.

Ready smiled at her. "You see, Miss Macklin? I always fulfill my promises. He's safe and sound and you're safe and sound." Then he addressed Celezon, "She's not a package, you black bastard—you can let go of her arm." Celezon almost frowned but stopped himself. He let go of Rita Macklin's arm.

"What was this about?" Rita asked Devereaux.

"His name is Colonel Ready," Devereaux said in his flat, distant voice. "He met me at the train station. I was coming to meet you. He said you were going to be here. I had to come."

"He told me you were here," she said.

"Lies, Miss Macklin, but only little lies," Ready said.

Devereaux considered the problem. The black would be armed, Ready would be armed. He would get rid of Rita and he would go with the two of them. They would expect him to be armed as well. Ready knew his tricks but Celezon did not. Celezon was big; it might be a matter of putting him between Ready and Devereaux's drawn pistol.

Rita Macklin touched Devereaux's sleeve. She saw the cold, dead look in his gray eyes, the old look, the look that had gone away.

"You fucking bastard," she said to Colonel Ready.

"She called me a fucking bastard many times," said Celezon.

"That's what we are, Celezon," Ready said, smiling at Rita. The white scar made the smile seem hideous and macabre, as though a corpse grinned at her.

"What does he want?"

"I don't know," Devereaux said.

16

"I want to talk to both of you, just talk to you," Ready said. "Celezon, why don't you go to the shops and buy some souvenirs for your whores in St. Michel?"

Celezon shivered. It was cold in this climate but they had come here before, and he had dressed warmly in a black coat. He did not understand why people lived in such cold places. Celezon said, "And the whores of Madeleine."

"Yes, both cities," he agreed.

"And they must be souvenirs of quality," continued Celezon. "All of my whores are ladies of the highest quality."

For a moment, the two men smiled at each other, sharing a secret. Then Celezon made a mocking salute that was part French Army, part wave, and slipped away.

■   ■   ■

The three of them sat at a square-top Formica table in a large café across from the lakeshore park. It was nearly empty. Ready ordered an expensive ecossé—Scotch—and Rita ordered Campari and soda. Devereaux sat between them. He did not drink. He waited and stared at Ready all the time.

"I need you for a job. It's a little job. I need both of you."

Rita didn't speak. She had retreated into the same coldness she saw in Devereaux's eyes on the dock.

"You can have me," Devreaux said. "For a little job."

"That's not good enough," Ready said and he sipped his whiskey.

"It will have to be."

"This isn't an English movie, Devereaux. You intend to kill me and kill Celezon as soon as you can separate Rita from us. I understand. I understand the idea and I understand you. But it isn't going to be that way." Ready's smiles and grins were gone; his voice was brittle and edgy.

"How is it going to be?" Quietly.

"That's better." Ready paused. "There is an island in the Caribbean called St. Michel. It is southeast of Haiti and there is not much to recommend it. The French gave it up after the war. There were bauxite mines and copper but they're played out. The people are played out as well. It's not much, but it's home."

"And what are you to St. Michel?"

"I am the chief of the army. Didn't you hear Celezon call me '*mon colonel*'? I have a nice uniform and a nice salary."

"And then there is the money you can steal," said Devereaux.

"Yes. It is amazing how even in a poor country, there is money worth stealing."

"What do you want me to do?"

"Not you, Devereaux. Both of you. I have to have your leverage."

"She isn't involved."

Ready looked at Rita Macklin and he smiled for a moment because the thought of her hatred excited him.

"I never thought he would give up the Section," Ready said to her.

Rita did not speak.

"It was love, wasn't it? He came to me six years ago and he wanted to run a check on your dead brother. To see if he was clean. He didn't trust Hanley in the Section to tell him the truth. He owes me for that. I remembered that, I put it away up here." He tapped his forehead again. "I thought he must have loved you to expose himself like that. It was simple once I figured that out."

"You fucking bastard," she said in a soft voice that might have been a prayer or a secret.

"St. Michel's thirtieth anniversary of independence is next week. Rita Macklin, the free-lance American journalist, will help cover the festivities," said Colonel Ready. "I have the visas, the ticket on the flight to Guadeloupe from Paris, the transfer to St. Michel. I have a reservation for you in our best hotel."

"Nobody is going anywhere," said Devereaux.

"Why don't you have a drink?"

Devereaux said nothing.

"You always drank. I thought you drank too much. But I

18

suppose that's because you're in love now, is that it?" Ready's voice dripped with mockery.

Rita Macklin sat very still. Her face was white. She breathed softly, consciously trying not to make a sound. He knew that she breathed that way when she awoke some nights in the darkness, lying next to him in bed. He would lie silently next to her, sleeping like a cat, his eyes closed and hands open and his defense uncoiled. He had learned to sleep like that next to her over the years.

"What do you want me to do?"

"Find out what side I'm on," said Colonel Ready.

"What side do you want to be on?"

"The side that wins."

"Is there a war?"

"There is always a war in a country like St. Michel. There are guerrillas in the hills because there are always such people. They are led by a man named Manet who is a Communist, I suppose, but it doesn't really matter. And there is the matter of the Langley Company. They want to know who's going to win as well."

"And you're going to tell them?"

"I will tell them if I have to. I want to be on the winning side. But what if Manet has the winning side? What if neither Langley nor Manet can win? Should I stay on my own side?"

"And you want me to go to St. Michel because no one knows me there."

"Yes," said Ready. "I am a little too visible. I need a spy. I need someone I can trust."

"You can't trust me," Devereaux said.

"You're wrong. You underestimate the situation," Ready said, smiling at Rita again.

"Who is for Langley there?"

"I don't know. There is a man there named Harry Francis. He is a comic spy, out of a Gilbert and Sullivan opera. I can't believe in him at all, he is so pathetic. Therefore, he might be very dangerous."

"What was his name in the agency?" Devereaux was

19

called November when he was an active agent. Harry Francis would be called something too, a code name, a clerk-created nickname.

"Hemingway."

"That's odd."

"A joke, I suppose. Harry Francis knew the great man when Harry worked for Langley in Cuba, before the Bay of Pigs. Harry gave Langley some good information but Langley chose to ignore it. Langley cut him loose a few years ago. Harry Francis writes novels. Do you know them? No, I don't think so. He hasn't sold a thing for years. He is a pathetic drunk. I don't trust that at all. I keep thinking that Harry might still be working for Langley."

"Why?"

"Langley cut Howard Hunt away from the Company three times that I know of. He wrote books too, little spy novels. Except I know he never left the Company, even when he was supposed to be working for Nixon and his gang."

"So there's Manet and there's Harry Francis."

"And there are other elements. A good agent can discover them. A good agent with a good cover. And all the while, Rita Macklin will be safe with me in the capital, covering our poor little thirtieth Independence Day celebration for her magazines and newspapers."

"No. Not her, Ready."

"Yes. Her." He looked at her as though she belonged to him. "Her because I told her about her brother, though it was you who asked. Her because I gave you two hundred thousand Swiss francs and it's for both of you. Her because she led me to you."

"Damn you," she said to him but her voice was as dull as night.

"I might kill you instead," Devereaux said. "There's the chance that I could do that."

"It's a possibility. Except that there are papers filed in a certain place. They are about November and where he lives and what he looks like. They would be useful to Langley. I'm surprised Langley was willing to accept your death. The R Section counts on clumsiness from its competitors."

Devereaux waited.

"And the wet contract. From KGB. To kill the agent called November. Canceled fourteen months ago because November was dead."

"If you know all that, you still work for Langley. If you know all that, they know it too," Devereaux said. "Then there's no reason not to kill you."

"I can think. I don't need Langley's computers," Ready said with annoyance. "It *had* to be a contract against you. That's why you 'died' in Zurich. Langley was after you in Ireland nine years ago but that's past. It had to be KGB. Besides, if I worked now for Langley, I wouldn't need you."

He decided then. "You can have me. You don't need her."

"Your word on it?" said Ready, starting to smile again. "Come on, Devereaux. We're agents, not boy scouts."

"Not her," he said and he realized Ready was backing him into a corner.

"It is all written down, about you, about her, all my guesses and my calculations, most of which turned out to be correct. Langley will get the file if I am killed."

"And if you aren't killed?"

"You will get the file."

"There's never an end to blackmail."

"Yes there is. I want one specific job. I want to know what side I am on. Then I never want to see you again, either of you. But first I need to know which side to be on."

"And who can tell me?"

"I don't know. But 'Hemingway' has a notebook and I want it. I know it exists but I don't know how to get it. I tortured him once before but he's tough. I don't think I would get it before I killed him. He drinks too much. If he were in good shape, I could probaby torture him until he couldn't stand the pain. But I can't take the chance."

"What's in the notebook?"

21

"Secrets, I think. I don't know. I've heard about Hemingway's notebook for years."

"What can one old man know?"

"What did the old priest know in Florida that was worth it to you six years ago?"

Ready stared suddenly at Rita and she trembled because he looked insane.

"What would you do with the secrets?" Devereaux said. His voice was without inflection and was very gentle.

Colonel Ready stared at Rita Macklin before he spoke. He felt her hatred shine like warmth on his face. He felt a stirring between his legs. She would not break her stare in return.

"It doesn't matter," Ready said to Devereaux. "You'll do the job for me to get me on the right side. Everyone talks about Harry's notebook. Even Harry. Except he keeps calling himself Hemingway. I think Harry is a little crazy, which you might expect after all those years in the trade. The notebook might be nothing more substantial than the Holy Grail but that doesn't stop everyone from looking for it. The notebook is power because knowledge is power."

"If Harry is on the island, you have all his knowledge now," Devereaux said.

"Harry is an old man and he drinks too much. He can't take too much hurt. If I torture him again he might die out of stubbornness and then he'd be worthless, wouldn't he? I have Harry and no notebook and that's a bad deal and it doesn't mean very much. But if I have a notebook, then I really don't need Harry anymore."

"And you can use it," Devereaux said. "How will you use it?"

"That's my business," Ready said. "You don't need to know that."

"I won't do it," Devereaux said.

Ready looked at him. "Yes. For your own sake. You like to be free of the trade, don't you? I know you, Devereaux. You slipped the traces and slipped both sides and your file is closed. But if it gets opened again with the kind of information I could plant at Langley, the Big Red Machine would have to acknowledge they had made a mistake about you, that you weren't really dead. November is dead and it doesn't matter who November is. The name is used once and never again. You're November dead and I can make November alive and you know I can. So you'll work for me, just a little job. I've tried my best with Harry, but I have a country to run." He smiled. "I can't spend all my time trying to find something that might not even exist."

"And if it doesn't exist?"

"Then you'll have to prove that to me. The burden is on you. It isn't fair, I know that, but it's the way I have to operate."

"Just me."

"No. I want leverage. You could be dangerous in the old days, Devereaux. You're slower now but so am I. And I'll keep Rita near me just in case you want to change the rules of the game in the middle. I won't harm her. In a little while, this will all be over for both of you."

"No," he said.

"What do you say, Rita?" Colonel Ready touched her hand and it was cold. "For his sake. For your sake." He looked at Devereaux. "You put this scam together and you have to see it through. You kill me now and you will be hunted again, believe me."

"What do you want me to do?" Devereaux said and Rita stared at him and did not believe his words.

"I am watched going in and coming out. I'll leave at noon. The next direct flight connects through Paris and Guadeloupe to St. Michel at noon each day. I will be on the plane Wednesday. Miss Macklin will follow on Thursday. And you will follow on Friday."

"No," Devereaux said. "I don't know St. Michel, but there are too many coincidental passages to your . . . island . . . from the same European port. She can follow in two days but not from Paris."

23

"There's a roundabout flight using Frankfurt to Miami—"

"Yes. And in four days, I'll leave from London."

Ready smiled. "You see, you always remember how to cover your trail. Instinct."

"I don't want to leave footprints," Devereaux said in the same soft and uninflected voice.

And Rita had stared at Devereaux as he made the plan with Colonel Ready and her face grew very pale and when she spoke at last, her voice sounded detached: "Kill him, Dev. Just kill him now."

Devereaux looked at her. His eyes were flat, without emotion. Ready looked at him and saw what the look in his eyes meant and felt contempt for Devereaux. He got up from the table and dropped a fat envelope of documents. "Visas," said Colonel Ready. "Press credentials. I expect you in two days, Miss Macklin. I know I won't be disappointed. Will I?"

"No," said Devereaux.

"There will be a reception in the palace. You can meet the president of St. Michel. His name is Claude-Eduard. And his charming sister. Keep away from the president, Rita, especially in dark rooms—he's reputed to have a three-foot cock."

Rita said, "Kill him now." Her voice was dead. "It doesn't matter. We can get away. We did it before. We can get away from him. If you won't kill him, give me the gun, I'll kill him. I know you brought a gun. I'll kill him and I'll run and it'll give you time."

But Devereaux only stared at the red-headed man and felt the impotence of the pistol in his belt.

"Damn you," Rita said. She was crying. "Kill him now."

4

KILLERS

Flaubert's chicken waited at the door of the café for a long moment and then minced inside. With each step, the hen stopped and seemed to stare at Harry Francis.

It was hot and bright. Humidity lingered on the walls of this café on the main road four miles south of the capital of St. Michel. It was the middle of the afternoon and nothing was moving on the road and Flaubert had gone back into his living quarters at the rear of the café.

Harry Francis had warned Flaubert many times about letting the chicken roam into the dining room. He had told Flaubert that it wasn't sanitary, that the chickens left droppings that carried disease. Flaubert always listened politely to Monsieur Harry during these lectures and then shrugged at the end of them. But this time, Flaubert was in the back and Harry Francis was drunk enough to do what he had always threatened to do.

The hen was scrawny and unevenly covered with worn red and white feathers. She was probably very old. Flaubert had no system in raising chickens, just as he had no discipline in keeping them out of the café. He killed the hens when he was hungry or when he served chicken to the customers. But a lucky fowl could live to an old age if Flaubert did not notice, because he always killed the chicken nearest at hand.

Harry Francis was drunk because he had been drinking with Cohn for two days in the café. Harry had known from the beginning who Cohn was and where he came from and why he had been sent to St. Michel.

The café was across the road from the long sand beach which stretched from the edge of St. Michel all the way south down the quarter moon of the island to Madeleine, at the southern end.

The sun was setting very quickly. The Caribbean was blue close to the land and further away, in the Gulf Stream, it was green. Harry Francis yawned. His eyes were red from too much vodka and too little sleep. The hen was backlit by the dying sun in the open doorway.

Harry Francis decided.

He bumped the legs of the chair across the floor and stood up. He pulled out an ivory-handled knife from the worn leather sheath on the wide black Garrison belt that was hidden partially beneath the blouse of his bush shirt. The shirt opened across an expanse of leathery skin that was cracked and burned and weathered by a life in the sun.

The hen paused, took a step, paused, and cocked its head to focus one unblinking eye on Harry Francis.

"She's inside, Cohn. You'd have to say she's inside," Harry Francis said in a rough, gravelly voice.

"Yes, Harry," Cohn agreed. His voice had grown rough along with Harry's from the days and night of vodka and rum. He saw the knife in Harry's hand and he didn't care. He was so tired.

"I told you I told Flaubert I'm not going to live like a goddamn nigger with chickens walking and crapping where I eat, didn't I tell him that?"

"Yes, Harry."

"So he leaves the door open anyway and he goes in the back because he knows a goddamn chicken is going to walk in finally. He does it to aggravate me. I know these people, I know people like Flaubert. I've lived in the islands thirty years. But you know that, don't you, Cohn."

"If you say so."

"And what does it say in my files?"

"I don't know, Harry."

"Martinique to Cuba, Windward and Leeward, Bahamas and Jamaica and St. Maarten, I've been on them all, worked on them all, I know them and all their fucking little secrets. I know you'd like to know everything I know. Everything I wrote down in the book. You'd like to know about the book."

"Jesus Christ, Harry."

"The trouble with these people is they never talk to you directly unless they want to say please or thank you but they don't mean it. I know what they really think—they have ways of letting you know what they really think. Flaubert wants to piss me off, Cohn, that's why he leaves the door open. Well, it's time to piss Monsieur Flaubert off."

Cohn said nothing.

"We're going to have chicken for dinner." Harry Francis crossed the floor. He held the knife in his left hand like a fighter. At the last minute, he rushed for the chicken but it fluttered with a squawk out of his grasp. Harry cursed.

Harry lunged again, moving more quickly than his big-bellied bulk might have indicated. The chicken squawked and flapped onto the tabletop. Its claws slipped on the dirty Formica and in that moment, Harry lunged again and reached under it and grabbed one yellow leg. The chicken made another sound and then was silent, waiting for death upside down, its wings spread. The weight of its feathered wings was too great to move.

"Not in here," said Cohn, feeling sick. His face was pale. "That's as bad as the other thing."

Flaubert opened the curtain that covered the doorway to the back of the café. He was a small, thin black man and his skin seemed oily in the heat. His black eyes glittered red at the edges of the whites. He wiped his hands on a soiled white dish towel.

"What it is, my friend?" he began in a singsong French that was part island patois.

"A fucking chicken. In here. I told you."

"I forgot. It was so hot in here."

"I know you forgot."

"You're going to kill it, Monsieur Harry?"

"Yes."

Flaubert shrugged and turned his back.

Harry Francis slit the head from the body with one stroke of his ivory-handled knife. It was so sudden there was no drama to it. The head fell to the floor with scarcely a sound. Blood spurted from the severed neck artery onto the floor. When the bleeding slowed, Harry Francis dumped the carcass on the floor.

A final burst of the creature's nervous system sent the headless body scurrying in a sudden dance across the floorboards.

Cohn felt frightened then; it was not pleasant to see a dead thing still moving as though it were alive.

And then it was over and the carcass collapsed and there was blood all over the floor of the Café de la Paix.

"Flaubert, get your chicken," Harry Francis shouted. His face was red and his eyes were shining. He wiped the bloody knife on his shorts and tucked the blade in its sheath.

Flaubert turned again, came to the carcass, and picked it up. He picked up the head as well and threw it out the window. "Philippe!" he called sharply and the boy with almond skin and light blue eyes came to the door from the beach. He stared at the bloody floor.

"Monsieur Harry has killed a chicken. Get the mop and wash the floor."

"Why did you kill the chicken, monsieur?"

Flaubert said, "Because he's drunk, *mon petit.*"

"Because your father is an unsanitary slob," Harry said and grinned and Philippe's face lit into a smile.

"Why did you do that?" Cohn said when Flaubert went into the back room. The child mopped the floor.

They spoke only English to each other. "I'm not subtle, Cohn. If I meant to give you a message, I would have just as soon stuck you myself."

"What message?"

"Cut the crap. You've been on St. Michel two weeks but you only found me two days ago. There are fifty thousand poor souls on this poor little island and only five thousand whites and we all live around the capital, so what was so fucking hard to find me?"

28

"Maybe I wasn't looking for you."

"Maybe. There are other games on this island besides me, I know that. But I know everyone is interested in my notebook."

"What about your notebook?"

"What about it, Cohn?" Harry grinned. "What about it is that I know things. Lots of things. Cheers, Cohn, up your ass." He took the expensive bottle of Smirnoff from the table and drank from the neck and wiped his mouth when he was finished. They had run out of ice long before. The clear liquid burned on the back of his tongue and the edge of his thought.

"I don't care particularly what you know," Cohn said.

The laugh filled the room. "Why don't you come out like a man and ask me what you want to ask me and stop this screwing around?"

"All right, Harry," Cohn said quietly.

"You're not even drunk," Harry said. "I admire that. You turn it on and off."

"As you did just now."

"Maybe it's only an act with me," Harry Francis said. Their voices were quiet, full of business.

Philippe stopped mopping the blood. He tried not to look at them. He tried to hear what they said to each other.

"You haven't written for a long time."

"Maybe I've been writing, maybe I just choose not to send the manuscript to a publisher," Harry Francis said.

"But you used to write letters home," Cohn said.

"And I've stopped. And you want to know why. Maybe because I'm tired of writing to people who don't read. The illiterate society and the illiterate government agency."

"We're very interested in your letters, Harry," Cohn said. "They were always informative."

"You thought they were lies. You thought I was making it up."

"How do you live, Harry?"

"That's my fucking business, isn't it?"

"Everyone back home is worried about you."

"I don't want them to worry."

"Can we make you an offer? On your next manuscript?"

"You don't even know what it's going to be about."

"We'd like to look at it, Harry. Whenever you have a few pages ready."

"I agree with Hemingway." A sly smile. "It's despicable for a writer to show pages until he's finished."

"We'd like to help you get published."

"It might be a true story this time."

"We always thought they were true stories, Harry."

"But this time, it might be even more true. The whole truth. And nothing but the truth. You know what Hemingway said, don't you?"

"What did he say?"

"He wrote it in *A Moveable Feast*. God, he got back at everyone in that book—he didn't have to do it but he wanted to. That's what I admire about him. He was a cold-blooded son-of-a-bitch right up to the end. He stuck it to everyone, even the ones who did him some good. It was the way he was going to end up being better than they were."

"Like you, Harry?"

Harry Francis smiled. "You're all so damned worried, aren't you? You'd like to know, wouldn't you?"

"What did Hemingway say?"

"You're patronizing me, but I won't be patronized. I knew him. I knew him in Cuba at Finca Vigia. I was in his army—we attacked the estates with an army with firecrackers and stink bombs. It was damned silly but it seemed fine at the time."

"What did Hemingway tell you?"

"He knew. He knew I was working for Uncle."

"Did you tell him?"

"You never saw him. You never got close to him. You couldn't lie to him. He saw right through you. He was like a surgeon. He could cut so easily it wouldn't even cause any pain, even if he didn't put you under first. Like a chicken waiting for slaughter. We just hung there with our wings out and if he wanted to kill us, he could kill us."

"What did he write?"

"Oh. It's not that, it's what he told me. I said I was going to write and he said the only things worth writing were true things and that when I started lying, I would never be able to stop. He said you had to write true things even if no one else would believe you. I did. I did that. I told them what would happen in Cuba. I told them that Castro knew but they went ahead and when it was over, they had to get rid of me. Hemingway knew it was going to turn out that way. That's why he killed himself."

"Is it?"

"I always thought that. He didn't want to be ruined. Like his father who killed himself."

"What about you, Harry? Are you going to kill yourself?"

Harry stared at him for a long time and did not speak. When he spoke, his voice was soft and almost purring.

"I can't, Cohn. There's the notebook to finish with."

"Would you like a publisher?" Cohn said carefully.

"I don't think I would have any trouble getting a publisher," said Harry Francis.

"I think we'd be the one for you, to give you the best audience, I mean. We have the resources, you know."

"I'll keep you in mind."

"Yes. Do that, Harry," Cohn said.

Philippe, who understood some English, listened very intently. He leaned on the mop and waited and it was as though he was not in the room with the two white men.

"You tell them I'm finishing the manuscript. You tell them that when the manuscript is finished, I'll keep them in mind. You tell them that."

"I will."

"You tell them about the line in *A Moveable Feast* as well."

"What line is that?" Cohn said.

"The one you'll have to look for," Harry Francis said.

■　■　■

The road from the café to the edge of the capital was dark. The street lamps in the south end of the capital usually went off at ten, and then the darkness belonged to the moon and the

31

stars that littered the clear Caribbean sky. The night also belonged to drunken white men, thought Cohn, who could not summon the strength any longer to be sober. He had been too long with Harry Francis and it was too late.

People here did not go out at night because it was dangerous. The danger might come from thieves and killers, from those who dealt in drugs and moved drugs about. It might come from the secret police whom the people called the *gendarmes noires*. But Cohn was not afraid of them. He was an American. He was protected by the consulate.

Cohn had not said good night to Harry. He left him in the café asleep, snoring, his head down on the table still littered with the remains of dinner, including the chicken. The chicken had survived Flaubert's slaughter for so long it had become old and tough and tasteless, and even Flaubert's sauce could not hide that.

It was past eleven. Flaubert had been in his underpants when he came out of the living quarters at the back of the café to unlatch the door for Cohn. He told Cohn Harry would sleep until four in the morning, that he would awake and drink anything that was left from the dinner, that he would stagger away and leave the door open. Flaubert said Harry always left the door open.

Cohn stumbled across a piece of driftwood and cursed it. He was walking on the beach. He felt terrible but he was glad to be away from Harry Francis.

The night was still and cool, and the sand was damp. Half of the moon sparkled on the water. Gentle waves lapped at the beach. Cohn walked along the beach instead of the main road because it was safer. Every now and then, someone would be reported killed on the road at night, struck by a car speeding north from Madeleine to the capital. The road was narrow and dark. Everyone in St. Michel deplored the state of the road, but the island seemed gripped by a fatal inertia and the road was the symbol of it. It ran from a small capital of slums and a few grand buildings to a second city of slums and whores and dealers nine miles south. It had always been like this. It would be this way tomorrow. Only Manet's soldiers in the hills above the long road did not accept the way it was.

The sand was wet under Cohn's bare feet because the beach narrowed at this point and the tide had gone out at sunset. Cohn carried his shoes in his left hand. A little breeze from the sea plucked at Cohn's dirty tan trouser legs.

Harry Francis was a sad case. Cohn would put that in his report. It was what they wanted to hear back in Washington.

"*Pardon, monsieur?*"

Cohn stopped, turned, and was surprised by the flashlight that suddenly blinded him. His face was pinched, fatigued, and he was annoyed. He suddenly wanted to relieve himself.

"Who the hell is that?"

"Monsieur?"

He repeated the question in the singsong French acquired at the Army Language School in California.

"Monsieur," the voice stated with flat authority.

Cohn thought he saw two of them.

They wore midnight-blue uniform shirts with empty epaulets and blue shorts with high black stockings and dark berets. The people of St. Michel did not call them the Special Security Force as President Claude-Eduard had dubbed them; they were the "black police." The *gendarmes noires*.

"Clowns," Cohn muttered in English.

"*Monsieur.* You are English?"

"I am an American."

"*Bon soir, monsieur.*" Politely and without sincerity. "Why are you on the beach?"

"I saw you yesterday in the capital. On Rue Sans Souci. I know you." He squinted in the light which hurt his eyes. "You know me. Cohn. With the American consul general."

"Monsieur Cohn." The black face was very close. The eyes blinked. He stared at Cohn as though he had never seen him before. "Do you have some identification?"

"What is this about?"

"A woman was raped."

33

"I didn't hear anything."

"It happened yesterday."

The second policeman who held the light smiled.

Cohn took out his wallet with his passport and visa and gave them to the officers. He was a public information officer. The larger policeman opened the wallet and looked at the money inside. He selected a ten-dollar bill. "There is a fine against using the public beaches after they are closed for the night."

"I'm not using the beach. I'm walking back to St. Michel. It's safer than the road."

"The road is very dangerous." The *gendarme* still held the wallet. "The woman was raped on the road."

"Amazing she didn't get run over."

"It was brutal," the policeman said flatly. "There were markings on her body after she was found."

Cohn shivered because of the slight breeze. The whole country was on edge. The tropical forest would take over tomorrow or the day after tomorrow; it would cover the road and there would be no men left on St. Michel.

No wonder Harry Francis had become crazy. He would say that in his report.

"I want to take a piss."

"The beaches of St. Michel are not a *pissoir*."

"I have to take a piss. I'll go by the road."

The large policeman shrugged. He put the ten-dollar bill back into the wallet and closed it. "It doesn't matter about the fine. You have diplomatic immunity."

"Even if you were to piss on the Palais Gris of the president, it would not matter," said the second.

"You could not be fined," said the first.

"You may even piss on the beach and not be fined because you have immunity," said the second.

"There would be nothing we could do," said the first.

Cohn took a step back. "All right then." He took the wallet and put it in his pants. "All right then," he repeated. "I can wait until I get back."

"No, it's all right. You have immunity," said the first.

"Yes. You are a guest of St. Michel. Please piss on the beach."

Had the wind risen? He felt cold.

"No," Cohn said.

"Please, sir," said the first. "We will turn away."

They turned and waited and Cohn felt a strangling sense of panic. He pulled down his fly and urinated on the sand. The sand smothered the sound of his urine striking the ground. When he was finished, he put on his shoes. He would walk along the highway.

The two policemen stood with their backs to him.

"I am finished," he said.

They turned slowly. They looked at him. The large one said, "Is everything satisfactory then?"

He began to speak.

He did not feel the razor. It cut from left to right, just below each earlobe, in a wide and grinning arc like the smile that children carve on a pumpkin at Halloween. Cohn did not feel any pain. He thought of something that Harry had said about Hemingway. He felt that something had happened that could not be reversed. The panic overwhelmed him.

It would be all right if he said something. He opened his mouth, and it filled with blood. He struggled to remain upright. Blood fell down his shirt and stained it; it soaked the white wet sand at his feet. He blinked because he thought he was going to cry. Perhaps it would be all right if he stood very still.

But he could not stand still.

He blinked again to see the *gendarmes* more clearly. The whiteness of the flashlight had grown to a whiteness that must have come from the blinding rays of the moon. He was certain of it.

5

THE IMPORTANT HOSTAGE

The flight drained Rita because of all that had happened before she left.

"Run," she said. "We can run."

"We can't run."

They had sat staring at each other in their apartment in Lausanne until dawn, speaking now and then, waiting for morning. They could not sleep; they could not touch each other.

"Kill him then."

"And then Langley will know I'm alive and then, in a little while, KGB will know again and the contract will be let again."

"So you're going to let me go?"

"He won't hurt you. He wants a job. It gives us a little time."

"It won't be that easy," she had said.

In the end, she had taken the tickets and visas and credentials and taken the long flight from Frankfurt-am-Main airport to Miami to Guadeloupe and transferred to the shuttle to St. Michel. She had been tired but she could not sleep. She had taken the first taxi from the line at the Aerodrome St. Michel.

The heat made her feel sick. It sapped her strength. Her stomach felt queasy. The ride in the ancient Renault was rough. The driver wore a colorful shirt that pictured palm trees and he spoke of the wonders of the capital city all the way into the town.

There seemed little wonderful about St. Michel. Cement-and-plaster buildings like dirty gray boxes squatted around narrow streets and squares. The streets were full of people who did not seem to move much. There was a grand promenade on the beachfront but the beach itself was littered with garbage. On the deep side of the harbor, fishing boats bobbed at wooden piers jutting into the water. The water was dark with oil and garbage.

"On the hill is the Palais Gris, where the president lives." The driver's name was Daniel. He said he was a teacher. He said he taught when he had the time and enough money from driving. Many visitors from other countries were coming to St. Michel now for the independence celebration, he said. He seemed proud of it. He was a very light-skinned Negro with reddish hair. He said he spoke very good English but phrased the statement as a question. She did not answer him. Her hair was damp and limp and she felt dirty and she stared out at the gray landscape of the sun-filled city around her.

"This is where we will build the museum," said Daniel. He pointed with an elegant hand toward an enormous excavation in the dry, cracked ground next to the road from the aerodrome. There was nothing in the hole. There was no sign of activity; no equipment, no workers, no scaffolding.

"It's a hole, just a hole in the ground," Rita Macklin heard herself saying.

"It is the idea of the half-empty cup," said Daniel with a quick smile into the rearview mirror. "Is it half full or half empty? At least the excavation has been made. It is a promise."

"What will be in the museum?"

"Many things. Artifacts of our society. And the traditional weaving of the women who live in the hills. Many things to interest important visitors such as yourself."

"Your shirt? Was it woven—"

"No," said Daniel. "I speak excellent English? I purchased this shirt when I lived with my aunt one year in Miami. It is from the J.C. Penney store. In time, there will be one such store here. Were you in to the J.C. Penney store in Miami?"

"No."

"The museum will also receive exhibitions." They were past the excavation, mounting a small rise from the harbor into the heart of St. Michel. Garbage was piled on the narrow streets. "The exhibitions will come from Paris. From the Louvre, I think. They made many speeches when they began to dig the excavation—this was three years ago. The French consul general said that the Louvre would surely loan an important collection of paintings to the museum of the Republic of St. Michel when the museum was completed."

"No one is working on the site," she said and her voice was far away from her.

"There are budget shortages and so work must cease. We have many problems on St. Michel, in all republics, like America. Money must be diverted to the army. The fight against the rebel soldiers in the hills must take precedence. Freedom is the constant price of being vigilant."

She shook her head to register the mangled quote. She closed her eyes a moment and the car jumped a pothole. The heat glued her blouse to her skin. Her jeans felt tight; she had worn them all her life. She wanted a bath, she wanted to sleep.

"And the cruise ships will come when the new pier is built," Daniel chattered on, turning into another side street hidden from the one they had been on. The city was a honeycomb of such streets but there was no great sense of urgency to the street life.

Devereaux had let her go two days after Colonel Ready left them. Devereaux had permitted her to become a hostage. Devereaux was to come in three more days, to slide into the island while matters were diverted toward the celebration. To probe the problem presented by Colonel Ready. A little job, he had said. And if he could get the book from Harry Francis that much sooner, all the better for both of them.

Devereaux had let her go.

The taxi coughed to a stop in front of a five-story building done in the classic French style with tall windows and small balconies. The building was a bright sandstone color. Over the portico was the name RITZ in script on a blue marquee. She smiled at that.

"This is quite the best hotel in St. Michel," said Daniel as though he had built it. He got out of the taxi and opened her door. "It is quite comparable to the hotel in Paris, don't you think?"

"I don't know. I never stayed there."

"You will be quite comfortable here," said Daniel with the air of a proprietor.

She took out a fistful of French francs—the currency of St. Michel—and chose two notes and then remembered that the schoolteacher named Daniel drove the taxi because he did not make sufficient money teaching school.

"What do the children do when you do not teach?"

"They wait for me," said Daniel. "I promise never to be away from them for too long. It is just long enough to make a little money."

Rita Macklin gave him four notes and climbed out of the Renault. Daniel had her bag and he carried it across the threshold of the hotel. He wore shoes and long pants and his beautiful shirt from Miami. He put down the bag at the lobby desk and waited for the clerk.

After a moment, a pale man with light blond hair appeared from the alcove. He looked at Daniel and at Rita and said in French, "*Complet.*"

"I have a reservation."

"There is no room."

"I have a reservation."

"It is impossible. *Complet! complet!*"

"From Colonel Ready."

"*Complet,*" said the bored young man and then his eyes opened wider and he took the profferred reservation form and looked at it as though it might be a forged bank note. He turned it over.

Rita looked at the lobby. The leather chairs looked old and unused but the lobby was clean and spare. There was a small bar off the lobby. A couple of men stood at the bar drinking with each other and speaking in soft French.

"Madame," said the young man. "I beg your pardon."

"Yes."

"We are expecting you, of course."

"Of course."

He rang the bell for the boy. He looked at the mail slot and found a card. He rushed around the front desk and shooed Daniel away. He picked up her bag. He waited for the boy who emerged from another alcove rubbing his chin.

The clerk spoke to the boy in imperious French. After a year in Switzerland, Rita Macklin had begun to understand the differences in the foreign language.

"We have your suite, Madame Macklin, and after you are refreshed, there is to be a reception for the friends of St. Michel—our foreign guests—at the Palais Gris—"

"I thought it was tomorrow night."

"No. It was changed."

"I don't understand."

"It was changed."

"When?"

"I'm not certain, but it was changed."

"I'm exhausted."

"*Garçon*, take the madame to her suite." The boy hefted the bag with thin arms and led her to the elevator cage. The cage was open. He pushed back the gate and they got on board and he pushed the button marked two. In the European style, it took them to the third floor.

The room was not a suite. It was a room furnished in an imitation French style with white painted tables and Louis XIV chairs that were actually fabricated in Mexico. The bed, she saw, had an elaborate headboard though no footboard at all.

She took a long, hot shower to stop her tiredness. The water had only a little pressure but it was enough. And it was hot.

There was no air conditioning in the room. It was

muggy. She wrapped herself in a towel and pushed open the large windows and caught a breeze from the harbor that smelled of sea and fish. It was a sweet rotting smell. She stared at the squat capital beyond her window.

There was a knock at the door. The clerk opened it without waiting for a reply. He was followed by the bellboy.

"Madame, my pardon," he said.

The towel covered her sufficiently but she did not move. The bellboy had a large oscillating fan on a silver tray. He placed the fan on the dresser and plugged it in. It whirred to life. The clerk carried a bottle of chilled Moët and a glass. "Madame Macklin, welcome to St. Michel."

She could only stare at him, at the fan blowing back and forth, at the bellboy waiting in attendance.

"Unfortunately," said the clerk, clearing his throat, "money for air conditioning was not included in the budget of the Ritz, which is only two years old and the most modern hotel in St. Michel." The clerk folded his hands in front of him. "There is every intention in the next budget to equip each room with air conditioning by the time the new cruise ships arrive at the new docks."

Everyone in St. Michel seemed obsessed with explanation, all delivered with cheerful regrets and an acceptance of perpetual failure.

When the two left, with more francs in their pockets, Rita sat in front of the fan and let it blow on her naked body and she drank a glass of champagne and tried to feel better.

Why had she come here?

Because she loved him. It was why she had done any of it. Devereaux had met her and used her and left her; then Devereaux had crossed her path a second time. They had fallen in love and had tried to run away once from his old life but there had been a contract against him from the KGB. Only when it seemed he had died in the hotel room in Zurich on the last business—only when R Section was willing to

41

bury his file—did it seem they were safe. He had relished his safety. He had lived with her and never wanted anything more. And one day, Colonel Ready had come down a hill in Lausanne and awakened him to his old life and now he said he thought he knew a way out for both of them. But it would take time. And she would have to play Ready's game.

"Ready is death," she told Devereaux.

But he had waited, he had not wanted to run again. The old dreams that had made him groan in his sleep when they first slept together and which had been banished by the peace of his dead life in Switzerland came back on those last two nights. He groaned and saw ghosts of dead men in sleep. He heard the chains of all the dead he had known and all the dead he had killed and all the dead he had tried to keep alive. The old life was in him again, cold and unfeeling and she had become a hostage for his life, for the chance he might be able to be dead again. He had said he had a plan. He was enacting it now . . . she would be patient.

The air from the fan felt cold on her naked body.

She put down her glass of champagne.

She pulled down the coverlet on the bed and felt the cool linen next to her skin. The sun sank inexorably. She fell asleep and did not dream; she had no old life to relive. He was her life. She slept until the evening when there was a knock at her door.

6

THE MORGUE

Cohn's naked body lay on the stone slab in the basement room used as a morgue. His face was blue and serene. The cut across his neck showed dark against the tissues beneath the skin which were already turning black.

42

Colonel Ready was dressed in his Class A uniform of the army of St. Michel. The light blue uniform was covered with piping and medals. He wore three gold stars on each epaulet.

"Where did they dump him?"

"Left him on the road," said Celezon, staring at the body with the same serene expression that showed on dead Cohn's face.

"There's always hell to pay for something like this," Colonel Ready said. "What about his papers?"

"Everything was missing."

"Why was he down there?"

"He spent the night drinking with Harry Francis. He'd been with Harry Francis for a couple of days."

"We knew that. Fucking Harry Francis, fucking rummy. All right, put on a show. Run him in and throw him in the dry cell until he gets reasonably sober. I'm not supposed to be a policeman, Celezon."

They had returned to St. Michel two days before. Rita Macklin had been observed by Celezon disembarking from the shuttle flight at Aerodrome St. Michel that afternoon. If Rita Macklin had not bolted, Devereaux would follow the plan outlined by Ready. Ready had been in a good mood when Celezon told him about Rita. It had seemed like a good time to tell Colonel Ready about the American who had been killed on the beach.

Colonel Ready stared across the naked body at his aide. Celezon was the nominal chief of the Special Security Police. The *gendarmes noires* were the most feared force on the island. Even the voodoo priests in the hills did not venture out at night very often when the *gendarmes noires* were combing through the villages allegedly looking for drug runners. The voodoo priests feared only the black power of the voodoo but there were those who said that blackness was most concentrated in the blackness of the evil of the *gendarmes noires*.

"We will discover the perpetrators," said Celezon.

Colonel Ready did not speak for a moment. His blue eyes were mocking and Celezon met his gaze with the dignity of a judge.

"How do you suppose it went down?"

"I don't know. Thieves. Perhaps it was one of the rebels—"

"Come on, Celezon. Don't tell me things like that. You start with Manet killing him and you'll end up believing Harry Francis did it."

"Harry Francis has a big knife. He killed a chicken the night Cohn was killed. He killed the chicken in Flaubert's café—he cut off its head like this." And Celezon made a slitting noise and drew his finger across his own throat. And smiled at Colonel Ready.

Ready returned the smile. "You tell them that this was not a white tourist—God knows we don't get many of those. Tell those morons that he was a Heap Big Man, you tell them that."

"He was a friend of the American consul."

"Fuck the American consul. Except I will have to hold his hand tonight at the reception for the president. I will have to assure him that Cohn was a victim of the unfortunate underworld of crime that is the only supportable crop on this godforsaken island. Cohn. I knew what Cohn wanted and I wanted him to get it from Harry so I could get it from Cohn. I just wanted to see the fucking book, to see if it existed. And one of your goons went and killed him."

"There are too many incidents of violence after lights out," said Celezon with gravity.

"That's not true and you know it. Even the voodoo priests stay indoors—they're more scared of your *gendarmes* than they are of the spirit of dead chickens."

"You don't understand the voodoo," Celezon said.

"Because I don't want to."

Colonel Ready turned and glanced again at the second slab. It was occupied as well, by the naked body of a young woman who had been raped and killed three nights before, not far from the road where Cohn was found. She had markings on her body, on her belly and breasts. The marks appeared to be geometrical symbols or astrological signs. They

44

had been cut into the flesh and the flesh was dried now and the marks were almost black. Her abdominal cavity was open because the medical examiner from the hospital had wanted to investigate the contents of her stomach; he was peparing a paper on postmortem digestive processes for a journal in Paris.

"Why must we arrest Harry Francis if you tell me that Harry Francis did not kill this man?" Celezon said in his flat singsong patois.

"Because we have to do all the usual things. Because it will give me something to say to the American consul tonight. And the American consul will radio that information to the spooks in the State Department and it will be digested in the intelligence community and there will be another black mark against Harry Francis's name.Maybe when Harry is in a corner, there will be a way to reason with him. Always think of the angles and make the best of a bad situation, Celezon."

"I will learn this."

"And learn this: Harry is the noisiest agent in St. Michel. In the whole fucking Caribbean. He's been a joke for a long time but that doesn't mean he isn't useful. To me. And to you. And to his keepers. The clown can hear as many confessions as the priest. And some of them will be truer."

"When does the gray man come?"

"In two days."

"Will he come to the capital?"

"I expect him. There's no other way except by air unless he wants to swim."

"I wish you would tell me what you really want from him—"

"That's none of your business."

"I am chief of security, *mon colonel*—"

"I made you that, Celezon." Colonel Ready came around the slab and stood very close to Celezon. "I can make you latrine orderly tomorrow, Celezon, so don't ever crowd me. And don't ever tell me that someone like Cohn has been slit by one of your goons."

45

"I am certain no member of the Special Security Force—"

But he stopped because Colonel Ready had turned away and was walking across the cement floor to the steps on the far side of the basement room. Above this place of death was the palace of the grand rooms. For a moment, Celezon let the hatred glitter in his eyes. It was only for a moment and only because Colonel Ready had turned his back.

From the bottom of the steps, Colonel Ready spoke with his back turned. "Tell Dr. Jobe to get these stiffs in the ground. I could smell them at the top of the stairs. We don't want guests at the reception tonight getting sick."

"*Oui, mon colonel*," said Celezon and because Ready's back was turned, he gave a large mocking salute with his big brown hand.

The morgue was in a wing of the gray stucco building called the Palais Gris. President Claude-Eduard and his sister, Yvette, lived in the part of the building that faced on the central court of the palais. In the basement, the *gendarmes noires* had their headquarters and their holding cells.

Which is why Harry Francis, when he was dragged to the cells around midnight, could hear the party sounds of the presidential reception floating through the open windows of the stately building.

7

THE TRAIL OF NOVEMBER

Hanley sat behind the government-issue gray metal desk and folded his white, almost translucent hands together on the desktop in front of him.

Lydia Neumann took her usual chair across from him. She was a large woman with spiky black hair cut in rough wedges. She wore a sweater because the windowless office was sixty degrees Fahrenheit. It was always cold because the temperature matched Hanley's pale, parsimonious nature.

Lydia Neumann was the computer expert in R Section. She ran CompAn. She had stumbled across November's trail twenty-three hours before. Now there was corroboration.

Hanley was operations chief of R Section, which was the name of an intelligence agency nominally under the director of Central Intelligence. The agency was coded in budget papers as an agricultural estimation service with an international intelligence mission. The code was not true and everyone knew it, including the Section rivals at CIA and DIA and the National Security Agency.

"Why is November awakening?" asked Mrs. Neumann. The people in Washington always spoke in slang, even the best of them. Agents went to sleep, never to cover or deep cover or even death. Agents rarely awoke independently.

"We don't know that he is. That is your interpretation of data. There's no contact with us. Maybe he went to London for a private job."

"He isn't free-lance."

"I don't know what he is anymore. Except dead."

"Asleep," she insisted. "He's waking up."

"Spooks never die, is that it, Mrs. Neumann?" said Hanley.

"Maybe he went to London to do a research project," she said. Her voice was very rough and raspy and when she added sarcasm to her words, the thrust was choppy and meant to hurt.

"It may be all coincidence," Hanley said. He studied his hands. He had studied them often in twenty years in R Section. The hands rarely contained answers. He did not believe in coincidence.

"Rita Macklin went to St. Michel. She went to Frankfurt and took a flight to Miami. She transferred to Air France to Guadeloupe. She transferred to another plane to St. Michel . . . a local carrier . . . ." She frowned because she had forgot-

47

ten the name of the line. "She is a more experienced traveler than that. She drew attention to herself, traveling in such a circumspect way."

"Yes."

"As though she knew we would be watching her and she wanted us to watch her very closely now," Mrs. Neumann said.

"Is that your computer analysis or your instinct?"

"Instinct."

"And we have a man in St. Michel," said Hanley.

"A dead man."

"Cohn. Cohn was pretty good," Hanley said.

"We have Cohn dead and—"

"Shh," said Hanley, putting one finger to his lips. Some things should not be said, even in rooms without windows that are cleared daily.

"And November is in London, checking out old friends and resources."

"Seeking information on the political and economic state of St. Michel," Hanley said.

"Coincidence," said Mrs. Neumann. Her voice was full of sarcasm again.

"Coincidence," said Hanley, staring at his fingers folded into the attitude of prayer.

Mrs. Neumann kept the computers. She filed the data, she did the research, she invented the programs for the one hundred people who worked for her in CompAn within R Section. She lived with the computers and was comfortable in their company. She knew what to look for when the computers spoke to her. They had spoken the day before to a routine GS-9 clerk who had brought the red flag to her immediately. NOVEMBER. But "November" was the nomenclature of a terminated agent. His file was not active; he was asleep, computerized into Archives, the paperwork backup of the floppy disks already grown dusty in the sub-sub-basement storage lockers.

But November was awake, the computer insisted. Awake and stirring.

48

"He had access to his friends in London," Hanley said for the sixth time that morning. "He could have used any name when he retrieved information from Economic Review. He wanted to signal us. That's why he used November."

"He didn't use the passport we fitted him with when he entered Britain."

"The bastard even had Economic Review bill us for the information he got. Effrontery."

"He put out all the flags."

"We're not under sail," Hanley said. "Hasn't he heard of safe phones? He could have called. Why not come here? He became a Sleeper through choice, his own choice."

Fourteen months before, to save his life, Devereaux had faked his own death. Hanley knew; Mrs. Neumann knew; the Old Man knew. And that was all. The file was filed in Archives and November was put to sleep.

Economic Review was one of those quasi-private companies that researches political and economic backgrounds of countries in the world. ER had 231 countries under constant monitor. Its service was expensive. The bill flashed forward to R Section in Washington was $7,312.14, authorized by November's old account number.

All of the strands of information had become confused in the last hour. Lydia Neumann had pushed her computers back and forth, scanning for confirmation of her hunches, of her instincts. Where was November going?

But it was obvious to her.

At 3:10 P.M. eastern daylight time, a Pan Am jumbo jet had touched down at Miami International on a routine flight from London. Two Watchers from R Section had been waiting at the customs shed. They knew who they were looking for but they did not know why. Mrs. Neumann had guessed corectly.

"Colonel Ready," she said now to Hanley.

"I don't understand it. It's like a masquerade inside a masquerade."

"A charade," she said. "He's signaling to us and to someone else. It's all sign language."

49

"He entered London with an American passport. Made out to Ready. But it's him, it's not Ready."

"And entered the United States with the same passport."

"And his hair. His hair."

"Perhaps he's become touched by vanity," she said, smiling because the sarcasm always upset Hanley. She liked to tease him.

"He dyed his hair red. I don't understand that at all," he said. "And then he disappeared after Miami. What is the game? He's going to St. Michel but I don't understand what this is all about."

"Neither did Cohn."

"Colonel Ready was CIA. Maybe he still is. Nobody ever seems to quit the old game."

"Like November," she said.

"Yes." He opened his hands and they were empty. "Like November. Except what side has he come in on?"

■ ■ ■

The shrimp boats and charter fishing boats sat deck to deck in the crowded deep harbor of Fort Myers Beach. The harbor lies on the east side of Estero Island, which is connected to the mainland by a steep concrete bridge directly over the harbor. The shrimp boats go out to sea down the channels east of the island to Big Carlos Pass at the south tip where the water is deep enough for them to make it out to the Gulf of Mexico on the west shore of the island.

It was late afternoon and the blood-red sun was shimmering across the gulf sea, painting red colors on the lines and masts of the shrimpers in the harbor.

The *Compass Rose* was overshadowed on one side by a sleek seventy-eight-foot charter fishing yacht with staterooms and on the other by a rust-stained old shrimp boat with peeling paint and the stench of the fish hold. The shrimp boats ranged the gulf all the way to Mexico from this spot on the west coast of Florida. Sometimes, they were gone for weeks and even months. Sometimes, when the shrimp were not plentiful, the boats found other cargoes, which is why the Drug Enforcement Administration kept at least two agents on full-time duty in the triangle of Estero Island, Sanibel, and Captiva islands.

The *Compass Rose* rode high in the water. Her wooden decks and hull were painted black, her cabin was low and close to the narrow deck. The boat was longer and deeper than it appeared because of the coloring. She carried a sailing mast and riggings as well as two inboard engines.

Devereaux, who only knew a little about boats, had learned this much from one of the yard workers in a boat repair shop behind the sea wall on the east side of the harbor. She's a good one, the sun-blackened worker had said, sweat across his brown forehead, but she's a bastard, like the one that owns her. Neither fish nor fowl. Not big enough for a commercial fishing boat, not fancy enough for a long-distance charter. But she had too much power for day cruising. The worker had stared at Devereaux for a long moment after offering these criticisms. He had meant to imply something about the boat and the owner.

Devereaux stepped onto the deck of the *Compass Rose* as the sun fell low enough to cause deep shadows across the deep, still waters. The day had been long and warm. Long enough for Devereaux to finish his preparations. The most difficult part had been finding the *Compass Rose*. He had flown from Miami to Key West in a twin-engine P.B.A. Douglas and searched for the *Compass Rose* in the old harbor of the old town. Finally, at noon, someone who said he had been a pal of Cain's said Cain couldn't afford the fees or life-style of Key West anymore, that he had gone up the west coast to Fort Myers Beach, that Cain was probably running stuff now with some of the drug pirates from Mexico into Tampa and north.

Everyone knew so much about Cain, but it was never enough to see him clearly.

Only enough to let Devereaux find him.

"You want something?"

Devereaux turned and realized Cain did not recognize

51

him. It had been twelve years, but Devereaux had made changes in the last twelve hours. He had red hair now, and gray, sick skin, the kind you can get from illness or from swallowing cordite to dull the skin tones. His gray eyes were blue. And there was a scar, a long wide scar that ran from the corner of his mouth to his ear.

"I want someone named Cain."

"Yeah? Who're you?"

Devereaux smiled. "You were in Nam, weren't you?"

"Everyone was in Nam."

"It seemed that way."

There was a pause. Cain was large, he had large hands and cracked, burned skin and large, empty eyes and an earring in his left ear and dark brown curly hair that fit tight over his large head. The empty eyes held the face before him and tried to sort it through the photographs of memory. There was something there.

"You remember Colonel Ready."

"That wasn't his name."

"That's what he was called."

Cain wiped his hands on an oil rag. He wiped them over and over. The day was peculiarly breathless and still.

"Are you going to a Halloween party?" Cain said. His voice was soft, too gentle for a big man. But there was strength beneath the cadence of the words.

"I don't look like him, do I?"

"A nice imitation. Good enough to fool someone who never saw him. But I know you, too, don't I?"

"Yes," Devereaux said.

Cain's puzzled look cleared then and he stared at the other man. He did not smile in recognition but Devereaux saw that Cain knew.

"What do you want?"

"A boat."

"There's lots of boats."

"Do you know St. Michel?"

"I don't go that way," Cain said. "I stick to the upper gulf. I go toward Mexico."

52

"But I want to go to St. Michel."

"There's nothing there."

"You ever there?"

"A couple of years ago. Think of Haiti on its worst day and then you got some idea of St. Michel at its best."

"I want to go there," Devereaux said. "It's a little business. It will take a couple of days."

"I won't go down there."

"You had to leave Key West. You couldn't afford it anymore."

"There's a lot of coast. And the sea is the same no matter where you start from."

"You're a poet."

Cain stared at him. "That's the literary influence. Being in Key West all that time."

"I remembered you were there. When you got out."

"You never get out. They just leave me alone."

"Until now."

Cain's dead eyes sputtered to life, like a flame lit in a dark wind, on a wet night. The flame died as suddenly as it was born. "Until now," he said. "What do you want?"

"I told you."

"You can't make me," he said.

"Yes. I can do that. You know that."

"I might just kill you out there," Cain said. "There's a lot of sea between here and St. Michel."

"Can you make it without refueling?"

"I can take on fuel at Key West. Then there's enough to get to St. Michel and enough to get back to the keys if we use the sail and get a breeze."

"I don't care about coming back," said Devereaux. "We can take our time. I want to get in quickly and quietly."

"There used to be a fishing village. Not a village, just a few shacks, on the road between St. Michel town and Madeleine. Halfway down the lee coast."

"Can you pull in there?"

"St. Michel has an army, but they haven't discovered a

navy yet. Sometimes a smuggler will go in there to rest for a couple of days."

"That's what you do. That's what they say in the boatyards."

"Everyone knows everything," Cain said with a dead soft voice to match his dead eyes. "I want five thousand. Your people have it."

"Yes," said Devereaux. "I want to leave right away."

"Where's your gear?"

"I have it in a car."

"We could go out after sundown. See those guys on the bridge? There. Just look at them, don't stare. DEA. They were at Sanibel last week, it's our turn. If I pull out, I don't want to come back with any dirt."

"This isn't about drugs."

"I don't want you planting some shit."

"This isn't about you."

"But you want to use me," Cain said, each word falling like a body jerked on a hangman's rope. The words dropped, kicked, were still, swinging back and forth. "This isn't about me, but it is because you're here."

"It's about Ready. That might interest you."

"What happened to him? You're working together now?"

"No," Devereaux said. "Ready is on St. Michel."

"Are you going to kill him?" Cain asked the question without any passion except curiosity.

"I don't know," Devereaux said.

"If you were going to kill him, that would be all right," Cain said.

"Yes. I knew that."

"Is that why you involved me?"

"Yes," Devereaux said.

"Damn you. Both of you."

"Yes," Devereaux said.

8

AN INTIMATE RECEPTION

Rita Macklin wore a blue silk dress that was quiet and very elegant. But when she entered the large reception room she saw that quietness was not a virtue to the women assembled. It was as though the presidential reception needed all the color it could get.

The colors were to erase the face of the large hall in this dreary, gray palace, on a hill looking down on the broken slum that was the capital of St. Michel. The capital surrounded a beautiful natural harbor that had no cruise ships. The realism of the city and the palace gave way in this room to the surrealism of the colorful dresses and gowns of the ladies of the foreign dignitaries.

On the green walls of the high-ceilinged room were huge oil portraits of unknown Frenchmen who had settled St. Michel, tamed it, brought slaves to it, worked its mines, taken its meager wealth, and departed. They had places of honor in the room on the walls but no one could remember all their names.

Fourteen soldiers in khaki uniforms of the army of St. Michel stood at attention around the room.

Colonel Ready grinned at her when she entered the room and came to her with a glass of champagne. His white scar was even whiter because in the two days he had been back in St. Michel, his suntan had deepened.

"I hope you had a good flight," he said. "Everything is satisfactory?"

She saw a look of amusement in his eyes. And something more, something deeper than the surface glitter of his blue eyes. "This is so bizarre."

"Everything about St. Michel is bizarre," he said. "You get used to it after a while. The bizarre seems commonplace. See that gentleman there? Sir Michael Blasinstoke. He's the British consul. He stutters and he hates the French, an interesting prejudice for someone posted to a former French colony."

She smiled despite herself. Colonel Ready was trying to charm her. She felt disoriented by the long flight, the time changes, the brief nap in the strange hotel. The hotel was nearly empty. She saw the keys in the mailboxes and she had turned the pages of the register and saw only her name and three others listed. Why had the clerk insisted the hotel was filled? Like everything else she had experienced here in a few hours, the reality of things seemed to exist separately in a compartment apart from the appearance of things.

"And that one is the French consul. Our president is constantly trying to prove his 'Frenchness,' but it's no use when it comes to the French consul because Mazarine went to the Ecole Polytechnique in Paris. Claude-Eduard will always be a hopeless rustic to Mazarine."

Colonel Ready was very close to her so that his low voice only carried to her. His blue eyes were full of humor and mischief and she felt a warm wave as she realized he was trying to impress her.

"You're very attractive, Rita," he said.

"And who is that?"

He turned. "Morgan. The American consul." Colonel Ready frowned suddenly. "I'll have to talk to him. You'll have to excuse me a moment." His voice became tight.

"What am I supposed to do?"

"You're a journalist. Report the story of St. Michel."

"Nobody is interested in St. Michel," she said.

He paused. "Yes, that's very true most of the time. And sometimes, it turns out not to be true. You can never be too careful. I mean, trying to make certain that you are always aware of when a thing is true and when it is not."

"That's why you want Devereaux."

"Devereaux." He stared at her. "Yes. That's what I told him."

"It was true, wasn't it?"

"You have only been in St. Michel a few hours. There are things that are true and there are things that might be true."

"Like that big excavation. For the museum."

"Yes. The museum. That's a good example, I suppose. The hole in the ground is there, the museum is . . . where? In people's imagination. I suppose you talked to Daniel."

"How did you know?"

"I know everything about you, Rita," Colonel Ready said, and it was not pleasant to hear him say it. He smiled then, to mitigate the words. "This place is full of stories."

"Nobody cares."

"Not today, then tomorrow."

"It is full of tomorrows."

"Don't forget Grenada. We have rebels in the hills. All island nations have rebels in their hills."

She was weakening in her hatred of him. His words were light and airy and full of self-mockery. He was the only thing she was familiar with on the island. "Are they really Communists?"

"Yes, of course," said Colonel Ready.

■ ■ ■

The reception droned on and became more listless, as damp as the muggy evening warmth that clung to the room. A small group of musicians played cocktail party music that recalled tunes played in New York hotel lobbies in the 1940s.

Rita Macklin never finished her first glass of champagne. Colonel Ready disappeared for a while with the American consul and then reappeared alone. The people of the room all seemed to know each other and talked in whispers, like members of a close, large family thrown into an unfamiliar territory. There were a couple of people who said they were

57

reporters, and at the hors d'oeuvres table was the archbishop of St. Michel.

Simon Bouvier had the face and build of a French peasant, which was what his father had been. The archbishop had been standing at the table laden with food and he had been eating and talking for nearly an hour. He nibbled at the sweaty side of salmon, at the melting aspics and the rum-soaked fruit, at the petit fours, at the rolls and crackers and various soft cheeses that were running on their plates.

Rita Macklin asked him about the religion on the island.

"Everyone is Catholic, of course," he said.

"Is the church very . . . involved?"

"In what way?"

"There are rebels in the hills—"

"Oh. They are Communists. The hills have many believers in many religions. Unfortunately, few of them believe in our religion."

"What religions?"

"The voodoo is in the hills."

"Really? Still?"

"And the Communists. Such a violent religion that is," said the archbishop and he shoved a cracker full of Camembert into his mouth and chewed loudly on it. He grinned at her. "Oh, yes. We have missionaries as well, but they don't bother me and I don't bother them. I am quite content with matters as they are."

"Catholic missionaries."

"Nuns who do not wear the habits of their order. Radicals and Communists as far as I am concerned. But then, I am a conservative." The archbishop smiled. "It is a comfort to me to be conservative."

She started to speak and could think of nothing to say to him for a moment. Here was another one. The bishop took a piece of dark bread and reached for the bowl of Russian caviar. The caviar smelled like rotted fish. The old prelate was sweating but did not seem to notice it.

"Where are the nuns? I mean—"

"I really don't know. They have no convent. They live like single women. Colonel Ready asked my advice about them but I said they were harmless enough. They want to convert the people in the hills."

"You said everyone was Catholic."

"Which means that hardly anyone is Catholic at all. There are no churches in the hills but the hills have many believers."

"In voodoo."

"Perhaps. Perhaps in other things. It is difficult to understand what people who stay in the hills believe in. In any case, it is beyond me." He turned back to the food table and dismissed her.

The evening ground on. Conversations came and went in fragments that mimicked the humid wind that failed to cool her. Once, near midnight, Rita went to a window in the reception room and looked down in the courtyard. She saw two policemen with truncheons prod a large, fat white man across the courtyard. Harry Francis looked up in that moment and saw her in the window and then disappeared behind a large metal door that led to the police headquarters and the cells in the basement near the morgue.

At five minutes after midnight, with nearly half the guests gone, the president of St. Michel and his sister appeared at the door that led from their private quarters. Colonel Ready had stopped once to explain to Rita that they were always late to their own parties; it was a calculated gesture, even as it was rude. Claude-Eduard thought it was sophisticated.

As they entered the room, the tired musicians perked up. The pianist mopped his brow and then began at fast waltz tempo "Begin the Beguine."

The president was very thin and tall. He seemed a nervous man with a long nose and watery blue eyes. His listless brown hair was combed straight back from his square forehead. His ears were long. He wore white tie and tails and a

59

medal given to him on the day he decided to become President for Life of the Republic.

His sister, Yvette, held his arm as they circled the room. She was fitted in a tight green dress that reached to her ankles. Her eyes were black and glittered with fierce energy, a dark contrast to her brother, whose features were indistinct. Rita was reminded of a hand-tinted photograph before the era of color pictures. That was it, she thought: They were out of time. Everything in this room was out of time.

Colonel Ready was suddenly at her side again as she stared, entranced, at the strange, glittering couple walking slowly around the room, stopping now and then to speak to this consul or that.

"They were orphans—"

"I read a little about them before I came here. About the island," she said and felt again the threat coiled in Ready's presence next to her.

"The last children of the colonialists. I think they believe this is still a colony. The president makes up to the French consul . . . do you see?"

She stared and did not look at Ready next to her.

"Yvette is the one with ambition. You can see it in the way she holds herself. A pretty enough package," Ready said, grinning, trying to distract Rita enough to look at him.

"Yvette is the reason Claude-Eduard stays where he is," said Colonel Ready.

"I thought you were, colonel."

"Well, I help."

"You have the army. You have the black police."

"You are informed."

"I wanted to be informed before coming to the enemy as a hostage."

"A guest, Miss Macklin. 'A hostage' implies a threat. There is no threat."

And Rita, no longer tired, remembered where she was and why. "I wish he had killed you."

"It would not have been enough. He would have killed

60

me in Evian if that would have ended it. His trouble is that he thinks too clearly. It was always his trouble. You can't calculate every step you take with an eye on the outcome."

Rita turned to him finally and saw the hungry, appraising look in his eyes.

"But you would have been dead," she said with a dull voice.

"And November would have been made alive," he replied. "And his girl. And if CIA knew it, then KGB would know it and some mechanism would snap in place in some third-level bureaucracy inside the Fourth Directorate and the wet contract would be issued again. This time, perhaps, to include you."

"There was no contract."

"There is no other reason to explain Devereaux's 'death' and his reluctance to be reborn."

"What if he doesn't come?"

For a moment, a flicker of uncertainty crossed Ready's face but it was soon gone.

"You're here."

"A guest, you said. I covered my tracks as well. I have three assignments from magazines here. Including my friends in Washington. They know I'm here, they know I'm at the Ritz. They know about you."

His face reddened a moment and then he grinned. "You are careful, Miss Macklin, but I assure you, no harm will come to you. When you write of St. Michel, I hope you will be brutally honest—but kind to us as well. We are a struggling people in the Caribbean basin, the impoverished of Paradise."

"How eloquent."

"Take Yvette, the president's sister. She is beloved of the blacks on the island. They think she is one of them. She makes cause with them and sympathizes with their poverty."

"She dresses like it."

"The people tolerate Claude-Eduard. But she understands power."

"She brought you here."

"Many elements . . . brought me here."

"You still work for Langley."

"No. I assure you of that. I'm retired."

"Honorably?"

"With a check every month from Uncle," he said. "Yvette brought Celezon into government—before I came. Celezon is useful to me. He has his own connections. There are rumors, always rumors, about Yvette, about the magic in the hills, about the voodoo—"

"Oh, come on," she said.

"Brother and sister. Neither ever married. Some say they are lovers, that she has had a child by him . . ." He was smiling, talking in the same strange way that infected everyone on this island of half truths, unfulfilled promises, endless tomorrows.

"Try that booga-booga stuff on someone else."

"Our people," Ready said. "The people of St. Michel. They live on rumors and scrawny chickens and the voodoo. Up in the hills, I mean."

"Where the rebels are."

Ready's grin was full of contempt. "Sometimes I just pity Manet, I honest to God pity the bastard, living up in the hills with his freedom fighters drawn from the ranks of that rabble, trying to foment a disciplined revolution with the likes of them."

"Manet has managed to elude you, though."

"Do you think so, Rita?"

And she realized again how she hated this man and had wanted to kill him that night in Evian because the cruelty in his manner raked her as casually as it raked Devereaux.

"The trouble with having ambition in a country without ambition is that you have to have enemies," Colonel Ready said.

She stared at him but he had turned.

"Look at Yvette. A magnificent woman. She should have gone to France with that ambition, not stayed here."

"Are you in love with her?"

Ready said, "What an odd thought."

But then the president was very close and his sister still held his arm and Colonel Ready was smiling at them. Rita Macklin looked in the president's watery eyes and saw a hunger that made her ill. She nearly flinched as the president smiled at her. She felt Colonel Ready's hand on her bare arm.

"*Mon president*," began Colonel Ready. "This is Rita Macklin, the American reporter I spoke of—"

"So?" He smiled like a cat licking milk. He inclined his head slightly as though expecting Rita to curtsy.

"And Mademoiselle Yvette Pascon, sister of the president."

"I'm happy to meet—"

"Colonel Ready, what an extraordinary man you are. You have promised to bring the world's journalists to St. Michel to record our celebration and you have done so. There are television cameras and reporters. And now, this journalist. She is not only an honor to St. Michel, but to your good taste, colonel. Mademoiselle, forgive me, but you are quite beautiful. Is she not so, Yvette?"

Yvette smiled. "As you say, my dear brother."

Rita felt her color rising.

"I must insist on giving you an interview, mademoiselle," Claude-Eduard continued. "A private and an exclusive interview, we two alone—"

"*Mon president*, another time, I will arrange it," said Colonel Ready, gripping Rita's arm. "She is too tired—she jetted in this afternoon from Switzerland."

"Why were you in Switzerland, dear one?"

"An assignment," she began again. She felt a little embarrassed, even ashamed. The president was so close to her that his body nearly touched her body. Damn it, she thought, it's not my fault. His breath smelled of sour milk.

She realized suddenly that he was wearing perfume of a strange, sweet scent that might have come from exotic oils.

His limp hair shone beneath the chandeliers as though coated with a thin oil.

She felt nauseated.

Colonel Ready said, "*Mon president*, Miss Macklin wanted to see you but she just told me she is feeling unwell. Would you forgive us if I took her back to the Ritz?"

"Colonel, mademoiselle: Permit me. If you are ill, I will have my physician attend you. We have a bedroom at the palace, many bedrooms—"

"No." The voice was sharp, certain of command. "Can't you see she is really tired, brother?"

Rita felt naked as they all looked at her.

And then Yvette turned to Colonel Ready and said, "Take her back to the hotel, colonel."

"Yes, mademoiselle."

"Claude, we have many other guests to attend to," she said. "The hour is late. The American consul has gone."

And then the president did a strange thing. He turned to his sister and his eyes seemed to glaze as though he were falling into a trance; his face was formed into the face of another person. "Who made us late?" The words were bitchy, uttered in a flat near-falsetto and Rita felt very frightened.

Outside the palace a few minutes later, in the still, humid air, she shivered. Colonel Ready understood. He took her arm again.

"They are frightening—"

"They should frighten you. *Mon president* wants you, I'm afraid." There was annoyance in his voice. "It's too bad. A complication."

"You knew this would happen."

"No. I can't predict the future. I don't anticipate the consequences; I act. I leave that for your friend."

"It would have been better to kill you."

"Yes," Ready said. "It would have been better for both of you. But that's too late now. He will fly in on the day after tomorrow and while we celebrate the anniversary of the republic, he will do what I asked him to do."

"You could have gotten anyone—"

64

"I wanted him."

"Why?"

Colonel Ready said nothing for a moment as he walked with her down the steps to the Rue Sans Souci that would lead back to the hotel. The city was dark and there were restless sounds in the darkness from those who did not sleep. They could hear radios playing and there was the sound of a guitar and the mournful voice of a very bad singer.

"Because I had to have him," Colonel Ready said.

"That's a threat."

"No. I never threaten. Only say what I will do."

"Then you're going to expose him in any case."

"Perhaps," Colonel Ready said.

She was very afraid in the darkness. She could barely see the outline of the wrought-iron gate that led up the stairs to the Palais Gris. There were sentries on the street. She saw their teeth form a grin, lit from the lights of the palace. Her knees began to buckle under her own weight. Colonel Ready held her arms and she could not move away from him.

"This is a nightmare," she said. She could barely stand up.

"No, Rita. It is much worse than that. Much, much worse," Colonel Ready said and his scar was white and as menacing as a knife across his face. And he leaned close to her and pulled her toward him. She felt his lips upon her lips and she felt her feet slip out from under her. The nightmare was upon her.

9

THE ROAD TO MADELEINE

They kept all the syringes and the needles in a sealed plastic box on the floor of the Jeep. The Jeep growled into a lower gear and the wheels grabbed at the slippery road that ran up the mountain. Beyond this last hill was Madeleine, the second city of St. Michel, tucked at the southern point of the crescent-moon-shaped island. Everyone on St. Michel believed the rebels owned Madeleine, even if there were some government troops billeted there.

"Why do we need to meet with a man like that?" Sister Agnes Kozowski had asked in St. Michel town, before the journey. She always asked the obvious questions.

"Because the mission is in the mountains again. And he has control of the hills."

"They aren't real mountains. Not like in Colorado."

"As you've told us many times." Sister Mary Columbo gave Agnes short shrift because Agnes, for all her generosities, had a sometimes whining nature. She had acquired it as an only child in a rich family.

The third nun in the Jeep, dressed like the others in simple khaki trousers and a cotton blouse, was Sister Mary St. John of God. She was the oldest of the three women but was not the leader. Sister Mary Columbo thought that she was probably a saint.

Sister Mary Columbo was sure that sainthood was not very close to her. She had been a nurse and skilled field medic in Vietnam. She had worked with a MASH unit in Vietnam more than fifteen years before. She was forty but she felt so old and despairing at times that she prayed herself awake all night. She was a practical woman. Sometimes, it frightened her to think that everything she did in the world did not matter.

Sister Agnes, on the other hand, knew she was making a difference by her actions and that she was saving lives. Which is why Sister Agnes was impatient about making the trip down the coast from St. Michel town to Madeleine to seek out permission from the rebels to cross into the hills that followed the line of the island on the windward side above the coastal road.

The nuns had medical supplies: penicillin and vaccines against scarlet fever and whooping cough—both diseases currently prevalent on the island among the children—and polio vaccines. There had been a polio epidemic in the hills the previous summer and more than a hundred children had died and many more had been crippled.

There were also books that contained prayers and stories. There were many rosaries as well because the people in the hills prized them and wore them as jewelry, which annoyed the archbishop down in the capital. Still, thought Sister Mary Columbo when she thought of it at all, bringing all those rosaries was a useful defense against the habit of ritual marking and the piercing of nostrils, earlobes, and sexual parts that was still practiced for ornamental reasons among the most backward of the hill people.

"It is too horrible sometimes," Sister Agnes had confessed one night during the summer, on their last mission in the hills, after another baby had died of polio.

"God is with us," Sister Mary Columbo had said. She had grown up in New York City, in the section called Hell's Kitchen on the West Side. The remarkable thing was that when she spoke of God, she believed all she said.

The Jeep was covered with dust so that the windshield was opaque save for the half-circle cleared by the wipers. The Jeep followed the last long blind curve to the summit. It was necessary to drive slowly here because a driver could not see a car coming from the direction of Madeleine; on the other hand, if you drove too slowly, there was a risk of stalling out the engine. Dense forests lined either side of the road. The tropical pines smelled sweet in the mountain air, and it was not so humid here. The road had been asphalt when it was built, but in too many places the asphalt had been broken up by neglect and the rains and the binding had dried up and the cinders broke away so that it was as treacherous as a gravel road. As the Jeep neared the summit of the hill that overlooked Madeleine, the road grew very narrow.

"Be careful," said Sister Agnes, who always said such things at moments like this.

Sister Mary Columbo bit her lip. She shoved the gear down the last notch and popped the clutch. The wheels spun and bit at the sliding asphalt base and nearly lost it and bit again and this time, they dug in. The Jeep protested the incline. The Jeep climbed the last hundred yards to the top of the hill, whining against the strain. The sound of the motor was so loud that they did not hear the first burst of the automatic weapons.

Sister Mary St. John of God, who had been sitting next to the supplies in the rear jump seat, saw the top of Sister Agnes's head blown off in a bloody clump. She saw this and was puzzled for a fraction of a second and then she could hear the sound of the weapons and she understood.

The bullets smashed the old nun's face and she fell sideways, still gripping the rollbar, still staring with sightless eyes now at the bloody bowl of Sister Agnes's head.

Sister Mary Columbo flinched at the firing because she had flinched for two years in Vietnam and even when she got home, she flinched at every sudden, sharp report. She did not look at Sister Agnes but pushed at the pedal and urged the engine up. The Jeep bucked and slipped again on the asphalt and then smashed sideways at a very slow speed into the soft wood of the pine trees at the side of the road. Sister Mary Columbo was slammed forward and cut her head on the windshield.

"I'm all right," she said in an odd voice to her dead companions. "I'm all right," she repeated and her voice was detached from her body. She felt no pain. She heard no sound, not even the firing that came from the men who were in the forest. She felt very calm. She stared at the trees.

The bullet struck her chest.

She spun around against the steering wheel. She saw Sister Agnes then. Blood covered her face and her dead, open eyes.

"I'm all right," she said softly.

The second bullet smashed into her back and she jerked like a puppet and fell out of the Jeep onto the soft undergrowth beneath the pines on the side of the road. She tasted blood on her lips.

The men came out of the forest then and took the plastic

68

cases of medical supplies from the back of the Jeep. They had to pull Sister Mary St. John of God's body out of the Jeep to get all the supplies. One of the men prodded at the body of Sister Mary Columbo at the side of the road and said something that made the other men laugh. Someone fired his automatic weapon again into the trees. The birds were silent. When the firing stopped, there was no sound at all. The engine had died in the soft crash into the trees and made no sound.

"Should we burn the Jeep?" one of the men asked in the singsong patois.

"No. There is no need to destroy it. It's always good to leave a vehicle like that. You don't know when it might be useful sometime."

One of them tore Sister Mary Columbo's blouse and turned her over. He took out his knife and cut her brassiere. Her wounds were still bleeding and there was blood on her lips. The man used the knife to cut a small mark above her breasts. It looked like a geometric symbol.

After a while, the men walked back into the forest, carrying the supplies in plastic boxes.

After a long, silent time, the birds began to speak again in the trees. In the undergrowth beneath the pines, insects buzzed and whirred and noisily continued the pursuits of their small lives.

It was the sound of the insects that Sister Mary Columbo heard first when she opened her eyes.

10

PHILIPPE

The boy missed Harry Francis.

The boy had awakened when the black police came after the blackout had begun. They had made a lot of noise at the door of the café. Harry Francis had answered the door and there had been an argument. His father had gone to the café to see what was the trouble. His mother told him to stay in bed. He had gotten out of bed and gone to the door and watched them take Harry Francis away. One of the black police took a bottle of whiskey from the table where Harry Francis had been sitting and snoring.

Philippe knew many things. He knew that Harry Francis was a drunk. He did not like Harry when the white man bullied his father. But Harry was the most fascinating man Philippe had ever known in all his eleven years. He studied the white man every day that he came to the café; when Harry did not come to the café, it was as though Philippe had missed school. Now Harry was gone and Daniel, the schoolteacher, was in the capital making money and there was an emptiness to the day.

Philippe had blue eyes that came from his grandfather who had been a Frenchman working for the copper company that had mined the island at the beginning of the century.

The copper had run out and the mines were abandoned in the hills. His grandmother had been a whore. That is what Flaubert, Philippe's father, had said. Her daughter was very beautiful; that was Philippe's mother. Flaubert had married her to take her away from Madeleine where it was certain she would have become a whore. Perhaps she already had been a whore when Flaubert married her.

The white man who had been Philippe's grandfather had gone back to France in the time before the European war. Philippe was told by his mother that his grandfather was a brave man and that he had been killed in the war in Europe. Nobody knew if this story was true but his mother wanted Philippe to believe it. Philippe thought perhaps it was a story for children.

Philippe was a solitary child because his color was wrong. He was too light and his eyes were blue. On the other hand, he was certainly not a white man, like Harry Francis.

Harry Francis had been gone two days.

Philippe thought again about him as he walked south

70

down the deserted beach, away from the café and even farther from the capital. Halfway between St. Michel town and Madeleine was a pier and two shacks where fishermen lived and which smelled of fish. There was a café there like his father's but not as clean. Harry Francis drank there sometimes when he was angry with Flaubert. Maybe Harry was angry now and had gone there instead. The black police would not keep someone like Harry for very long; when they had arrested him once before, they had kept him only two days and he had come back from the jail very weak and very tired and his skin had been very white.

He came over a rise of sand and saw the white man sitting on a piece of driftwood, waiting.

The white man had red hair and dark skin and his gray eyes glittered in the light. He was large but he sat very still with his hands on his knees.

The beach was brilliant in the sun, the sand white and glistening but the tides threw up the remains of squids and man-of-wars and the beach which was littered with driftwood.

The white man did not speak.

"Who are you?" Philippe said. He did not move closer.

"*Gamin*," began Devereaux. His language was not of the island, Philippe saw. "You are Flaubert's son."

"Yes."

"Where is Harry Francis?"

"In jail."

"Why is he in jail?"

"I don't know. It is about Monsieur Cohn, I suppose."

"I don't understand."

"Who are you?"

"*Gamin*," Devereaux said again, "I talked to one of the fishermen down at the dock. He said that you were a friend of Harry's."

Philippe blushed. He felt proud that the fishermen would understand that Harry Francis valued him as a friend.

71

"Harry was arrested by the *gendarmes noires* two days ago. At night. After the blackout."

"Why?"

"They ask him about Monsieur Cohn. No one has seen him since he left my father's café many days ago. I think six days."

"Who was Cohn?"

"Another white man. He drank with Harry but he wanted something from him."

"What did he want?"

"A book. No. It was in English. A word that is . . ." Philippe bit his lip. "I don't remember. A nun-book."

"Notebook."

"Ah, *oui, d'accord*. Notebook."

"Did Harry give him a notebook?"

"No. Everyone talks to Harry about his notebook. But I don't think he has one. I told him once I would like to see it and he said he would show it to me some day. When he was finished with it. But I knew he was not telling me the truth."

"How did you know."

"Because I could see it in his eye. When he tells me a lie, his eye does not look at me."

"The notebook is a lie."

"He said it is all the secrets. How could it be all the secrets—there are so many of them?"

"You heard him talk to Cohn."

"When I cleaned the blood. Monsieur Harry had killed a chicken and I had to clean the floor."

"Harry is in jail then," Devereaux said, staring at the sand, his gray eyes distant with thought.

"If he is not with the fishermen."

"No."

"Sometimes he goes there when he is angry with my father."

"Where does Harry live?"

"Toward the hills. That way."

"You've been there?"

72

"Yes. Sometimes I go to see Harry and we talk."

"You like Harry."

"Yes. We are friends."

"Will you take me to his place."

"Do you think he's there?"

"I don't know, *gamin*."

"Why do you want to see him?"

"To find out about the book."

"The nun-book?" Philippe smiled. "Everyone wants the same thing and all leave without it. Even the *gendarmes noires*."

"They wanted the notebook."

"The first time. A long time ago they took Harry to jail and when he came back, they had hurt him. He told me later that they had wanted the notebook and that he would not give it up. That's when I thought there was none and that Harry was too ashamed to say that he had not written the book."

"Ashamed?"

"He is a writer. He showed me the books he wrote. All of them a long time ago. But he has not written for a long time."

Devereaux stood up. "Show me the place."

■ ■ ■

They climbed for a half hour and the house was half hidden in the trees. The place was old and ramshackle. There were two rooms and outside, a privy. The walls of the shack were very dry. The wood was bleached and the tarpaper on the roof was thin and peeling. They had passed a half dozen shacks like this, all of wood, unlike the concrete huts in the town and along the beach.

Devereaux opened the door of the shack. The boy stood on the porch and watched him. The place smelled of Harry. He had lived there for six years, since he first came to St. Michel.

The larger room was full of books. They were stacked on shelves and on the floor. There was a large and dirty cotton rug on the floor. There was a big easy chair of cracked vinyl near the window. Next to the chair was a tray with an empty vodka bottle on it.

The place had been searched not very long ago, Devereaux saw. Some of the books were strewn, some had been replaced on the shelves. Dust had been disturbed and it had been so recent that a new layer of dust was still in the beginning stages. Perhaps a couple of days, about the time Harry was arrested.

When Rita Macklin came to St. Michel.

It was the second thought—the one about Rita—that had filled him from the moment the boy said Harry Francis had been arrested. If Ready did not need Devereaux to find Harry's secret for him, he did not need Rita Macklin. Why had he involved them at all, why go to Switzerland and set a trap to get Devereaux to this island?

Rita had asked him the questions that night in Lausanne and he could not answer them. He had to walk in darkness with flat, uncertain treads on uncertain surfaces, hoping that he would eventually have light and a solid foundation to stand on. Ready wanted a spy as good as Ready.

The boy said, "He has not been here."

"No."

"He must still be in jail."

"Where is the jail?"

"In the capital. In the basement of the Palais Gris."

"What's that?"

"The presidential palace. The jail is in the basement. You can hear the prisoners when they are screaming."

Devereaux was looking at the books, opening them, closing them, going through the careful routine in the hot, still room. "Why do they scream?"

"Because they are in pain."

"Do the police torture prisoners?"

"They tortured Monsieur Harry. The first time. They thought they had killed him. Harry said it was why they let him go, they did not want to kill him, they only wanted to frighten him."

"Was he frightened?"

"Some people think he is a buffoon, but Monsieur Harry is not. He is a brave man," Philippe said of his friend.

Harry's titles were few. They were espionage novels all written more than a decade before. The covers of the novels were lurid, with men with guns and women with long legs and frightened faces. "By Harry Francis." He had been working for the Langley Firm then. They had approved his work, even encouraged it, Devereaux supposed. The intelligence agencies had writers who wrote novels that planted disinformation in the minds of the Soviet agents who read those novels for clues to what the Americans were really doing. Harry was part of a long literary tradition of spies turned writers.

And he had known Hemingway and he had become "Hemingway."

Devereaux spent a careful hour in the two rooms. He worked slowly and tried consciously not to hurry in his task. He touched every object in both rooms. His fingers turned over books and notebooks and canister jars full of caked salt and a Zenith transoceanic radio and bedclothes that were strewn around an unmade army cot. It was the home of a lonely, middle-aged man who had gathered some treasures and comforts and then had abandoned them because they were not enough.

There was nothing in the house.

Devereaux walked outside and stretched in the muggy air. The sun was filtered by trees here and it was not so hot as it was down on the beach.

"You see," said Philippe with triumph in his voice. "No one can find Monsieur Harry's notebook."

"Because it does not exist."

"That is what I think," Philippe said. But he had lost the attention of the white man, who was crossing the bare, sandy yard in back of the shack to the privy.

Devereaux opened the door and was assailed by the dank stink of rotting feces in the holding tank.

"What do you look for?"

"The same thing the other men looked for."

"Commander Celezon."

"And Colonel Ready."

"Once Colonel Ready came here. I know. Alone. I saw him. He was like you. He looked in the toilet. What are you looking for?"

Devereaux made a face and stood still until he became accustomed to the smell. Then he took a stick and poked at the underside of the toilet seat, which was a wooden shelf with a hole cut in the middle. There was nothing.

He expected to find nothing. But it was the way you did a search. The way Ready would have done a search.

He dropped the stick.

The stick dropped into the filthy holding tank and struck something. The sound was hard, wood on metal.

He looked at Philippe, who was staring at him with wide blue eyes in a wonderfully old and cynical child's face.

Devereaux reached under the seat and pulled at the nails that held it to the support boards.

The nails screeched and the board came up. The holding tank was open but there was nothing to be seen but the murky filthy water and the bits of paper and leaves and the rotting feces.

The stick floated on the scum.

Devereaux made a face. He took the shelving of the toilet bench and poked the surface of the water. He felt a hard object beneath the opaque scum.

He put the toilet seat back on the boards and stepped out of the privy. He stared at Philippe and the boy returned the stare. The boy knew, Devereaux thought. He had known when he had watched Colonel Ready alone go through the search and miss it. He had known when he saw Celezon and his men tear up Harry's place and miss it. He had known.

"How does Harry get it out?"

"I don't know what you mean."

Devreaux shrugged. He walked back to the shack. He

found it in plain sight. Fishing poles and bits of tackle and leaders and reels. Also an old net.

And the net on the pole.

He went back to the privy.

The box was wrapped in oilcloth and it was dripping with scum when he lifted it out of the holding tank. He dropped the box on the ground. With the end of a stick, he opened the oilcloth. He took the box and wiped his hands on his trousers and they streaked his trousers with filth.

He was sweating and the boy was watching him but from a little distance.

"This is Harry's secret place isn't it?"

"I don't know," the boy said and he took a step back.

"Is that true?"

"I would not lie."

"You would lie to protect Harry."

"I would protect Harry anyway."

"If I open the box and you see what it is, what will you do?"

"Nothing."

"You might tell the police."

"You don't ever talk to the police. You don't know that? But you are white, so you don't have to know that."

Devereaux thought he understood. Besides, what would the boy know?

My God, Devereaux thought. A secret. Harry has a secret after all. It was the last thing he wanted.

He wanted only to have enough time to put a finger on Colonel Ready, set the trap he had already baited with his gaudy performance in London and Miami and in Fort Myers Beach. And now there was a secret.

Devereaux opened the lock with a knife. Inside the tackle box was more oilcloth. He opened this and took out the contents.

There was a photograph. It was pasted to cardboard to make it stiff. It was a little faded. The photograph showed a large, bearded man with a large belly who wore a white shirt and shorts. He was a handsome man with a straight nose who combed his hair forward to his forehead, as though he might be going bald.

Philippe came close. He stood near Devereaux, who was crouched on the ground. Philippe was overcome by curiosity. He came and looked at the photograph. He said, "This man looks like Harry but it is not him."

"No," Devereaux said.

"Who is this man?"

"A writer named Ernest Hemingway."

"Harry told me about Ernest many times. He said I would like this man, he was a man who knew many children."

"And this man is Harry when he was young."

They both saw it. They stared at the young man, thinner, wearing a black mustache, taller than Hemingway, also clad in shorts. The two men standing on a dock somewhere. Perhaps in Cuba, when Harry had worked for the Langley Agency there. The writer and the spy.

Carefully, he put down the photograph on the grass and he picked up the notebook.

It was bound in good calfskin leather. The thin pages were yellowed by the years.

"That is Harry's book."

"You know about that."

"Everyone has heard of Harry's book. It is magic. But no one has ever seen it. The *gendarmes noires* came here many times and they never found the book. And that is the book and you have found it." Philippe was impressed.

Devereaux opened the book and he saw the first page covered with numbers in rows. The numbers were grouped in sets of five. A simple number code. Row after row of numbers. The kind of numbers sent in simple ciphers before the war, before the invention of machines that could invent random codes that could not be broken without another receiving machine.

He turned the pages, kneeling on the grass.

Thirty pages were filled in a methodical way with the numbers, each neatly copied, each set of five followed by a precise space that led to a second set of five.

There could not have been a notebook; Devereaux had thought the notebook was a ruse from the beginning, a fabrication created by Harry or by Ready to use against Devereaux. Devereaux had realized sitting in the café in Evian that Ready meant to kill him and he had not understood why he had not killed him then and there. Why lure him and Rita to this island with an elaborate explanation about Harry Francis and his secrets and about spies and about "operations" about to commence. No one cared about St. Michel.

Except there was a notebook in code and it changed the rules of the game and changed all of Devereaux's expectations.

The damned thing should not have existed.

"What will you do, monsieur?"

"I don't know."

"You will take the book that everyone speaks about."

"Yes."

"It belongs to Harry."

"I'll give it back to Harry. When he is released. From jail."

"What if they beat him again as they did before and this time he tells them where the notebook is and it is not here when they come for it? They might kill him."

"Did he tell you they beat him?"

"Yes. Twice. He showed me the marks."

Then that part of it was true as well. Ready really had wanted the book, really believed in it. And he had power over Harry Francis but only up to a point. If he didn't have the notebook, he had to be careful with Harry.

"I could tell them you found the book," said Philippe and then he was afraid because of what he had said.

Devereaux stared at him a moment, the eyes going cold and dead. "Yes." And then the color changed in his eyes, as though he had decided something.

"Yes," he said. "Tell them if you want. They might kill him in that case. But you can tell them."

"You are not afraid?"

"No," Devereaux said and it was a lie.

"What is the book? What are those numbers?"

"I don't know."

"Harry said once they were looking for the wrong book." Philippe blurted this out because this man impressed him. This man was not afraid. Even Philippe's own father, Flaubert, was afraid. But this man did not talk too much as Harry did and even though Harry was white, he was afraid of the *gendarmes noires*.

"There's another book?"

The boy stood unblinking but a little space away from Devereaux. "He said this and laughed. He pointed to his head. That's all he said. I said there was no book. He laughed at me and said there was a book but they were all looking for the wrong book. The one that counted was the one that was hidden in plain sight. I did not understand him. He said this in French to me very clearly but I did not understand him."

11

THE STRANGER AT THE SQUARE

Simon Bouvier, the archbishop of St. Michel, felt his stomach growl in protest because the morning had not been full of food. He ignored it for once. He blessed the crowd first with holy water so vigorously that a few droplets clung to the face of the president who stood in the front row at the foot of the steps of the cathedral. And then he raised his right hand again to make the sign of the cross over the multitude. His stomach rumbled and even the president heard it.

The square in front of the white adobe cathedral was filled. All in the square blessed themselves, even the people who had come down from the hill and who bore marks of the voodoo on their bodies. All blessed themselves except two of the American reporters who had flow in from Miami and the reporter from the newspaper in Havana. The Cuban reporter explained to everyone, over and over again, that he was an atheist.

The people had been brought in from far neighborhoods of the capital city as well as from the junkyard-strewn suburbs that led into the hills above the squat roofs of the town. The *gendarmes noires* had gone out very early in the morning, when there was still fog clinging to the damp coastline and the town, to find enough people to fill the square. They had brought them down in flatbed trucks. The trucks growled through the ghostly, foggy streets for hours, bringing down people and going back empty to find more. Some of the people even came on their own, like the people from the hills. It was a national holiday to mark the independence of St. Michel.

In the center of the square was an obelisk of granite erected in 1919 in memory of the men of St. Michel who had volunteered to fight with the French in the first European war. None of them had ever returned, though not all had died. There were twelve names on the obelisk and some said that at least three of the names were fictitious. But the war was lost in a long ago memory and no one cared that some of the names might not be real.

The square and the memorial were the sites of all official celebrations on the island. The flag of St. Michel, adopted from the French tricolor, was red, white, and blue, but superimposed on the white third was a round orange disk that represented the sun.

The cathedral was Norman with two towers, one of which was finished with a pointed roof, the other of which was flat. Bells in the tower rang. They rang on all forty-one feast days and days of national holiday in the calendar of St. Michel.

The president stood as the French consul general walked stiffly across the square and stopped in front of him. He carried a box containing the medal of the Legion of Honor. He said something to the president and the president nodded and said something else that no one could hear. There were loudspeakers but they continued to play music. The president bent his head and the French consul general hung the award on a silken band around his neck and kissed him on each cheek.

Then there were to be speeches. The music stopped and the first scratchy voice came over the loudspeakers and no one could understand what was being said.

Rita Macklin had gone to a café off the square with a fellow American she had met in the crowd. He was Anthony Calabrese and Rita thought Anthony was a much more fascinating event than the one in the square. She had felt alone and afraid for nearly four days; Ready had not contacted her again after that night he had kissed her in the darkness at the bottom of the hill from the presidential palace. It was as though he had wanted her to feel her isolation. She would have welcomed seeing him if he had called her; she wanted another voice or even the familiar face of a man she loathed to soothe the aloneness.

Because Devereaux had not come.

Anthony Calabrese bought her a beer in the café and ordered a glass of Perrier for himself. He said his stomach didn't drink before noon, even if he wanted to. He had said a lot of things she thought were funny. Maybe she missed laughing with someone. Maybe she was only very afraid of being alone.

"Come on," he urged her, taking her arm and leading her to the café. "Nobody is going to do anything until the fat lady sings. Besides, you can fake it in your stories. Everyone does."

Now he sat across from her. He had olive eyes and dark skin and dark, glistening hair and a golden chain around his neck. His face was broad but not without interesting depths. His cheeks were high and he might have been her age.

"You're a reporter, huh?"

"Yeah, a reporter, huh."

He smiled. "You got the wrong story."

"'Wrong story.' What story should I have?"

"The nuns. Those are the people you oughta be writing about. Up in the hills, giving medicine to the tutzons. That's the story. Sisters of the Holy Name. Sister Mary Columbo, my cousin for Christ's sake, I didn't even know she was here until I was down here a couple of times, my Aunt Rose says your own cousin, the nun, she's down here in this place called St. Michel, she's working for the poor. I never even told my Aunt Rose I was down here, I musta let it slip, who talks about St. Michel?"

"You're a travel agent."

"A packager." He smiled. "Hell, maybe I deal dope, you never know. Everyone does."

"Do you deal dope?"

"No."

"Is that true?"

"Yeah. But what the hell, how do you know if I'm telling the truth."

"You wouldn't lie to me, would you?"

"Baby, I love red-haired broads, drive me crazy. Of course I'd lie to you. I'd tell you anything you wanted to hear. Salut." He raised his Perrier and drank a sip. "Frog bubblies. You go in New York, pay three bucks a pop for seltzer as long as it comes from France. People want to be robbed, you know? They walk around with their pockets open and money stuffed in their noses."

She laughed then and it was in relief, to hear a human, cynical voice of another American cutting through this claustrophobic nightmare on the island. She had dreamed of Ready and it had not been pleasant. She had felt an ache where Devereaux should have been, next to her.

She sipped her beer.

"Girlish figure, you drink beer?"

"I run."

"Everybody runs. Sickening. You shouldn't drink outa a glass here."

"Why?"

"Germs."

"You do."

"Honey, I drank tap water in Mexico. I got no feelings inside."

She stared at him, trying to understand him. He seemed more exotic because he was so much more out of place than anyone else in St. Michel. He was a story, St. Michel was not. She tried to think of a story, not of Devereaux.

"These people are filthy. They wash once, when they get baptized. They want tourists here, they gotta shape up. People don't want filth coming off a cruise ship. They want local color like they see in a movie, they don't want to smell it. They'll take niggers but they don't want dirty. Even French niggers. The best of both worlds."

"Why are you here?"

"I told you. Travel."

"No ships come here. A cabdriver said they don't have a deep harbor."

Silence for a moment. She waited.

"Fucking want to build a new pier, dredge the harbor, bring in cruise ships. So they pop for me to see what they're doing. They do nothing. See that hole in town? The museum. Shit. I'll build a museum before they do. Besides, what do people want with a museum?"

"Cruise people."

"Right. This is free port? They got whores? So what? Whores are on the ship, pardon me."

"Gambling," she guessed.

"Gambling," he said. "You see the program."

"You represent someone?"

"I represent me."

"No. Gambling interests," she said, interested.

"Always a possibility, you gotta say that. But you gotta have a clean act. Go down to the Bahamas, they play that English kind of craps, different rules, pisses people off. American craps, American tables. I mean, these mopes think they're gonna get frogs coming here?"

"I don't know about gambling."

"Take Atlantic City," he said. "They clean it up. Atlantic City, pardon me, is for shit. I gotta cousin lives there, gotta be the last white man in a hundred blocks. For shit, all of it. The best thing ever happened to that town since Monopoly is gambling."

"I know."

"But you keep it clean even when the city is for shit. They keep the garbage tucked away from the casinos. You go to Atlantic City, you don't even have to see the town for Christ's sake. You eat inna hotel, gamble inna hotel, drink inna hotel, get laid inna hotel, and bam, you're back on the bus and home before you know it, explaining to the old lady how you blew ten dimes in two days."

"I know. You're going to do the same thing for St. Michel."

"Me? I'm a small fish," said Anthony Calabrese. "People want to listen to me, I tell them things. I scrounge up tours, I take freebies to get my own tan. I booked the Caribbean by now for the season, I take a few days off. But nothing is going to happen in St. Michel."

The words echoed oddly to her. She sipped her beer. From the bottle this time.

"Why'd you come to do this story?" he said suddenly. He was very alert. She felt tension between them. She put down the bottle and lied to him with her eyes.

"I do what I can get paid for. That's free-lance work."

"You must not be very good to have to work a story like this."

"And you must be a crackerjack travel agent to be here," she said.

85

He smiled, leaned back, broke the string. "So I lie. So you lie to me. So it tells us something, right?"

"What?" Her voice was cold.

"We got reason to lie to each other," he said.

"You work for Colonel Ready?"

"No."

"You know him."

"Sure. There's fifty thousand people on the island and maybe fifteen are worth knowing. Sure, I know him, he knows me. But I don't work for him."

"Everyone lies in a place like this after a while," she said.

"Yeah. That's right. It's a haunted island. The French pulled out when the mines went and they've got ghosts. And Claude-Eduard is a ghost. And the voodoo—"

"In the hills," she said.

"Ghosts and spells and chants. All nuts but all ghosts and goblins. You ever meet Harry Francis?"

"Who?"

"Harry Francis. He lives here. He's an agent."

"What do you mean?"

"He's a spy."

"Why are you telling me this?"

"He's fun. Everyone knows he's an agent. The upfront agent, you might say. He's a ghost, too, you know." Anthony Calabrese was smiling, twisting his necklace between his index finger and thumb, his olive eyes shining with cynical amusement.

"His own ghost."

"And Hemingway. The writer. I told you. The only good story here is the nuns. Up in the hills. Not Manet and his rebels, not Ready, not nothing else." He dropped his chain on his chest and leaned forward again. "You don't want to write about ghosts. Nobody would believe you. The nuns. That's what you want to write about."

"And maybe Anthony Calabrese," she said. "You're real, aren't you? I mean, you exist."

86

He smiled. "No. Not really," he said. "You want another beer?"

But the music was finished in the square and the president's speech was to begin and Rita declined. She went back to the square and scanned the crowd while the president spoke, and she thought of everything Anthony had told her and wished that she would see Devereaux's face in the crowd, to have one chance to speak to him now. She felt lost in unreality. She felt trapped by the island heat, by the island mentality, by the shabby poverty around her, by the threat of Colonel Ready against her existence, against Devereaux's. She would only have done it for Devereaux, she thought at first, but there was her own peculiar curiosity as well. St. Michel had secrets in layers, but which ones were important?

The nuns, she thought, half listening to the speech. Maybe the nuns had the secret worth knowing.

12

CAIN

The *Compass Rose* was six miles east of St. Michel and moving away and the beaches had disappeared into the shimmering horizon formed by water and sand. The hills above the coast road were dusky in the light of the afternoon sun, neither green nor brown, just colored dark against the changing sky.

The *Compass Rose*'s sails cut easily into the steady, low wind. The sky was full of clouds sailing in lines of war before the wind. The color of the clear water changed as the light changed against the sea, filtered through the various clouds. Here it was green and there it was a color almost like a vein of gold, running a zigzag into the steady waves that slapped the stern of the *Compass Rose* as she turned in the water toward the south point of St. Michel island.

Devereaux sat on deck and studied the book. He turned to each page and stared at each one for a long time and then went on to the next page.

The book was 192 pages long. Thirty pages were filled with the patient rows of numbers.

Devereaux sat cross-legged on the deck while Cain stood in the open cockpit and watched the sea roll before him. The wind snapped the mainsail and there was an agreeable sea odor of fish and canvas and dampness on the wooden deck. There were no sounds but sea against sail and wood and the cries of gulls following on a trailing wind.

Devereaux took out a red-handled Vercingetorix Swiss Army knife and opened the penknife. He slid the blade edge up the book endpaper and broke the ancient bond of the dried glue. He slid the knife very slowly and carefully up the end-paper so that he did not cut it.

Devereaux wore light blue shorts. His naked body was tanned not because of the sun but because of the six tablets sold to him by the reliable chemist in Baker Street in London, the one the Section always used. Hanley would be billed in a few days. The tablets turned his skin almost black. He wondered whether Hanley had been contacted yet by Economic Review for the information he had purchased on St. Michel.

The trail he left was intended to be just obvious enough, something to interest Hanley and Mrs. Neumann but not enough to make them act.

Devereaux stared at the writing his knife had uncovered on the inside of the endpaper.

Six rows of numbers now but written with more hurry, broken into words. And signed, this time: "Papa."

In plain English.

But who was Papa? A demented Harry Francis or was it a real signature. Someone would know who knew those things but he was 225 miles from Key West. It would wait because Devereaux still had no leverage on Colonel Ready.

"What do you want to do now?"

Devereaux frowned at the book in his hand and then glanced up at Cain. He left Cain for a while and went below decks. When he returned, he had a notebook in his hand.

Cain's empty land eyes seemed full of calm on water, reflecting the sea life around him. He left the emptiness in the harbor of Fort Myers Beach, in the darkness, with the two DEA agents at the bridge watching the black hull of the black ship *Compass Rose* creep out of the harbor. When they crossed from the channel through Big Carlos Pass to the open gulf, the same two agents had been at the open bridge, watching the passage of the ship.

And Cain had waved at them and the two men in business suits and open collars had stared at him until the *Compass Rose* was on the far side of the bridge of Big Carlos Pass. Then Cain had given the two men the finger. They had just kept staring until the boat was a dot in the open gulf, heading into blackness from lighted darkness, into the evening chill of the sea. "I have to land at Madeleine." It was the town at the southern tip of the island.

"There's the johnboat. I can take you around to the windward side. If there's a storm, the boat'll break up and then I don't know how I get you off the island."

"I'll get off the island," Devereaux said.

Cain stared down at him. The *Compass Rose* swelled on the water.

"I could leave you," he said.

"And leave five thousand dollars."

"It's not that much money."

"Only if you don't have it," Devereaux said quietly. Twelve years is a long time gone to judge a man again. He had needed Cain because Cain was in the right place and because Cain would have to do what he said. Up to a point.

"I been thinking," said Cain in that soft voice that barely carried above the sound of the wind on the sails.

Devereaux waited.

"Colonel Ready was with Langley Firm," said Cain. "I

knew that much. Even knew how you spooks talked about each other. Langley. The Company. The Section. The Opposition. A fucking game right in the middle of the war you started."

Devereaux sighed and glanced at the book and then slipped it into the waterproof bag and zipped it and stood up slowly. He was in his middle forties. His body had a tautness that was earned, not expected as it was in youth. His belly had two scars and there were peculiar soft scars like belly buttons tucked into the soft flesh beneath his rib cage. That was when he had been shot once by someone behind him whom he had trusted. The last agent he had trusted for either side. There was the faint trace of a scar across his neck, from the time in Belfast when he had been garroted. He had too many scars, Rita once said. He had agreed.

"Ready and you. I don't know which one I hated more. Then."

"It wasn't me," Devereaux said.

"You can say it now. But I never knew. None of you tells the truth."

"It doesn't matter," Devereaux said just as quietly as Cain.

"You're not working for Section, are you?"

"No."

"And Ready?"

"I don't know."

"What do you want?"

"I want to finish a job. I want to get away," Devereaux said.

"From who?"

"Ready. Or the Section. Or Langley. Or all of them."

"You quit, huh?" In that sun-black face was the trace of a smile. "Just the way I was let to quit."

"You weren't part of us," Devereaux said. "We used you. We had leverage."

"You had Susan Minh," Cain said. "And the boy. You

got them out. You did that. I agreed to the rest because you did that."

"You were just a soldier. It wasn't your game. I followed the case. After. I was sorry about Susan and Thau."

The names seemed to break Cain apart. He shuddered and turned and jumped from the cockpit to the open deck. Devereaux had expected it. He turned into the big man and reached for the soft parts of skin beneath the armpits and let the big man hit him as he threw him toward the rail. Cain hit the rail with his belly and made a sound. And Devereaux pushed him into the water.

The *Compass Rose*, freed from a hand on the wheel, yawned toward the port side, the mast dipping and pointing at the sun like a rifle barrel.

Cain came out of the green clear water and pounded the water with his open hands.

Devereaux turned the wheel in the cockpit and spun it against the port dip and the *Compass Rose* forgave the men on her and righted herself.

Cain could not pull himself out of the water.

Devereaux lashed the wheel and threw out a lifeline. He dragged Cain aboard.

They did not speak for a moment. Cain sat on the deck in a puddle of water, gasping for breath.

He looked up at Devereaux. "You had to pull me out. You couldn't handle the *Compass Rose* yourself."

"I don't know that."

"You're not a sailor."

"And you're not one of us," Devereaux said carefully.

"I betrayed her. And her family. That's why she killed herself."

"Yes. Perhaps."

"I wanted to have her too bad. I squeezed her like you squeeze a bird and you kill it in the palm of your hand."

"Yes." Devereaux thought of himself. Was his palm open or closed? Who would die if he made a fist?

"All right. I made my own choice." Softly, words often spoken to himself. "All right."

"I need to go to Madeleine."

"I won't help you," Cain said.

"For money," Devereaux said.

"To hell with you. I just wanted to get both of you and kill you—"

"There is a woman," Devereaux said. "Her name is Rita Macklin. On the island."

Cain breathed harshly and watched Devereaux.

"Who is she?"

"Mine."

Cain's eyes opened wide.

"Yours? A woman? And Colonel Ready has her." Cain smiled. "Thieves fall out. You bastards deserve each other."

"You're a fool, Cain," Devereaux said. His voice was weary, flat, edged with anger. "Self-pitying fool. The Minhs were traitors. For you and for the woman and the boy, we got you to do what you should have done. Your sense of personal ethics only bothered you when Susan wouldn't let you win. I'm tired of you. Pull by the island and I'll take the lifeboat and you can go back to Florida. Go run dope or whatever your conscience allows you."

"You won't get off the island," Cain said in a distant voice. "Not if Colonel Ready doesn't want you to leave. Not if you don't have the *Compass Rose*."

"Then I'll die there," Devereaux said.

"It's that easy."

"Easier than trying to deal with people like you," Devereaux said.

"What am I that's so bad?"

"A burned-out case. I don't have any use for you."

"What about this woman?"

"Don't worry about it."

"What will Colonel Ready do to her?"

"Nothing. I think." He stared through Cain. "I think he

92

won't do anything once he finds out what he wants to know. Once he has me."

"You walk into it."

Devereaux felt chilled in the bright hot sunlight of the open deck. The black boat turned slowly into the wind, the wheel straining against the lashing.

"It was a private matter," Devereaux said. "I was out of the old business."

"And now you're in."

"Ready came for me. I thought I didn't have a choice. I let her be hostage to give me time. I rationalized everything."

What was he saying? But he was not talking to Cain. He did not see Cain at all. He stared straight into him and through him. A moment before, when he saw Cain, he realized everything.

"I was willing to risk her. I wanted her bad enough for that," Devereaux said. "And now I see you, twelve years later. And I see me."

Cain stood up and walked past Devereaux to the wheel. He untangled the crude lash and pushed the *Compass Rose* into the wind again and began to make for Madeleine.

Neither man said a word. Devereaux went below and hauled up a seabag after a few minutes. He wore jeans and a light blue work shirt. His hair was still dyed red but the other pieces of disguise, including the white scar, were gone. He put the waterproof bag with the notebook into the seabag and went to the rail and watched the approach of land. Once, Cain tried to speak but Devereaux did not look at him. Cain's eyes were empty now, as they had been on land, as they had not been at sea until this moment.

Devereaux lowered his bag and his body into the dirty white dinghy and Cain released the lines and Devereaux's oars bit into the waters on the empty windward side of the island toward the rocks and the ground that fell steeply into the water at shore. Madeleine was around the bend of the hill.

Here all was peace, pine trees, emptiness, sea and land and the murmuring crash of waves.

"Devereaux," Cain said. It was the first time he had spoken his name. But Devereaux was working the dinghy hard. Perhaps he was too far away to hear him.

"The hell with both of them," Cain said. He lowered the sail furiously and he started the engines and the black bulk of the *Compass Rose* turned and began running to the north and west, away from the island.

13

HARRY'S TROUBLE

Celezon gave the orders without shouting, with the skill and calm of a surgeon preparing for a routine operation.

They followed the orders just as calmly.

They took Harry Francis out of the drunk cell in the basement of the palace in the morning. He smelled very bad. He had slept on the cement floor in his filthy clothes.

They put Harry in another cell with tile walls and a tile floor and two drains. They left the door open and Harry huddled in the far corner and tried not to look at the open door. When they came back, they sprayed him with a fire hose until he nearly drowned. The water hit him like a continuous clubbing. The water bruised his skin and when he tried to breathe, he breathed water. He fell again and again and banged his head on the wall. He was bleeding and gasping for breath. He could hear them laughing at the door as they sprayed him with water. When they were finished, they told him to remove all his clothes.

He sat on the floor of the tile room exhausted and shivering. He was there for a long time.

When they came back, they brought a wooden chair into

the tile room. They put it in the middle of the floor. One of them tied him with wire to the chair. Harry said he was cold and they smiled at him.

One of them tied a positive wire to his left testicle. He felt the thin strand of wire wrap around the sac and felt sick to his stomach. One of them slapped his penis and said something that made the other one laugh. The second man seemed nervous and he tied the negative ground too tightly to Harry's right testicle.

The two wires were connected to a device like a hand crank with a flywheel and copper points. First one and then the other turned the crank, faster and faster, trying to outdo each other.

When the crank was turned, there was an electrical charge that burned Harry Francis's testicles and seemed to explode his stomach.

He was knocked over, still tied to the chair. He passed out with a scream.

One of the two men frowned then. He went over to Harry's naked body and held his ear against the chest of the prisoner. He heard Harry's heart fluttering beneath the chest wall.

"He's all right."

"We went too fast."

"Celezon told us to use the hand machine, the battery machine was too powerful."

"This is too powerful as well. He can't feel anything if he's unconscious."

"What a heavy pig. Help me lift the chair upright again."

"The trouble is, it's different for each one, depending on how strong they are."

"Yes, but I think we turned it up too much."

"My arm is tired."

"I could do this all day."

"Remember the skinny one last week. He looked like he couldn't take it very much."

"Yes. But he was a man after all. He had courage. Macho. Such little balls he had."

"He never betrayed his comrades."

"He was brave, all right."

"The women."

"That's different, all right."

"Sometimes they're stronger than you think."

"This man smells so bad. He never bathes."

"Sometimes the women are stronger than the men."

"Well, Celezon didn't say how many times to do it."

"I was just getting started."

"Maybe we ought to leave him a while, until he gets awake again before we do it."

"Yes, I suppose. But I was just getting started."

"Still, we aren't supposed to kill him."

"No."

And they left Harry alone for a while.

■ ■ ■

"How are you, Harry?"

"You know how the fuck I am. My balls hurt. Those bastards fried me. I swear to God they were going to kill me, I didn't think you wanted to kill me."

"I didn't order that. Believe me. I've had business with the ceremonies. Our independence celebration, Harry. You missed it."

Harry said nothing.

Colonel Ready put a package of Lucky Strikes on the table. "Go ahead, Harry," he said.

Harry was still naked but he was dry.

He reached for the cigarettes and his hand trembled.

"I told Celezon he was a baboon. He is a baboon. I put the two men who did it in the hills. Let them eat grasshoppers for a couple of weeks."

"I wish you had just killed them."

"Harry, violence begets violence. I need discipline. You can't run an army without discipline."

Harry inhaled. The smoke hurt. His hands shook. His head hurt. He was cut and bruised. And his testicles were bloated and angry red and they burned all the time.

"Harry, we didn't bring you here for violating the statute on public drunkenness. That's why Celezon got carried away, I think. I say that in defense of him."

"I'm glad it was something serious, seeing my balls were practically burned off by those spooks."

"Harry, you take yourself too seriously." The cold eyes narrowed, the scar was bright against the dark face. "You're here in St. Michel on tolerance. I wouldn't show such animosity to the authorities."

Harry took another drag. He coughed. He was so tired.

Colonel Ready took his time. He was careful; he always finished one task before starting another. The nuns had been found outside Madeleine that morning. The journalists were on their way to the story. The president was annoyed. Ready was furious but it did not show in his face. The nuns were not supposed to have been killed. If they were all killed, there would be no one left to tell the story. There was no discipline in the country.

But he took time now to speak to Harry with patient tones.

"What do you want?"

"What did you tell Cohn?"

"I didn't kill him. They said he was killed, I didn't kill him—"

"You didn't?" But it was not really a question. Colonel Ready stared with perfect calmness at the naked man. He let time pass.

"Did you tell Cohn about the notebook?"

"I didn't, I—"

"Harry." Gently. "Harry, we listened to his code transmissions back to Washington. We know you told him."

Another time was allowed to pass.

"Yes," Harry Francis said.

"Good, Harry. I wanted you to tell him about the notebook. But did you tell him what was in it?"

"No."

"Good, Harry. That's good."

"I threatened him with it."

"Good, Harry." Almost a lullaby.

And another time passed. The room was silent. The tomb of the jail was damp and still.

"What do you want from me?"

"I already have what I want from you, Harry. Except for the notebook itself. When are you going to give me the notebook?"

"And when I give it to you, you'll kill me."

"Yes. Our little impasse. It never changes, does it, Harry?"

He was so tired. His beard was soiled. His belly was folded with fat.

"I want you and I want the notebook. But if I have the notebook, I probably don't need you. And if I let you go, nobody needs you, so you choose your voluntary exile on beautiful St. Michel. You choose me over death and I choose you because I must. It's so neat, so well balanced, isn't it, Harry?"

"And there might not be a notebook at all," Harry Francis said, and there was a sudden bitter smile that broke his face.

"Yes. That's a possibility as well. Celezon searched your place again. While you were our guest."

"And didn't find it."

"I don't think Celezon believes it exists."

"Do you?"

"I don't know, Harry. I really don't know. But I have to keep protecting you."

"If your goons had protected me any more, I'd be singing soprano in the Vienna Boys Choir."

"Yes. But if I torture you enough, I get the notebook."

"Or you kill me."

"And there's no notebook and no Harry. I like for there to be one or the other."

"Or both," Harry Francis said.

For minutes, they sat in silence again. The problem between them was almost an agreement. Ready was patient. Celezon would have become angry at Harry and killed him accidentally. Or on purpose. Ready didn't permit anger in himself.

"Perhaps, in a little while, I won't need you, Harry," Colonel Ready said.

"We all get used up. I'm fifty-nine. Hemingway was sixty-one when the end came. I have two more years."

Ready said, "Not that long, Harry."

And Harry Francis shivered because it was cold in the cells.

"Things are happening, Harry. Don't you feel them happening?"

"It's cold in the cells."

"Put your clothes on, Harry. I don't want you to catch cold."

"Until you don't need me anymore," Harry said.

But Ready did not speak.

Harry understood completely.

14

FROM HELL'S KITCHEN

Mary Columbo opened her eyes.

The pain was on her and inside her. But she had fallen in and out of consciousness so often that the pain was expected. It did not seem as intense. Perhaps they had given her some of the drugs they had stolen.

They had removed one bullet but the second was near her spine.

She remembered that and tried to move her toes. She could feel them moving. But the pain was all around her.

"If we remove the bullet, it may kill her; if we don't, then she might be paralyzed."

The voice, in the rough French patois of the country, had come from above her and behind her the last time she had been conscious. She had wanted to speak and tell them that she did not want to be paralyzed.

Another voice: "Don't kill her. Even if she's paralyzed, she's more useful alive."

She blinked and saw she was in a tent now.

I'm all right, she told herself. She told Sister Agnes. But Sister Agnes was dead.

She would not be afraid.

For Thou art with me. Thy rod and Thy staff, they comfort me.

She dreamed of helicopters clattering down out of the sky, the wounded strapped to the sides of the copters, the wounded on buses. The wounded had torn bodies, the wounded were always asking her if they would die. Sometimes they asked without speaking. No, she said, and didn't know.

Will I die, nurse?

Yes. But don't be afraid to die. Fear no evil. God is with you. He comforts you.

It didn't play, Charlie. Nobody wanted to die. It didn't play in Peoria, sis.

They wanted to live and listen to Janis Joplin on the Sony box bought at the PX and wanted grass to ease the pain after the lingering, humid, terrifying afternoon. They wanted music to drive the sounds of death out of their heads. They wanted a fox from Saigon in her little itty-bitty to sit on their laps in the stench of a Saigon bar and open those thin thighs again, smelling Brother Jack Daniel's and Brother Johnnie Walker and they didn't want no cunt telling them they were going to buy a bag and take the big trip home. Man. Nobody wanted to die.

Fear no evil, said Sister Mary Columbo.

She had prayed to fear no evil.

When she had finished, it was not perfect and she often thought she would drop over the edge of her faith at any moment. But she was Sister Mary Columbo now and there was peace for her, a temporary truce to ward off waiting for death. To stop those hopeless, homesick eyes of Vietnam warriors coming into O.R., asking: Am I going to die?

She groaned. She saw the outline of a man in the tent next to her. She asked for water. She asked twice, in English, and then she heard him speak in the French patois and repeated the word in his language.

He left the tent.

She waited a moment or a day. When the flap of the tent opened again, it was another man.

"Water," she said again.

"Here."

He lifted her head in a gentle hand and gave her water from a plastic cup. She drank until she choked.

He wiped her lips with his fingers.

He had large, luminous eyes and he was watching her. His hair was dark and cut close to his head. He had one blue eye and one brown eye and a mustache rode above his broad lips.

"Why did you come up here?"

"To see you, Manet. Again. For permission."

"I told you the last time. Colonel Ready uses you."

"And you use us and it doesn't matter if we can save the children at least."

"Your other nuns. Dead."

"I know."

"You're very tough, sister."

"Did you ambush us?"

"No. It was someone else."

"Not Colonel Ready. He gave us permission—"

"Colonel Ready is a man of his word, sister."

"None of you are," she said. "The medical supplies."

"Gone. Everything was gone. Only the Jeep left. We brought you up in the Jeep."

"Whooping cough vaccine. Polio."

"It doesn't matter," Manet said. "We had nothing before. We still have nothing."

It was all taken. She felt tears darken her sight. She squeezed her fists and thought of Sister Agnes who talked too much and Sister Mary St. John of God who never spoke at all. How sad it was the supplies were gone.

"Did you bury them?"

"Oh, yes. We buried them and arranged a funeral mass and we took them to the cemetery in St. Michel. We asked Colonel Ready for an honor guard."

"You bastard."

"A holy woman should not say such things," Manet said. He stared at her and did not move. His face never changed expression and his words, covered with sarcasm, were delivered in the same monotone.

"You left them in the road."

"For the army to bury. Let the dead bury the dead. The army killed them."

"How do you know?"

"If not the army, it was Celezon and the *gendarmes noires*. One or the other."

"Or you?"

"Yes. We killed those two and only wounded you and now we save your life. Why is that? For practice?"

"This cruel place."

"The world, you mean, holy woman? Or just the people of St. Michel? They cut you on the breasts, there was a small infection. We wasted some of our penicillin on you."

"Why?"

"Marks of the voodoo? I don't know. The army knows. Colonel Ready knows."

"Why do you hate us?"

"I don't hate you. You're nothing. You're a wall to walk through. You save this child so that he can die more easily the next time. If you want to save the world, start in les Etats-Unis. Don't you have black people there to practice on?"

"Why did you save me?"

"So that you will not blame us. So that you can tell the people in Washington we are not filthy niggers in the hills who rape white women and kill nuns and spread communism to Florida."

"I never spoke of the rebels."

"No. You did us no good."

"And no harm."

"Damn you, Mary Columbo, sister and holy woman. You do harm when you do not choose. You save their lives and not their souls, these people here."

"You shouldn't speak of souls."

"People don't know what they want, they do not sacrifice until you show them it is right to sacrifice. You give medicine to babies so they will not die until they can become starving children. Give children food so they can grow to listless, toothless men without hope, so they can have more babies, so that you can save them. . . . You disgust me, you and your order, all you nuns and priests disgust me. You try to make it easy for these people. To accept the world as it is."

"If you hate me, why save me?"

"To take you to the journalists here, so that you can tell them Manet and his filthy rebels saved your worthless life. So that the engaged ones in the press will ask themselves questions about who kills nuns in the hills of St. Michel. Who will ask the questions in les Etats-Unis in time."

"For what?"

"Before the Armageddon. It is coming, Sister Mary Columbo." His eyes were distant. "Perhaps soon or late for the world, but it is not too much longer for poor St. Michel."

The pain was beneath her. It no longer covered her. She felt the words like ice. Fire and ice, she thought, the end of things.

"When will it come?"

"Very soon. In days."

"What will happen?"

"I don't know," said Manet.

"Death."

"Yes. Death and destruction and an end to old things."

She closed her eyes. She thought of herself before she had become a nun. Sitting in the cramped living room in Queens, far from Hell's Kitchen where she had been a little girl. Sitting in the living room after she had come back from Vietnam, watching Walter Cronkite describe the continued slaughter of innocents in that land. Her family did not speak when she watched the evening news. It was a religious moment for them. She only watched and wanted to scream because she would be inside that box when the images came on the screen. From Hell's Kitchen into hell and now into hell again. Wasn't there ever heaven?

"If war is coming—"

"It is here," Manet said.

"If the end is coming," she said, "why did Colonel Ready let us go into the hills?"

"Yes," Manet said. "Ask yourself. And then tell the journalists when they see you that all these things have happened and that you have no answers. And perhaps the journalists will forestall the end of the world for a little bit longer."

15

A WOMAN OF PLEASURE

Devereaux heard about the dead nuns when he got into Madeleine. He went to the Green Parrot, drank, and listened. There were many sailors in town, English sailors and Americans.

He spotted two of the Americans and turned away when he saw them. There should not have been Americans in Madeleine. He knew they were agents and they did not seem to bother hiding themselves. They were enjoying themselves and watching the harbor. For what?

Madeleine was Manet's stronghold even though it seemed to be in the hands of the government troops who patrolled the streets. He had come to Madeleine to find Manet because he had not believed in the notebook, and he still did not know what it was and what the secret of it was.

Manet might know, Manet might trade for his knowledge. And then he'd have leverage enough against Colonel Ready to hold the trap open until he could remove Rita.

And himself.

"*Encore*," he said to the bartender in rough French. He put the glass down and let the other man splash in whiskey. He wanted the whiskey to warm him. He had seen himself in Cain, seen himself in that bitter man who had not survived the war after all. He would survive Vietnam finally and all he had done since. Even if it killed him. But he wouldn't be a man with dead eyes sailing on a shallow sea, waiting for all the bitterness to poison him.

He had seen himself in Cain, or what he might really be. He had been chilled by the vision. And chilled still when he beached the dinghy on the wooded side of the crescent-shaped island. Cain was gone and there was no way to get off the island.

Unless he made a way.

He had found the notebook. He could go to Colonel Ready with the notebook and remind him of the promise and Colonel Ready would release him and let Rita and him leave the island. He could do that if he believed Colonel Ready would let him go.

She had been prepared to play the dangerous game because she loved Devereaux. And Devereaux had let her be the hostage because he needed time to set up a scheme against Ready, to rid himself of the red-headed man for all time.

What did that make Devereaux?

Two Americans were on the island in the rowdy town of Madeleine and they should not have been there, just as the notebook should not have existed.

His way off the island with Rita might lie with Manet. The rebel was in the hills. The whores of Madeleine were all operatives of the *gendarmes noires*, of Colonel Ready, and they were all in contact with Manet. Manet must be Colonel Ready's creature as much as Devereaux. Everyone on the island belonged to Ready. But perhaps Manet was reluctant, as Devereaux was reluctant, to serve the red colonel.

It was not the kind of risk they taught you to take in the spy school in western Maryland where they trained the recruits to R Section. But this was not training and there was no clear way to get out.

Devereaux had laid the trail to Ready. Now Devereaux would have to become invisible and jump the trail and get Rita away at the same time.

He felt the coldness filling his body; he had betrayed Rita to gain the time to set a trap for a red-haired fox.

Two Americans. What did their presence mean?

He found a whore in the Green Parrot and she led him to her room in an old building behind an alley called the Street of the Blue Pleasure. Madeleine was noisy in the last light of day. The sun was down behind the hills above the port. The sky was red and it was streaked with blue but the port was already in purple darkness. There were sounds of dogs barking in the darkness.

Her name was Mimi. She wiggled her behind at him as she climbed the stairs to her room. He gave her money inside the door of the room. He did not touch her. She pressed her shiny dress against him and he went by her to the window and looked down at the alley.

"What is wrong with me?" In the high, insulted voice that only carries its tone in French.

"Nothing."

"If you won't fuck me, I have to go out. I don't have time to wait. Maybe you only want to look at me?"

"Sit down, Mimi."

"I could open my legs and let you see."

"Sit down, Mimi."

"Who are you?"

"Someone who told you to sit down."

She was skinny and wore a tight dress. Her face was long and quite lovely in the dim light of the room. In the morning, it would look tired. She was seventeen and her lips were broad.

"How about this instead?" she said, coming over to him, kneeling next to him.

"Mimi. I gave you a hundred dollars. Here's another hundred dollars. Now sit on the bed and be a good girl."

"You're a sissy?"

"Yes. I'm a sissy. Now sit on the bed."

"Even sissies like that."

"Shut up, Mimi."

"What are you watching?"

"Shut up, Mimi."

She sat on the bed and was quiet for a while. It became night. He saw the one American pass the lights of the Green Parrot. He took the Python out of the seabag and unwrapped the oil rags carefully, as though he was unwrapping a baby's diaper.

"Mary, Mother of God, I don't want that," said Mimi.

"Be quiet. It'll be all right."

"Who do you want to shoot?"

"The American in the alley."

"He has been here for two days."

"What else?"

"He came in a boat. Right to the harbor with the other one. It's there."

"The white boat?"

"Yes. Fishermen. Sport fishermen. I took care of one. The little one."

"Good, Mimi. Maybe we'll take care of the big one first."

"Why do you want to kill him?"

"So that I won't have to kill you," Devereaux said. She was quiet after that.

The American stood by the light of the Green Parrot until the little American came along with a girl in his grip. The girl pointed down the Street of the Blue Pleasure in the direction of the building where Mimi and Devereaux waited in the darkness.

"That's Eliane. She saw us go in here."

"Yes."

"Why did you let them see you?"

"I wasn't sure. If they saw me, it works just as well to get it over with now. If not, I would go away."

"Will you kill me?"

"Not if you are quiet, Mimi."

"I would do anything for you, I would be your slave—"

"Be quiet, Mimi."

One waited in the street while the little one went up the stairs. The little one waited outside Mimi's door for a while and then went back downstairs. The two of them talked to each other for a moment. They looked up at the window. Devereaux did not move in all that time.

They decided to go upstairs together.

"If they knock on the door, tell them to go away."

Mimi's eyes shone in the darkness. "But I'm not supposed to."

"I bought your company. Remember, Mimi, I have a gun."

But they didn't knock.

They were in the room, one left, one right, and their pistols were out. They had expected darkness but darkness is always a surprise when you find it.

Devereaux fired twice.

The little one wasn't dead. Mimi was screaming.

Devereaux opened the little one's wallet and took out a card that meant nothing; an American Express card without raised numbers or letters or expiration date. Everything was printed on it flat. The card was a copy which when inserted into one of 311 machines in the world identified the bearer. R Section knew of them; tried to duplicate them; never had them. Langley still had toys that R Section only dreamed of.

Because the little American was not dead, Devereaux asked him, in English, his name. It was peculiar to ask, Devereaux thought, even as he spoke.

"Felix Summit."

"Who do you work for?"

"It doesn't matter. Are you going to kill me?" The voice was nearly choked with blood.

"No, Felix, you're dead."

"Who are you?"

"No one."

Devereaux got up. There was no time at all. If they were here, open like this, there was no time at all left. But he didn't know what for.

"Mimi, I want to see Manet."

She sobbed. A woman from an apartment across the hall peered into the darkness of Mimi's room, saw the bodies, saw the man with the gun standing. The woman said nothing. She watched. The halls were filling with people but none came into the room.

"I don't know what—"

"Come on, Mimi. I don't want to kill you."

"Don't kill me," she said. "I'll do anything for you."

"I want to see Manet."

"The soldiers."

They heard whistles in the streets.

"What do you say?"

"We go in the back, through the Rue Madeleine." She decided because the whistles were very far away and the gun was very close.

16

THE AFTERNOON AND THE EVENING

She opened the door of her room.

Colonel Ready stood there in his uniform. He smiled at her. She wore a blue cotton dress of rough fabric of the sort that women call "comfortable" to explain why they wear a shapeless garment to hide their bodies.

"It is refreshing to see you again," Colonel Ready said and he grinned at her, at the room, at the little fan whirring away bravely in the humid, still afternoon heat. "You know about the nuns now."

"I heard the news," said Rita Macklin. "Everyone has heard."

"Everyone has heard and is deeply shocked," said Colonel Ready. He stepped into the room and closed the door behind him. He kissed her.

She did nothing. She stood very still and when he was finished with her, his face was red and his eyes burned into her. He held her.

"This wasn't your promise."

"To him? But he's going to die," said Colonel Ready.

She took a step back, toward the window. The fan blew against her shapeless dress and gave it some form.

"It doesn't matter. Not now," said Colonel Ready and he did not move toward her again. "I came for you because there was to be an interview with the president in the Palais Gris and—"

"Why do you go on with this? It's a sham."

"Everything is. All the more important that we keep playing our assigned roles."

He sat down suddenly in a side chair near the dresser with the fan. The fan bathed his face with a damp breeze. "I want you to understand."

She stepped back again.

"You have just heard about the nuns. I have heard other things," said Colonel Ready. "Devereaux is on the island. He went to Harry's shack."

She only stared at him.

"Alive but dead," said Colonel Ready. "I know everything about him. He even found the notebook, and that's a very clever thing for him to have done. I sent Celezon down there a dozen times. I even searched that holding tank in his privy once myself and I didn't find it. And he found it the first time out. He's a lucky bastard, isn't he."

"He's on the island." She said it slowly to make sure the words registered.

"But dead. As I said. He's landed a dinghy at Madeleine. I expected him to find another way to come to the island but I didn't expect that. The child. The child we talked to. He said the American had red hair. But I knew it was him. And he has the book. What do you think of that."

She said nothing. Her face was as white as chalk or sand.

"There was a book after all and the bastard has it," said Colonel Ready. "I wasn't even sure about that. It's a small island and it won't be long until I find him."

"If you wanted to kill him, you could have killed him in Switzerland."

"No, not at all. He's useful to be a dead man still walking around St. Michel. I told him. I told you. I need ways of escape and you are part of it. Did you ever play gin rummy?"

She shook her head.

"You play the cards against your opponent, not for your own benefit. It's a blocking game if it is played well. You begin to see the shape of the cards your opponent holds. One on one, man to man, hand to hand. Every card is a chance given to you or to him and you have to decide which chance you will take. It's a blocking game."

"Don't kill him."

"Why? What does he mean now to you? He gave you to me. He let you come here."

"There's a plan."

"Good. I hoped he'd had a plan." Colonel Ready smiled. "It would have been too easy otherwise."

She was staring at him now and the fascination of what she saw was filling her cheeks with color again. She was breathing, she was alive, she was trying to think.

"I have him blocked at every point. Except for details like your plan. What was it?"

"He didn't tell me."

Colonel Ready waited a long time and then let the moment end with a crooked smile. "Perhaps," he said. "We'll talk about it another time."

"What are you afraid of?"

The question was followed by silence but the smile faded.

"Nothing. Not of you or Devereaux, in any case. Well, you'll be late for your interview with the president. I arranged it myself. I have a lot of things to do, but I see to the details. If you see to the details, the big things work out."

"You're crazy, you know that?"

"No, I don't think so. There are games in games here, Rita. There's the president and there's Celezon. I thought for a long time that Celezon had found the notebook and was holding it out, but he never mentioned it and he would have. And I thought there was no notebook."

"You didn't need Devereaux."

"Devereaux. Devereaux blocked me three times in Vietnam. Devereaux. And you. Blocked me once again. In the matter of the old priest in Florida. I hold a grudge, it's my weakness. But I didn't use it against you until I needed you. I need martyrs and I need victims. I didn't expect the nuns but their deaths were welcome."

He was mad, she thought, the island was mad. And it was better to say nothing to any of them because in their madness, they controlled the world she inhabited at the moment. She was Alice, fallen into a wonderland in which nothing was as it seemed. Except—at last—Devereaux was here finally.

"I play six games at the same time and each opponent thinks it is the only game I am playing. It's useful to put the world into compartments. You and Devereaux, your lover. You thought you were that important to me. But you were only a little important."

"I won't go with you."

"Of course you will. That's why I came for you myself. You must bring your notebook. President Claude-Eduard has prepared for the interview all morning."

She stepped back and this time, she touched the sill of the window.

He came to her and handed her a notebook. "Do you have a pencil? Or a pen?"

"Goddamn it, I hate the sight of you."

He kissed her. She resisted this time and pushed at him but he held her for a long time and pressed his lips against her mouth until she could not breathe and she opened her mouth and he put his tongue against her lips for a moment. She tried to bite him. He slapped her then, very hard, across the face.

"Come on." Voice cold, face pale. "I have to show you a few things. Maybe by the time we go to the morgue, we'll have your friend on a slab."

He took her arm and hurt her. Four *gendarmes noires* waited for them outside the door and they could not hide their smiles.

■ ■ ■

"Good of you to come," said the president in English.

She was in a white room with a dirty white carpet on the floor. The ceiling was blue and there were gold cherubs hanging around the base of the chandelier.

On the way to the palace, she had noticed the streets were empty except for soldiers and the police. She sat next to

113

Colonel Ready in the back seat of the Peugeot which bore no license plates.

"Where is everyone? Where are the reporters? I saw some in the streets before . . . you came to my room. Where is everyone?"

"The reporters were causing a disruption. We took them back to the airport. And the people had to leave the streets. This is very upsetting to us, that the rebels have killed the nuns—"

"You can't do this—"

"Rita, in the time after the Second World War, the government of the Soviet Union killed thirty-three million people. Do you understand what I have just said? They killed thirty-three million people for a number of very good reasons. All we have done is inconvenience a few American reporters for a few hours. Do you suppose we can get away with it?"

"This isn't Russia," she said.

"No." He smiled. "We'll give them their story in a little while. About the dead nuns. About the dead American reporter who was possibly ambushed with the nuns. Do you suppose you would like to be a heroine?"

"He'll kill you," she said.

"He had his chance. Now he plays my game and dances to my tune. The trouble with wanting something in this life is that someone else is always able to deny it to you. Devereaux wanted you and he wanted to be left alone. I was in a position to deny both things to him. But I left him an out. I let him have his three or four days to prepare to come after me. I wondered what game he would play against me. But I always had you."

"I might not have followed."

"Then I had both of you in any case because the KGB would have been informed of your . . . existence."

Now, in the palace, she waited to speak because her voice was dry and not sure. When she found it, the president was next to her on the white couch, staring serenely at her with pale, watery eyes.

"Your colonel brought me here," she began.

"I asked him—"

"He is working against you. Did you know that? He said he plans a revolution against you."

Claude-Eduard smiled as though she might be a child or an idiot. "No such thing," he said. "There is no revolution. Even the rebels in the hills under Manet understand that. Everything is as it is in St. Michel. Nothing will ever change from that."

"He means to kill me. I'm an American citizen." Her mouth was very dry and she could smell his cologne and it was as damp and stinking as the heat of the late afternoon. "I want to see the American consul."

"Of course," said the president. "Has anyone denied you?"

"You have reporters under guard at the airport. The American government won't put up with this—"

"The American government is so great and we are so small that I am certain they could not care about our actions. If the Americans come as friends, we are friends; if they come as our enemies, they will be destroyed, just as Manet will be destroyed."

The voice was so calm, she thought, and it sickened her because Claude-Eduard seemed to be speaking to himself.

"The Communist whores in the streets. They all work for Manet—"

"They all work for Celezon," said Rita Macklin. "In Switzerland, I heard Ready tell Celezon to buy trinkets for the whores, they all work together, everyone is part of the conspiracy against you—"

"My dear, it is common, I understand, for paranoia to rule American reporters. You have so many conspiracies in your country."

She couldn't talk to him. She thought of a nightmare she had suffered as a child in which she spoke again and again to others and they did not understand her, no matter how clearly

115

she spoke, and she was tolerated by everyone, as though she were mad. But she wasn't the mad one now; the world was.

"Do you know what they say about me, the whores, the Communist whores who work for Manet, in the street of the whores in Madeleine?"

She stared at him. He was changing colors like the sea. He was close to her. He was azure and green and a streak of gold dancing on the water.

"They say I sleep with my sister. To have intercourse with her, I mean."

It was the horror she could not resist. She dropped her pencil on the white rug.

"It is disgusting and unnatural," he said. "But I would sleep with you." He reached his hand between her legs and she hit him and stood up.

"I am sorry," he said. "I'm much affected by events."

"The nuns."

"What nuns?"

"Colonel Ready killed nuns."

"I'm sure you're mistaken. There are no dead nuns on St. Michel that I know of."

"They're in the morgue."

"In that case, let us go there."

And she saw Devereaux in front of her eyes. He would be on the slab in the morgue, naked and dead. He was dead. Colonel Ready knew everything, saw everything, he could not be resisted.

Down the halls and stairways. The president tugged at her arm.

She held back like a reluctant child.

Down and down and the rooms were cooler beneath the ground.

And there was a sweet odor mixed with the damp in the basement and the president pushed open the door of the morgue.

The naked bodies were on the tables and a large portion

of Sister Agnes's skull sat in a metal tray next to her large and flabby body.

Before she fell to the floor, she saw there was one empty table in the morgue.

17

ANGEL

Frank Collier tried to sit perfectly still, tried not to tap his fingers, tried not to jiggle his right leg which he always did when he was nervous, tried to listen to the words and accept them calmly.

He was in Room 236 of the Pier House hotel near Mallory Square in Key West, Florida. It was 6:34 P.M. Peter Jennings, the anchor of "ABC World News Tonight," was speaking in that clear, crisp Canadian accent, almost without inflection, and on the screen there were still photographs of three women.

" . . . The nuns, all Americans, had been ambushed apparently by rebel guerrillas outside the city of Madeleine on the southern tip of this impoverished Caribbean island. Meanwhile, Reuters reports that correspondents from ABC and the other networks, as well as newspaper reporters dispatched to St. Michel, are being held in custody at the St. Michel airport. . . ."

Operation Angel was fourteen hours old. It could only be aborted with minimal casualties now. It could not be put on hold; it could not be reversed. Another abortion. Like the Bay of Pigs.

Frank Collier could not help himself.

In the darkness of the room, sitting in his boxer shorts and black socks on the only upholstered chair, he began to

117

jiggle his right leg up and down in a frenzied telegraph. That was when the phone started to ring. He let it ring six times and then he reached for the receiver. Peter Jennings was speaking of London now, where there had been a car bombing.

"You heard," said the voice from Washington, D.C.

"What do we do?" Frank said. He saw it all wasted, thirteen months of planning, of making deals, of setting up all the actors in all the right spots. And getting the funding through . . . that had been a miracle itself. No one had a clue to this operation except the principals and six men at the highest level of Central Intelligence. And, of course, the president's senior adviser.

"That's what the director wants from you," the voice said. "He called a session at four P.M. We don't know how this affects us, to tell you the truth. We were aware of missionary work—"

"I know that, I know all about the goddamn nuns—what I want to know is what do we do? All we can do is abort or push on—"

"We want other options, Frank—"

"There are no other options. We've got Task Force Alpha in transit, out of radio contact, we have One, Two, and Three set to perform their functions at the right time—I see Two at dawn at Fort Myers, so you tell me—"

"Frank, if we abort—"

"If we abort, we can't do this again in six months. No one is going to trust us a second time around. We do it now or we lose the chance to ever do it."

"What does that mean to us? That's what the director has been asking. What does it matter if we abort?"

"The Company, that's what it matters. We've taken shit for twenty years down here. Nicaragua, Panama, Salvador, Cuba—it started with Cuba."

"Grenada," said the man in Washington. The line was very clear and very safe.

"That's a start." Jesus. "I'm supposed to get a signal at

118

twenty hundred hours from Nine." The numbers referred to the principals in Angel. In this case, Nine was an American CIA caseworker (as field agents are quaintly called) who was bleeding to death at that moment on the floor in Mimi's room off the street of the Blue Pleasure.

"Everything is moving," Frank said, and he thought he sounded as if he were pleading. Maybe he was. It was the big-bang chance and there wasn't going to be another one on St. Michel. And maybe not another one for Frank Collier either. He had sixteen years in service and six years in grade. It was time to move up or start thinking about how to squeeze out retirement on GS-12-level pay.

"I'll be in touch," said the voice. "After you hear from Nine and I get back to the director. But Frank, who did it?"

"I don't know. It was Manet but he must have gotten wind of Angel. Somehow, he knew something was coming up and he wanted to stop it—"

"It wasn't very smart of them to stop the media at the airport—"

"What would you suggest? Send them up to the hills so they can film Angel?" Frank said. "Fuck the *New York Times*. We'll explain what happened later."

"Frank."

He paused before speaking: "Yeah?"

"This has to work. I'm pushing you on this. I took care of you up to this point and now it has to be you alone." His rabbi was drawing the line; it was bar mitzvah for Frank.

"I understand."

"I want you to make it."

"I understand; I will."

"I think you will, too. But this is all on you, Frank."

"Don't worry and I appreciate. Don't worry, we've got too many fires lit for all of them to go out. Believe me."

He replaced the receiver and shivered in the chill of the air-conditioned room. Peter Jennings was speaking of health care facilities in Cincinnati. Who cared about the nuns? They were ninety seconds on the news. Send the reporters back to

119

Miami and let them stew there until it was over. They'd take baby food spooned out to them if that was all there was to eat. They'd learn to like it.

"Too many fires," Frank Collier said aloud, reassuring himself.

18

THE COMMUNIST, THE NUN,
AND THE AGENT

There were too many fires, Devereaux thought. Everything about Manet's camp was wrong. Yet he had to see Manet, to see if there was a way to use him to get himself and Rita off the island.

He had been led up the hills by Mimi, who had walked barefoot on the carpet of the forest, who had seemed—after her first fears—to relax as a child relaxes in the grip of the countryside. The forest was cool and green, and the air carried the scent of unseen flowers, of the tropical pines.

Mimi had taken him to the edge of the camp and turned back to Madeleine two miles down the hills. The hills were complex because the trails led nowhere. Some trails were wide and they stopped very soon. Others were narrow but tangled round and round and turned in on themselves. There were no reference points because the hills were irregular, without distinguishing marks, like certain ridges of low hills that run through western Pennsylvania. Devereaux felt disoriented. He could not see the lights of Madeleine from the place where Mimi left him.

He had buried everything with the dinghy except for the waterproof, which he had taped to his belly. The waterproof held the notebook, the photograph, and ten one-thousand-dollar bills. There was also a letter from Krup-Zema, the international arms dealers in Zurich, explaining everything about him.

The brown-skinned man in camouflage had been there all along. Devereaux had sensed his presence in the bushes not far from the place where Mimi left him. He had studied the camp and not moved while he waited for the guerrilla to come out of the bushes.

"Come on," the soldier said and he pointed at the center of the camp with the tip of his M-17. It was unprofessional to use a gun as a classroom pointer but Devereaux did not think to move on the soldier's mistake. He noted it. He noted the make of the submachine gun as well. The piece was new and was showing signs of neglect. The soldier did not keep it clean, but it was new enough not to matter yet.

He did not search Devereaux and seemed unconcerned whether Devereaux was armed.

In the encampment, there were three fires, which Devereaux thought were three too many. He had worked in Vietnam and Laos and Cambodia for the Section for five years. He knew the way a guerrilla lives who does not wish to be spotted or captured. He wondered for the first time what Manet was, besides what he appeared to be.

"You're one of the journalists," a large man with luminous eyes said. He came from around a tent near one of the fires. The camp was full of men and women. Some were sleeping, some were cooking, some eating. The camp was around the entrance to some kind of mine long since abandoned that was sunk into a low hill.

"Yes," Devereaux said in English.

"We have the nun, she is well, we did not kill them," Manet began in a careful, rumbling, prepared speech. "Are you with the *New York Times*?"

"Yes," Devereaux said, caught in a sudden trap of wonder. He was prepared for almost anything but this. He stared at Manet.

"Do you want to see her first or do you want to know

121

what happened first?" said Manet. He spoke carefully. "I'm glad you are with the *New York Times*. You will tell the truth about what has happened. The truth must be known soon. Very soon. Before the end begins."

Devereaux said he wanted to see her. He didn't know who she was. He did not know about the slaughter of the nuns two days before. He did not know that Rita Macklin, at that moment, was being led to the autopsy room in the basement of the capital to see the dead bodies of Sister Columbo's companions.

He looked at the wan face of the nun swathed in bandages and bedclothes on a camp bed in the tent.

"My name is Devereaux," he said in a flat voice. "I'm with the *New York Times*. What happened?"

And she began to tell him and he listened and felt Manet's presence next to him in the small tent. He had brought no notebook or pencil and Manet had commented on that. Devereaux had tapped the side of his head with his index finger. Manet had not been so certain of him after that but the nun told of her mission, of her interview with Celezon and Colonel Ready in St. Michel for permission to go into the interior, of the ride down the coast road to Madeleine.

"I was in Madeleine," Devereaux said. "It's full of soldiers. How could it be your headquarters?" Devereaux looked at Manet.

"It is always the same. We have the countryside, we have Madeleine. The soldiers come and we move away. Sometimes, we fight, but mostly we move away. The soldiers wait and then they are recalled because there are not enough soldiers to maintain them all the time in the field. And then we move back again."

"But when did the soldiers enter Madeleine in those numbers this time?"

"Three days ago," Manet said and stared at Devereaux shrewdly. This journalist knew that matters were about to unfold. He would be useful to Manet if he could tell his story in time. There was so little time.

122

Sister Columbo watched the dark-skinned American with red hair while he spoke to Manet. And she broke in without thinking: "He's right. He didn't kill Sister Agnes and Sister Mary. It wouldn't make any sense to kill them. Besides—"

Devereaux turned and looked at her.

"He wasn't in Madeleine. I didn't know that until now. Until you said the soldiers had been there for three days."

"How do we get Sister Columbo out of here?" Devereaux said.

"I don't know. I don't think it is wise to move her in any case. There is a bullet very close to her spine and we have no facilities to operate on her—"

Devereaux looked at the nun. For a long moment, he thought of plans, rejected them, created new ones. But there was no way. He was trapped on the island. If he could escape Ready, it would have to be out the front door, with Rita, out of St. Michel town. And he would never be able to rescue a wounded woman in danger of death if she were moved.

"Something can be done. At least to tell the truth," said Devereaux because that is what Manet wanted to hear. And then he saw tears in the nun's eyes and misunderstood. "I'm sorry," he began.

"No. That's what I want as well. The truth. Tell the truth about the murders, about the attack, about how Manet saved my life."

"Yes," Devereaux lied. "I'll get the story out. And I'll get you out in time as well. Don't worry about that."

■ ■ ■

He and Manet talked outside for a long time. They sat at a small fire near the entrance of the abandoned bauxite mine and they drank wine and now and then, Manet would stop and ask Devereaux to repeat something the nun had told him and Devereaux would do so.

"It is extraordinary to have such a memory," Manet said with a smile. "In your profession, I mean."

Devereaux said nothing. He probed Manet without

123

seeming to. He watched the camp life while they talked. Everyone seemed so unconcerned, as though it were family camp out in the woods. There were men with M-17s—all of them he saw were American-made M-17s—but none seemed on guard. Manet watched his eyes when Devereaux looked out at the camp and he finally spoke.

"You think we should be more on guard, Monsieur Devereaux?"

"I've been to other rebel camps," he said. "In Laos, Vietnam."

"They faced a different enemy. One with great ruthlessness and great resources."

"You do not," said Devereaux.

"I know my enemy."

"Is he Colonel Ready?"

"That is one. That is not all."

"There are Americans in Madeleine," he said in a flat, even voice and he watched Manet's eyes. Manet's eyes grew larger but the calm of his face did not change.

"Journalists."

"I don't think so."

"What were they doing there?"

"Watching the harbor. As though they were waiting for something."

"Then it's begun."

"What?"

"The Americans. The Americans wish to destroy us. They are in league with Colonel Ready. He has had American money."

"And you have had it," Devereaux said. It was dangerous but Manet seemed to be taken aback by the presence of Americans in Madeleine.

"St. Michel is a threat to freedom," Manet said. "If St. Michel becomes a socialist country, I intend to invade Miami within six months."

Devereaux watched the impassive face and let the sar-

124

casm fall without response. "St. Michel is a dagger pointed at the heart of Alabama," Manet said.

"Where do your arms come from?"

"From Colonel Ready."

Devereaux held his breath a moment.

Manet turned his lazy eyes to him across the fire and smiled. His eyes glittered in the fire. "Four months ago, we raided the barracks. The soldiers fled and we took out four cases of weapons and ammunition. What do you think of that? A gift from Colonel Ready."

"Do the soldiers always run away?"

"No. It surprised me. We never intended to get so much. So many riches."

"Perhaps Ready wanted you to have the arms."

"Yes. I thought of that later. But what would be his purpose? The news of St. Michel is not very important to the world. If we rebels are armed, what does it matter to Americans? They don't care about me, about my men, about this country. So what would be Colonel Ready's purpose to let me arm myself so well?"

"Perhaps to permit an American invasion," Devereaux guessed.

Manet smiled for the first time. He seemed too amused not to smile. "Will you write your guess in the newspaper? Will your editor permit this?"

"I don't know. You know the *New York Times*."

"Yes. I do. I read it extensively. All the time. I have read it for ten years, monsieur. And you are not a correspondent for that paper. Not in the Caribe, not in Asia. I waited a long time to see what it was you were but you didn't tell me. Except to count my fires and to notice my weapons. So you are CIA then and you are very brave or very foolish."

"Neither," Devereaux said. The voice was steady and that was training. He sat very still and that was training.

"Then tell me another story, monsieur. Convince me of who you are."

125

Devereaux did not speak for a moment. He could construct another lie, but Manet had already guessed.

He thought of the camp and looked across at the lazy width of it and he thought he would be shot before he got fifteen feet.

"I'm from Washington," he began.

"And your name is not Devereaux."

"My name is Felix Summit."

"All right. That's correct. You were in Madeleine three days. Mimi had sex with you two nights ago."

"Yes."

"And Mimi brought you to me tonight. Why did you want to see me?"

"To make an accommodation," Devereaux said.

"It's too late. The Americans are set to invade. Operation Angel. I know about this."

"How do you know?"

"Because Havana knows. Because I know. Because Colonel Ready knows."

"But which one told you?"

"Who murdered the nuns?" said Manet. "Colonel Ready will betray you. Colonel Ready is not your friend."

"But you are, right?"

"If you didn't think that was possible, Monsieur Summit, you would not have come to my camp alone."

Devereaux waited a moment. He let the self-delusion sink into Manet. All lies need believers and believers are those who have to believe in something. Manet was on the verge. The eyes revealed themselves now in the red glare of the fire. The eyes were worried, were desperate. The wine and Devereaux's lies had opened them up.

"Can you stop Angel?" Manet asked.

"It's stopped. On hold," said Devereaux.

"Why?"

"The nuns. Something's wrong."

"It would not be like you." Manet turned suspicious again. "Murdered nuns justifies an invasion."

126

"But we're not sending in marines, are we, Manet?" Devereaux guessed.

"No." He made a face, spat into the fire. "You are sending in Gautier's contras. Those expelled from the country. The freedom fighters." Manet spat again. "Trained at your CIA camps in Louisiana. Trained to create civil war and kill their own people."

"What do you create, Manet?"

"Hope," he said, almost lyrically. And then frowned to realize it was the same word he had used in accusation against the wounded nun.

"Perhaps we can make a deal," Devereaux said.

"What deal?"

"Uncle Sam doesn't want to be played for a chump," Devereaux said. He paused, trying to be certain he remembered his lies and could separate them from all the information that had suddenly been rushed at him. Manet was telling him everything as though Devereaux already knew the truth. There was too much information about too many things. "We came down here three days ago, we were waiting for Gautier, made sure everything was right—"

"And Colonel Ready crossed you."

"Someone did. Someone killed those nuns. This isn't the kind of attention we want."

"No. You want a fait accompli. To send in the reporters after the fact as you did in Grenada."

"And why did Colonel Ready let you have all those weapons?"

"To kill Gautier at the beach, I suppose."

"And then what?"

"I don't know. I don't understand it."

"If Gautier fails, do we try again?" Devereaux prompted. He was going on logic, on what he would have said if he had been the CIA agent named Felix Summit who was dead on the floor in Mimi's room.

"No."

"Then what?"

127

They did not speak. The camp was quiet. The fires burned low. There were whispers in the camp and low voices. The night was full of the sounds of insects and owls and the rustle of the evening wind through the thick trees.

"Nothing," said Manet. "We are here three years and we have not received anything from Havana. Twice we sent emissaries. They never returned. Why do you suppose that is?"

"Havana doesn't trust you. Havana thinks you're a CIA invention."

"Why do they think that?"

"Perhaps it's true," Devereaux said.

Manet stared at him and the fire caught an emotion in his eyes that Devereaux knew was hatred.

"I hate everything you are, Monsieur Summit. I hate the United States and you cannot understand the depth of my hatred. It is not that we are poor and you are rich. It is that you are so certain of your rightness. You cannot understand that even a poor country in a lost cause can be right. If you are great, then we are wrong. The equations are bent to suit your rules."

"And the nuns," Devereaux said, pushing it, wondering where it would make Manet go.

"Fools, of course. Misguided, of course. But they were nothing to me until the ambush outside Madeleine. Someone has betrayed me."

"You had an arrangement. With Colonel Ready."

"No."

"You have open fires, you are not so difficult to find, you have guns that are left behind when you raid a barracks . . ."

"And I have thought of all these things as well and cannot explain them."

"You're a poor rebel, Manet. Colonel Ready keeps you around to do his dirty work for him."

"Perhaps I know that," Manet said in a soft voice and Devereaux was startled.

"Perhaps I have enough intelligence to understand a trap. And enough intelligence to use the trap until I can spring it on my own terms, for my own safety."

Devereaux stared. It was what Devereaux had expected to do as well. Manet and Devereaux were in traps of Colonel Ready's making and both thought they were smart enough to turn the trap on the man who set it. How many other traps were set, traps within traps, each set to spring when the other failed? Colonel Ready had always left himself an out in Vietnam, no matter how dirty the deal or complex the arrangement. He had nearly left Devereaux in one trap and then, almost in a gesture of noblesse oblige, had come back to extricate him. And Ready had set the trap for Cain and Devereaux had backed it when it seemed the only way to get Susan Mihn and the boy out of Vietnam. Traps in traps in traps, each more clever than the first. Ready loved games, loved puzzles that seemed to have no solution.

"Should I kill you now?" Manet said.

Devereaux stared at him still without speaking. Both men seemed caught in the same thought. They were in traps in traps and now they were not sure that it had all been arranged this way, that someone had decided these things.

"No," Devereaux said softly at last.

Manet waited.

"You will give me Sister Mary Columbo."

"Why will I do that?"

"You will give me the nun and one of your men with a gun to my head and the Jeep and we will go down into St. Michel town tonight to the American consul. And she will tell them everything she told me and told you."

"And you will kill her."

"No. And the consul will not kill her. But it's the only way out for you. Killing me solves nothing for you."

"I trust you?"

"No. That's why you watch me all the way to the consulate."

"It's a trap," said Manet.

"You have the nun but Colonel Ready is not going to release her. You know that. You should know that. He thought all the nuns were killed. She wasn't supposed to survive."

129

"Yes," said Manet. "But I can't trust you."

"Don't trust me. Trust yourself. And stop trusting Colonel Ready," Devereaux said.

Manet had a pistol in his hand. He had produced it so easily that Devereaux had not seen the move, only the shadow of movement.

■ ■ ■

Manet gave his orders. Two soldiers took his gun and led Devereaux down the hillside a little ways away from the camp.

The first had an M-17 and the second had a shovel.

"Dig here," he said and gave Devereaux the shovel.

Devereaux looked from one to the other. He dug into the heavy, wet earth. The digging was not so hard, but in a little while, he was bathed in sweat. He felt the waterproof packet cling to his wet skin beneath the shirt. He decided to hit the one with the submachine gun first.

He waited too long.

He bent over to grab a spadeful of earth and there was a single shot and he felt the pain and he plunged forward, blood on his head.

The first soldier said, "It was deep enough."

"Manet does not want anyone to find his body."

"It was deep enough."

"Turn him over. Let's search him."

They found a waterproof packet around his neck and opened it. They found a book and opened it.

"Numbers," said one.

"He was a spy," said the other. "That's what Manet said."

"Then give this to Manet, it will be of use for him," said the first one, the one with the submachine gun.

"Come on, let's get this over with."

They covered the body quickly with clumps of earth and with branches. The grave was shallow but the body was covered and there was enough dirt to do a good job.

"*Adieu*," said the first one.

The second one said, "I wonder what's in the book?"

"Manet will know what to do with it."

They clumped away through the vegetation back up the hill to the camp. There were no sounds but their footsteps and the cry of insects and the sounds of owls hunting in the night.

19
MEETING AT SEA

The beaches were empty, the dawn sky leaden with the threat of rain. The white yacht growled out of the channel from Captiva Island into the open gulf. The DEA agent followed it for a long time with his field glasses and when he saw it disappear on the far gray horizon, he went back to his car parked behind a grove of scrub pines.

"KZA seven-five-one calling KZA seven. Over."

"KZA seven. You're up early."

"Our friend decided to take a sea trip."

"Nice day for it. We're getting rain in Fort Myers already."

"It's clear here."

"That's because that's where rich people live," said the dispatcher.

"You wanna notify coast guard?"

"Roger."

"Approximate heading five degrees south by southwest from the harbor."

"Roger."

"I'm going home. Get some shuteye. Signal went off at three that he was moving. Old fart, what's he doing at dawn?"

"Will notify CG. Ten-four KZA seven-five-one."

"Ten-four."

Coast guard headquarters in St. Petersburg relayed the message from KZA 7 of the Drug Enforcement Administration to the *City of Akron*, patrolling fifteen miles off Naples, but the message —requesting surveillance of the white yacht that had left Captiva at dawn—was ignored. *City of Akron* was on Priority One out of Washington. No one in St. Petersburg realized that. The secrecy was intended.

■　■　■

The white yacht bobbed against the swells of the sea. White caps were crashing across the bow and washing the ship down in salt water to the aft deck. The yacht was seven miles southwest of Captiva now. The whitecaps charged like soldiers, in rows racing across the plain of the sea.

In the main cabin, a large man with brown, loose skin and gray hair sat at a table playing blackjack. The second player was a woman with long blond hair and very shrewd eyes. Her skin was brown and tight and her body was meant to be seen and touched. She wore bikini pants and a button-front silk blouse that was unbuttoned.

"Stick," she said.

"Nineteen," he said. His name was Theodore Weisman and he ran dope and women and gambling on the west coast of Florida. The east coast had long since been divided by old alliances in the family, going back to Meyer Lansky, the man who fixed the World Series once. Teddy Weisman was of a younger generation. But he was nearly sixty years old and the years weighed on him because there was not enough time left to do all the things he wanted.

Dee dealt the cards again. She had dealt in Vegas for a while, looking for a break. The break came unexpectedly, when Weisman decided to give her a place to sleep. Right next to him.

They played out of boredom. They played because it could not occur to them to do anything else while they waited in the gray morning light in the middle of the shallow sea.

"Hit me," Teddy said.

"Stick," she said.

She had two queens. The large man took the first hit which brought him to fourteen. He had to gamble on that. He called again and another queen fell in front of him. She took two dollars and left two on the table and he pushed two to the center and she folded the cards and dealt again.

Again and again. The only sound in the cabin was the sea pushing at the Fiberglas hull, slapping in regular beats. And the sound of the cards slapping on the table.

The door to the cabin opened. A man with black hair, wearing a white shirt and designer jeans, stood in the hatch. "They're here."

"'Bout time."

"Had the same problem we had in this sea."

"It always rains in Florida, Tone," said Teddy, not looking up from the cards. He had seventeen. It was enough. "Okay, Tone," he said, dismissing the big man. "Dee, get to the galley with Tone, make me some sandwiches. And a couple of Heinekens."

"Maybe he don't drink beer for breakfast," said Tone.

"I give a fuck what he drinks," said Teddy, taking the money. Dee sidled out of her seat and took her money and shoved it in her panties.

"Dee, you disgust me," Teddy said. "Putting dirty dollar bills next to your snatch like that. You get a disease."

Tone, behind Teddy, grinned at Dee as though they had private jokes.

She glanced at him and then at Teddy who wasn't smiling. "I got no pockets."

"Button your blouse, you look like a bimbo. I mean, you may be a bimbo but try not to look like one when I got visitors, okay?"

"Don't start on me."

"You got it wrong, Dee. I already started. What you want to watch for is the finish."

"Come on, Teddy." She gave him a squeeze. He smelled

133

her body. She pressed her belly to his face for a moment so that he could smell how young she was.

"You know I hate weather like this."

He smiled, patted her bottom. "Afraid I'm gonna let you drown? This boat ain't gonna sink, that's for sure. This boat sinks I'm on it, I sue somebody," Teddy said. He was trying to make it light.

"That's what they said about the *Titanic*," Dee said.

He laughed like a big man. He had a hoarse chuckle. He had been a big man when he was in his forties. He had problems now, all kinds of problems. He wasn't big anymore. He didn't have time to do all the stuff he wanted to do.

"Wash your hands before you make the sandwich. Make BLTs. Couple of them. Get the glasses frosted, Tone."

"You got it, Teddy."

"Good boy, Tone."

Tone and the woman crowded into the galley and closed the hatch door. Dee smiled at Tone and bumped him with her pelvis. He smiled and touched her breasts beneath the silk. She shook her head and washed her hands.

The coast guard cutter was white with red-and-blue piping on the bow. Two of the yacht crew took lines from the cutter and the distance between the two boats closed. A man appeared on deck, covered against the spray with a yellow foul-weather jacket. He climbed the rail of the cutter and dropped five feet to the deck of the yacht. Then he ducked belowdecks and the crew of the yacht released the lines and the cutter growled away, into the pewter sea.

The sky was dark and lower than it had been at dawn.

"Okay," Teddy said into a microphone to the pilot. "When we got the cargo, head on back but slow."

The receiver squawked and Teddy shut it off.

Frank Collier ducked through the hatch into the main cabin. He had seen Teddy Weisman many times before they had connected for business reasons.

"You look good, Frank. You look like you wanna be a sailor," Teddy said in his growl.

Frank nodded, shook hands, and took off his yellow jacket. Frank Collier had a strong grip when he shook hands. He was from Notre Dame, one of the few to make higher rank in CIA. The FBI usually recruited from the Catholic colleges. The CIA was the domain of the Protestant eastern establishment.

Teddy's hands were strong as well. He had started as a juice collector in Chicago forty years before. He had known how to use his hands and be strong and never show weakness. Even now when his flabby body was betraying him.

"I like boats," Frank said. He felt close to the old man for some reason. A lot of people didn't trust Teddy. Maybe Frank didn't trust him either. But he liked the old man. "Sailed in my uncle's yacht on Lake Michigan when I was a kid. He was in construction."

"Tom Collier," said Teddy.

"That's a good guess," Frank said.

"I never guess, kid," said Teddy. "Your uncle was a crook."

"Yeah, I know," said Frank Collier.

"Hey, all right. I like you, Frank." The old man smiled. "I like you from the start. Only reason I do business with you people again, I trust you. Fucked twice in Cuba, I ain't gonna be fucked again, ain't gonna be holding no douche bag this time."

"Everything is all right."

"Except them nuns got killed."

"Yeah. But that'll blow over. That won't touch this. Gautier's men are on Island Begin, waiting for Z-hour."

"I love the way you guys talk, like you was being overheard by the G making a bet on the phone. Z-hour. The fuck, I can't help it, I like it." He grinned and it was meant to overwhelm Frank. Frank wasn't a fool; he knew what charm was for.

"Everything is Go."

"So when is Go, Frank?"

135

Frank stared at him. He was part of Angel but he wasn't part of it. "Everything is Go," Frank said again.

"What are you now? Gonna start playing games. Fuck you then, I thought we knew each other."

"Six hours, Teddy. Six hours and a hundred guys on the beach. The best. Trained men. Tear the country a new asshole in forty-eight hours."

"And my guy is set," said Teddy. "There. In the pocket. He's got twenty guys now in the capital.

"That's the deal," Frank said. He couldn't help it. It was getting to him. His leg started jiggling up and down under the table. There was a vibration. Teddy said, "You got to go to the bathroom or something?"

"Nothing," said Frank Collier. "Nothing. Everything is set on your end." He said it like a wish.

"Everything. One of my main."

"Anthony Calabrese," said Frank.

"Yeah. You know mine and now I know yours. Trust. That's what we didn't have in Cuba. Everyone fucking everyone else."

"Lack of guts. We pulled back when we shouldn't have."

"Yeah," said Teddy and his eyes were lazy now, remembering, trying not to show anything.

The hatch to the galley opened. Dee came in with a tray of sandwiches and two green bottles of beer and frosted mugs. She put them down on the table. She looked at the government man. She didn't like him. She thought he was a pussy. She told Teddy that once. Teddy said he had a wife and three kids. That explained it, Dee had said.

"The bread's got holes in it, I tole you," said Teddy.

"Holes is for him, not you, Teddy. I made the sandwiches. Your bread ain't got no holes in it."

"Okay. Just so my broad's got holes in her," said Teddy, trying to smile, annoyed because the bread with holes stared at him. The holes were eyes. He hated bread with holes, hated to sit at a table where someone ate bread like that. It turned him off. She knew it.

136

"Ignore the holes," Dee said.

"Maybe Frank don't like bread like that neither."

"No, no, it's okay. Food is food. I didn't eat." He wished the woman would go away.

Teddy watched Frank Collier. "Okay, Dee, beat it."

"Gee, 'Thanks for the sanwiches, Dee,'" said Dee.

"Thanks," said Frank. His leg was jiggling again.

"Beat it," said Teddy.

"Some people are polite," Dee said.

"Some broads know when they got it good," Teddy said.

Dee closed the hatch behind her. Teddy made her mad. Tone grabbed her breast and tried to kiss her. "Go away, Tone," she said. "We're on the fucking boat."

Teddy and Frank ate for a moment in silence. The beer was cold and the bubbles broke on the back of their throats.

"Six hours, Frank," said Teddy, making a salute with his mug.

"Six hours."

"Anthony takes out Ready, takes out Celezon. Nobody can function. Gautier makes his move on Manet, then he's got a wide road to the capital. Just that easy."

"The first wave in six hours. The second assault eight hours later, on Madeleine itself. We've got two men down there, been there three days."

"Who killed the sisters, Frank?"

"Manet."

"Naw. Manet didn't have the road. Who killed them?"

"Why would it be Ready? It doesn't make sense."

"What about Celezon. What about his voodoo cops?"

"If they did it, then Celezon wants to move on Ready. That's just as well. Let them kill each other and Anthony Calabrese kills who's left."

"Okay," said Teddy, biting the sandwich. "Just so you thought about it."

"Gautier is in our pocket. Your pocket. You'll have a casino in six months. You'll own the island."

"Like Havana in the old days."

137

"Better. More money. More tourists. Everyone gambles."

They chewed and drank beer. "Drugs stay there," said Frank.

"That's the deal. I don't screw you, you don't screw me. Everyone needs a partner sometimes. A good partner takes what's his and leaves what ain't. I got no interest in drugs. Everyone is smuggling. I get squeezed, I got so many chumps to deal with, it drives me crazy. I'm ready to consolidate. Business. Caribbean Amusement Investments. Banks. Nice and legal and very pro Uncle."

"They secure the southern half of the island, rip Manet apart. Manet is a paper company. Ready lets them be rebels. But Ready got too greedy. His army is paper too. He steals too much, he makes too many trips to Switzerland. He should have kept the army up."

"He should of," agreed Teddy. "You guys got good sources."

"It isn't that hard," said Frank and he felt good about it. Nothing was that hard when it came down to it.

"Still, you got good sources."

"He's blown out of the water when he comes down the coast road to take on Gautier. Calabrese sabotages the capital, kills Ready or Celezon or both if he can, whatever is left of that army and the security police—well, it's not enough. Gautier'll have two hundred and fifty men within twelve hours of the first wave."

"Eighteen hours from now."

"That's it," said Frank Collier.

"And Gautier is sure." They had gone over these things a hundred times. They spoke to reassure each other. It was the waiting. Frank jiggled his right leg again under the table.

"Gautier loves America. He loves us. We've got a base there."

"And we got Gautier," said Teddy. "He loves money, too."

"Who doesn't?"

138

Teddy tried a growling chuckle. "Who doesn't. Right." They sat for a moment and stared out the porthole at the gray, swelling sea. The porthole was streaked with spray and rain.

"There wasn't supposed to be a storm. We checked all that. That's what I hate when you do the homework and something fucks up anyway," said Frank.

"He's coming from twelve miles off. This ain't gonna stop him," said Teddy. "Don't worry, Frank. Gautier'll be there on time."

"I got to worry, Teddy. You got no worries. If nothing happened, nothing came off, it costs you nothing."

"It cost me Anthony. It costs me what I been doing on St. Michel, getting in with Ready and those people. It costs me, Frank, don't think it don't."

The white yacht pushed through the waves with authority, rising and falling. In six hours, at Ismaralda Key in the middle of the chain that stretched from the mainland to Key West, Frank Collier would debark and get in his rental car and take the drive back to his rooms at Key West. The first signal would come by the middle of the afternoon. By midnight, it should all be under control. By dawn, it should all be over.

He couldn't help it. He drummed his fingers on the table and stared out the port.

But no one was on the stormy gulf on the long trip down to Ismaralda Key except for a couple of commercial fishing boats and a peculiar black ship with black hull and deck and a sailing mast pushing down for the keys. The two boats ran parallel for a while about half a mile apart but the black ship was fast and more skillfully piloted. It pulled ahead and before they all reached the keys, it was gone.

"Who'd want weather like this," Frank asked at one point.

Teddy, playing solitaire, looked up and realized what Frank was talking about.

"Dope runners," said Teddy Weisman. "I know that boat. I used it a couple of times."

"I'll keep that in mind."

"No, Frank. This is business. I tell you things, you keep that out of mind unless I tell you to remember."

And Frank Collier, for the first time, caught in a boat with this strange man on a shallow, stormy sea, felt he was not in control.

20

YVETTE

Rita Macklin awoke and gray dawn surged against the window panes. It might rain. She felt very warm beneath the covers and she realized she was naked. She blinked in the darkness of the room and could not see where she was.

She had dreamed of the nuns all night. She had dreamed of the metal tray, gleaming with bone and brain mashed into the bowl of the skull.

She sat up in bed as the door opened.

Yvette wore a silk dressing gown and crossed the large room to her and sat down next to her. Yvette's face was pale. Her hand was cool to the touch.

"Celezon brought you here," she said.

"Where am I?"

"In the palace. Colonel Ready wants you detained."

"I'm a prisoner?"

"No. Celezon brought you here. I told you."

Rita felt the chill of madness settle around her again. They were all mad. Which only proved that she might be the mad one after all.

"I think he means to kill you. Now that he has your friend. Was your friend an American agent after all, as Celezon told me?"

"What do you mean?"

"Devereaux. It is French, no? He was killed this morning

about two in the morning, I think it was. Celezon said the people in the hills brought the notebook."

She had remembered how it had been for her when she had discovered her brother was dead in Laos long ago, when she had not wanted to believe the words of the telegram or the sympathy offered by the priest who came to the house afterward. And, for a long time, because they never found his body, she believed he was alive. If you believed them when they told you the truth, the bleakness of the truth would twist your heart more than if you lied to yourself for a long time and let the lie replace hurt until the hurt could be measured in small doses into yourself. It was the only way to take truth as a poison so that it did not kill you.

But she wanted to die.

"Who killed him?"

"Manet. In the hills. And then he sent that notebook to Colonel Ready. Colonel Ready has replaced all authority, all decency. Even the faith of the people." Said with a strange and glittering madness of tone. Yvette's dark eyes fixed her in the gloom of the unlit morning room. "Celezon brought you here, it was all right until you recovered. But you have to get out of St. Michel, you have to tell someone what is happening here before everything is destroyed."

"Where is Devereaux? Is he in . . ."

"The morgue? No. I see you love him. I understand." She touched Rita's hand absently. "They buried him in the hills."

The sob broke the soundless room and Yvette put her hand on Rita's mouth then and forced her to lie down and she held her hand over Rita's mouth until the great sob might only be little cries of fear and hurt.

"I'm sorry. But we are hiding you at great cost."

"Who?"

"Celezon. Me. The patriots. Ready has taken our country and killed the faith of the people." Said with simple madness.

"I don't believe any of this."

141

"Here," she said.

And it was the ring that she had given Devereaux once. He would not wear a ring or any jewelry, but he had taken the ring and bought a chain in Ouchy and worn it around his neck like a talisman. "Dogtag," he said once, smiling to her. They had smiled about the ring. The ring reminded him of her, he once said, in the way of perfume or a remembered evening shared when they both listened to a sad *chanson.*

"Who is Colonel Ready?"

"An American agent. He is a renegade, I think now, but he was. He was brought here. He took . . . over . . . the . . . country." Slowly, almost painfully. "Celezon is my brother."

Rita said nothing, trying to think.

"Celezon. We were children once, brother and sister. And then there was the brotherhood of the true religion, the one of the hills, not the false religion of that fat old priest from France."

"Your mother and father—"

"No, of course not. We were made brother and sister when we shared our blood."

She smiled, paused.

"And our bodies."

Smiling still, through the horror of the gray morning room. "You must tell of what Colonel Ready has done, how he has perverted this country from the true ways."

"I have to get out of here," she said.

"Yes. There's a way. Four miles south of the town is the café of a man called Flaubert. You will be able to find Harry Francis there. Or you will find a child who can take you to his shack."

"Why must I find him?"

"Because Colonel Ready has the notebook now. Harry's notebook. It is all he needs. Harry will understand that. Harry will find a way to take you off the island. You have to escape to tell the truth. If Colonel Ready finds you, he will kill you. Remember."

"I—"

"No. Nothing. Now you must flee. I'll give you francs, a new cloak to wear—you have to go now while most of the soldiers are drunk or sleeping. . . ."

TELLING HARRY

The clouds built high above the island and blotted out the gray sky to the east. The black clouds blustered about rain, and the wind shifted and the waves began to pound at the beach outside the dining room of the Café de la Paix.

Harry's bones ached. Philippe watched him at the table. Harry drank coffee laced with rum. Once he said, "Did you miss me, kid?"

Philippe said nothing.

Philippe saw that Harry's face was flushed with drink but that the cuts were healing. They had let him go the night before.

"When you were in prison, a man came to find you."

"What man, little one?"

"He had red hair."

"It was Colonel Ready."

"Another man."

"What kind of a man."

"A white. Like you. And an American. He said he was your friend."

"I don't have any friends." He tousled the boy's thick hair. "Except you."

"He went to your house."

"He did, huh?"

"He asked me to take him there."

"So you took him. What'd he do, bribe you?"

"You weren't there. I thought he might be your friend."

"I don't have no friends, I told you that."

"The police had been there before. I didn't think it mattered."

"What didn't matter?"

"He wanted to find your notebook. I told him you were in the prison."

"You're a regular chatterbox, you know that?"

Philippe said nothing. It wasn't right yet.

"They all want my notebook, Philippe. It's the thing that keeps them going."

"Yes."

"Get me another bottle, will you?"

"Yes," said the child.

Then: "Monsieur Harry?"

"What do you want?"

"I thought they might kill you."

"So did I at the time."

"He found the book," said Philippe.

Harry paused. He put down the cup. He stared at the child.

"He found the notebook. In the pit in the *toilette*."

"Jesus Mary and Joseph."

"He took a net and took out the box. There was a picture of you, monsieur. And a monsieur named Hemingway."

"Jesus Mary and Joseph."

"The notebook was full of numbers," said Philippe.

"Jesus Mary and Joseph, son-of-a-bitch."

And Harry grabbed Philippe by his scrawny neck and squeezed until he felt the breath leaving the body of the boy, felt the muscles straining in the thin body against his hold.

"Who is it, you whore's son? Who was this man that took the box, you son of a fucking whore, you black nigger bastard?"

The eyes of the child bulged.

Harry meant to kill him all right. Flaubert saw that.

Flaubert was at the door of the back room and he had a cleaver and he thought for a moment if he should kill Monsieur Harry because Harry meant to kill Philippe. He stared at the tableau.

And the front door banged open in the wind.

Rita Macklin, in dark cloak, stood framed in the gray storming light.

Flaubert said, "Don't hurt Philippe."

"Who took my book, you little nigger brat?"

"Devereaux," she said.

Harry Francis opened his hand and let the child breathe and Flaubert let the cleaver fall to his side and they all stared at the woman in the doorway. The wind blew into the room and the door banged on its hinge.

"Who the hell are you?"

"Devereaux took your book. And now Colonel Ready has it and Devereaux is dead," said Rita Macklin. Her face was flushed. She had dodged her way from the Palais Gris through the shuttered town, past the army patrols, down to this place and she thought she had no strength left. She had run for no other reason than to run from the nightmare that Devereaux's naked body was on a slab in that building, that his brain was splattered gray on a metal tray.

"Who are you?"

"I came with him. I'm a journalist. You're Harry Francis and Colonel Ready is going to kill you and we have to get off this island."

"Who was Devereaux, who was I to him?"

"Like you. An agent in the trade," she said in a controlled voice that was as loud as the wind. "And he died in the trade and you're going to die and that's all there is. I want to escape—"

"Who told you this?"

"Yvette."

His face blanched. She saw he thought it was true.

145

Yvette would know. He knew about Yvette and he knew that she told the truth. She had the ring in her fist, it was the truth to her that Devereaux was dead, but her words were enough for Harry Francis.

"He took my notebook." Slowly and sadly. Harry stood up and there were tears in his dead eyes.

And the first *gendarme* was in the door and he hit Rita Macklin across her back with his short baton. She stumbled and he took her by the hair and hit her again, and the pain fell in folds down her back.

"*Allons,*" he said to her and pulled her and the second one was in the door with handcuffs. Harry Francis took a step forward. The first policeman hit him in the ribs. Harry grunted. He swung again and Harry went down to one knee. He swung again and Harry cried out. And the third one was in the door and he did not know who to hit so he hit Flaubert because Flaubert had the cleaver in his hand. The cleaver fell on the floor. Philippe screamed and the third one hit him with the baton and Philippe was knocked out. Flaubert said nothing and tried to stand still and the third *gendarme* hit him again because he was standing still and doing nothing. The first one hit Harry Francis across the back twice and the second one pulled at the handcuffs so that Rita's arms felt numb and her footing was bad and she slipped and the second one hit her again.

Harry said, "You bastards."

The first policeman grinned and said, in French, that he would probably be back to arrest Harry later but that all they wanted now was the white woman.

They shoved Rita into the open Jeep. The rain washed down the seats and one of the policemen held her because she could not keep her balance in the open Jeep. The Jeep turned sharply around and headed north back four miles to the center of St. Michel town and then up to the Palais Gris where the prison and the morgue were in the basement.

Philippe groaned, rose, ran to the door, stumbled, held the jamb, watched the Jeep.

He turned to Harry Francis and he said, "I'm glad they have the notebook. Because now they will kill you too, along with that woman."

22

DEVEREAUX'S GIRL

They took her down into the cells. She crossed the courtyard of the palace in the rain, crossing from the front to the side basement door as Harry Francis had been dragged across five nights before. She felt the arms push her but felt nothing more. A sereneness had come to her on the road to St. Michel. Thomas More had watched the prisoners led to the execution dock and said, "There but for the grace of God go I." God's grace ran out for him in time; and her. She thought these things because they comforted her.

When she was led into the cells, they took her clothes. One of the men said he had to search her then. He put on a latex glove and he explored her. When he was finished, he looked at her and smiled and she saw he had only blackened teeth. She said he was a bastard and his mother was a whore.

He hit her and smiled and hit her again very hard. They put her in the cell then with the tile walls and the tile floor and the two drains. They turned on the hose and beat her with the steady stream of water. She thought she was drowning.

She was inside the cell for an hour. It was raining. She heard the thunder though there was no window in the cell to see the rain. Devereaux was dead. In a little while, she would be dead as well.

A man came into the room and told her to stand up. She

stared up at him. He kicked her below the ribs so that she vomited. He told her to stand up. She stood up. He told her to keep standing. He went out of the cell.

When you are cold and wet and naked and a prisoner, you lose your defiance because dignity is too heavy a burden to carry. When your body is not your own, there is no dignity. You only want to be what you are not—warm and dry and safe and clothed and free. But the least of these things is freedom. You will give up freedom to have the other things. All of the manuals of interrogation agree on this, whatever their language. The lesson is the same in Dzhersinski Square in Moscow or in Havana or Salvador or in the little safehouses off the beltway in Virginia where people are not seen and cries are not heard.

Pain is useful, the manuals agree, but that is later. The process must begin with humiliation. The process begins with nakedness. In the United States federal prison system, the new men are called fish and are stripped of their clothing first and forced into mass showers and are inspected in their orifices and are issued clothes that do not fit well and then are thrown to the mercy of the general prison population. The prisoner has to understand his situation from the beginning.

Rita Macklin thought to fall down as though she had fainted as she had fainted the night she saw the naked bodies of two dead nuns in the morgue.

But the *gendarme* had been quite specific when he kicked her and made her vomit.

She was to stand.

23

IN THE LAND OF THE DEAD

The rain washed the ground in the hills.

The rain fell through the trees, broke apart on the branches, fell softly to earth between the trees and soaked the ground and ran down the earth, down the hills, back to the sea.

He lay for a long time awake but with his eyes closed and when he felt the rain, he tried to move his arms. They were heavy, his body was heavy. He moved his arms and they pushed up and then they were free.

Devereaux groaned and tasted earth in his mouth and coughed and pushed up again.

There was less than six inches of dirt over his body; also leaves and branches and clumps of grass. An animal had awakened him from death. It had dug in the earth and found his finger and bit it and he had felt pain. He moved his finger and the animal—he never knew what it was—bit again.

Pain and pain.

Then he felt the curious detached pain in his head and realized he was alive.

He rose from the grave and stood a moment, leaning against a tree. He felt giddy and weak but he was standing and the tree was solid and he did not think he would faint. He closed his eyes and opened them again to see if the world remained.

There was rain above his head. His face was black with dirt, his body was caked with wet dirt, his hands were dark. There was blood on the finger that had told him he was alive.

He touched his head.

There was a wound, of course, but the bullet had been

fired carelessly, perhaps as he bent over for the shovelful of earth. It had caused a lot of bleeding and flattened him into the grave and they must have thought he was dead.

Devereaux smiled. His teeth were perfectly white against the darkness of his features; he grinned like an animal. He was very alive and he felt the rain and opened his mouth to wash the taste of earth from his tongue.

It was daylight. He had been dead all night.

And then he realized the waterproof packet was gone. The notebook. The photograph.

And her ring.

"I won't wear a ring," he had said.

"I know." She had smiled. *"Just have it anyway."*

They never spoke of it again. He never left it. He carried it with him. Sometimes, when she had been away on an assignment, he would take the ring and hold it like a talisman. He would conjure her in memory.

He blinked again. The pain in his head was not his, as though it belonged to another person. He heard the rain but heard it imperfectly, the sound of rain made on an old-fashioned radio. Everything he heard was curiously flat.

He shook his head and it hurt very much, and he thought he might vomit. He stood still until the hurt stopped, until it went into another person.

"All right," he said and his voice sounded strange to him. "I'm all right."

■　■　■

Devereaux could not guess the time. The sky was sullen with clouds, the rain pitched straight down. He had started in the direction of Madeleine and become confused. Now he was on the hill behind Madeleine. At the base of the hill, he had beached the dinghy.

His head throbbed and his ears were ringing. He sat down under a giant pine and huddled against himself. He was wet and tired and dirty and the strength seemed gone from his legs.

150

All of his guesses about St. Michel and what he would find there had only trapped him. He had been wrong to think there was no notebook; now it was gone. He had been right to believe that the whores of Madeleine knew Manet, had access to him. It was why he had chosen one of them. Something Colonel Ready had said in Evian that afternoon to Celezon: Go and buy some souvenirs for your whores in St. Michel. And Celezon had answered: And the whores of Madeleine. Colonel Ready somehow controlled the rebels—he had been sure of it from the beginning when he read the Economic Review report on the island. The rebels were small in force, disorganized, financed haphazardly. Ready would have been more than a match for them.

He had explained none of these things to Rita Macklin. They were all just guesses based on hunches, guided by everything he could find out about St. Michel in thirty-six hours in London, guided by everything he knew about Colonel Ready.

And because they were guesses, he had confronted Manet and fallen into Manet's clumsy trap. For the first time in a long while, he felt a wave of self-pity and it disgusted him. He'd end up no better than Cain.

He pushed the pity out of himself with an almost physical effort. He sat very still and let his mind fill with plans and new guesses and an idea of what he had to do next. The self-pity retreated.

There were three problems: Rita. The notebook. Escape from the island.

The trees around him protected him from the brunt of the morning rain. He could look out through the trees at the churning, dangerous waters of the gulf. The Caribbean was not a gentle sea anymore. It heaved for breath like a gray old man, full of impotent rage.

Rita was in the capital and there was nothing to be done until the escape could be arranged. In any case, Colonel Ready would let her go on her own. There were reporters on the island because of the nuns; Manet had said so.

151

And there were CIA caseworkers and that did not make any sense at all. Unless Ready was still with the Langley Firm.

Or Harry Francis.

Harry Francis. The name insisted.

Devereaux picked up a blade of grass and broke it off and put it between his teeth and tasted the sweetness. His eyes were staring through the trees at the sea. Harry Francis. The notebook. Everything had to begin and end with Harry Francis. Colonel Ready somehow wanted the notebook badly but not badly enough to kill Harry Francis for it.

Because he needed Harry Francis alive. Or he needed the notebook. Both of them. Or one or the other.

And Manet had a notebook. He could bargain with Ready for it if he knew it was what Ready wanted. Or he could give it to Ready and Ready could kill Harry Francis. Or use Harry to interpret the book.

Devereaux closed his eyes. Guesses and guesses. But everything involved Harry and the notebook, the leverage was in the notebook. That was what Ready wanted from Devereaux, the thing he couldn't find himself. And Devereaux had given a notebook to him through Manet.

Damn.

He stood up then. It was a matter of finding Harry Francis if he was still alive.

He finished the thought and started to turn and stopped. Something had caught his eye again, something he had not been looking for.

He saw a small flotilla of white boats bursting across the gray, heaving sea, flailing the waters with shallow wakes. The boats bumped over the ridges of waves and each boat was bristling with men. Men with guns.

They were coming in very quickly and he could hear the faint buzz of their engines. Where the hell had they come from? Who were they?

And then he thought of the two dead agents in Mimi's

room. He had understood then the warning found in his London research. He shut his eyes and saw it again verbatim:

ECONOMIC REVIEW: ST. MICHEL, REPUBLIC OF:
. . . . In 1979, during the Carter administration in the U.S. (ER 12/79/382), approximately 240 exiles from St. Michel were accepted into the U.S. following a decision of the Pascon administration to expel them for "seditious, traitorous acts" against St. Michel, its government, its people. Henri Gautier organized a paramilitary command (Saviors of the Republic) with evidence (ER 12/80/383) of covert CIA funding. . . .

Approximately the time Colonel Ready came to St. Michel. And the time that Harry Francis surfaced here.

The first boats were docking and men were wading in the shallow surf at the base of the hills toward the shore. Devereaux watched a moment longer and then turned. He began to thread his way through the forest, down the hill, in the direction of Madeleine.

In under a half an hour he saw the low roofs of the town. With the lights off, Madeleine seemed sullen in the rain, expectant, waiting.

When he reached the streets it became clear that the soldiers were gone. Everyone had withdrawn. Colonel Ready had anticipated the invasion by passively allowing it.

Devereaux found an ancient Renault parked in the Street of the Blue Pleasure. He opened the door and the key was plugged into the ignition. No one stole on St. Michel because there was nothing to steal; no one stole because there was no place to run to and enjoy the stolen wealth; no one stole because the penalty for theft, like the penalties for other serious crimes, was the same.

Devereaux turned the ignition and held his foot on the floor and the 2CV engine whirred into life like a sewing machine. He punched the gas and found first gear and the Renault bucked down the narrow alley, jolting itself over the cobbled streets.

Devereaux was at the top of the hill on the coast road, heading north out of Madeleine, when the first wave of Gautier's men entered the town.

24

IN DISTANT PLACES

Radio silence broke at 2:12 P.M. eastern daylight time. Frank Collier picked up the telephone as soon as it rang. The other end of the line was in Alpha 4, an expensive ship-to-shore hookup that only a government could afford.

"Angel landed at o-nine-hundred hours," Gautier said very clearly despite the storm and the crackling distance between St. Michel and Frank Collier's room in Key West.

"At noon," Frank said. His leg began to jiggle on its own. "Noon."

"The storm here. Altered . . ." The radiophone connection faded a moment. Frank pressed the receiver to his ear. "We have Madeleine."

"Casualties," Frank Collier said.

"None. Repeat: none."

His mouth fell open.

"No resistance."

"Damn."

"Pardon?" He heard Gautier's puzzled voice. He stared at a bad painting of sunset in Key West on the wall of his hotel room. The day was evil with rain and darkness and waves of clouds pinning down the flat island to the sea all around. The palms were bending to the force of the wind and the narrow streets of Key West were all empty, the houses shuttered against the blow.

"Where is the army?"

"Gone, vanished."

"It's a trap," Frank Collier said, the fear rising in him like sickness in his throat. He wanted to gag. "Trap."

"I can't . . ." The voice faded. "We proceed against Manet—"

"Trap," Frank Collier said.

"We will trap them, yes, and—"

"No, no, no, no," Frank Collier said.

"Hello? Hello? Hello?"

"Trap!"

The radio connection went dead. He put down the receiver. He stared at the painting of the sunset in Key West. It was very beautiful when the sun set in the Caribbean and people went to Mallory Square at the waterfront to celebrate and drink and watch the street musicians and clowns and con men perform on the square for the rich tourists.

The painting in the room caught none of these qualities of sunset in Key West.

Frank Collier got up and went to the window and stared at the storm. He thought of the last sixteen years. He thought of the options they had wanted yesterday. No options. Abort or Go. He pushed for Go.

No options left at all.

25
DEVEREAUX'S RUN

He came along the coast road slowly, looking for the turnoff into the scrub pines that the child had showed to him. He would try to find Harry Francis first because he had to solve the problem of Hemingway's notebook to survive. To survive with Rita. To escape this damned place.

He pushed toward the fishing village, which was midway between Madeleine and St. Michel. The village was three shacks of tin, bits of stucco, wax paper on open windows. The boats were all in the small harbor, old buckets with sails and leaking hulls, patched together by old men who had nothing better to sail in to find the fish that gave them enough life each day to wait for tomorrow.

He stopped the car and went inside the shack that was used as a meeting room for the sailors. The room was full of tobacco smoke and the smell of warm beer. He had stopped there the first time, when he had been brought in by Cain, when he had found Philippe and Harry's notebook.

He nodded to the half dozen men sitting at the table. They stared at him but did not speak. He was an apparition, in rags, caked with filth, gaunt and bloody. But they were men who had seen many things and they said nothing. They only stared at him.

"I've missed the road. The turnoff to Harry Francis's place," Devereaux said in French.

Nobody moved.

"Can you help me?"

No one spoke.

"I have to find Harry Francis."

"Monsieur Francis is not there," said one finally. "Go down to the Café de la Paix. I saw him go there an hour ago when the *gendarmes noires* came."

"Did they arrest Harry?"

"No. Only the American woman." The man smiled. He had very white teeth and a very black face. He was thin and tired and the fishing was not very good, it had not been good for a month. He had his woman and three children and he sometimes thought he should take the old tub and sail north until he either drowned or reached Florida. Even in prison in America, there was food enough to eat. He thought of the white woman and this white man before him.

Devereaux spoke in a gentle voice. "Who was she?"

"An American. They struck her, she spoke in English."

"All right," Devereaux said, sickness in his belly. He stumbled at the door.

"How did you get so dirty, man? You look like a nigger now," said the thin fisherman. And the other men laughed at that.

Devereaux stopped at the door. "What about the woman?"

"She was a white woman. A couple of *gendarmes noires* took her. I wonder what they did with her?" He smiled and the others smiled as well.

Devereaux felt anger for a long moment and then let it pass. These men didn't mean anything.

He got back in the Renault and continued up toward St. Michel. Two miles south of the town, in the blinding rain, he pulled up in front of the Café de la Paix.

He stepped inside the door.

He stared at Harry Francis.

For a moment, Harry did not look up. He was staring at the bottle of vodka in front of him. He was staring at it as though he saw his future in it. When he saw Devereaux, he said nothing. Devereaux took off his shirt and dropped it on the back of the chair. Philippe came out of the rear of the café where the family lived. He saw Devereaux and thought he resembled a ghost.

"Devereaux," Harry Francis said then.

Devereaux felt the sickness overwhelm him. He felt as though he would never move from this spot.

Harry Francis had his name.

"You killed me, you bastard."

"I don't care about you, Harry. Why did they arrest the woman?"

"I don't give a damn why. I had the notebook and you took it and that's the only thing that could have saved my life."

"How did you know I took it?"

"This traitor." He nodded to the boy. "And now Colonel Ready has it and we're all going to die."

Devereaux almost saw all the pieces now. The connections were not so blurred.

"And that includes you," Harry said and he got up from the table and took out the long knife on his Garrison belt. He held the knife well, away from his body, tentative and yet strong, like a knife fighter.

"You don't want to kill me," Devereaux said.

"You're wrong, friend. I want to do that very much. Why did you think to look there, in that foul outhouse? The stink is enough to kill you—"

"Tricks of the trade," Devereaux said, standing easily flat on both feet, his hands quiet at his sides, ready to move right or left. His head was still ringing but the pain was clear now, localized, not general. He blinked and watched Harry carefully with gray, arctic eyes.

"What trade is that?"

Harry took another step.

"The same one," Devereaux said.

"CIA," Harry said. "He's going to wring your neck as well. You can't trust him."

"Ready needs that notebook."

"Maybe he does and maybe not. He can't read it, not yet, but that will come in time. There isn't a code that can't be broken."

"Even Hemingway's," said Devereaux in a very soft voice, as though he wanted to attract attention to what he said. The rain was steady on the roof now, the water dripped from his shirt on the back of the chair onto the floor.

"How did you know that?"

"Under the endpaper. 'Papa.' The book was old enough. You were in Cuba with him."

"Damn you." And then Harry paused. "Damn you." He let the knife fall to his side. "You're good at it, you know that?"

"Yes."

"Damn you. You got that and they'd been over my place a hundred times. Never thought to look in the toilet."

"Because it stinks."

"I kept moving it. I had three places."

158

"I looked in the other two."

For a moment, Harry Francis smiled. "I bet you do know where they are."

"Are you going to kill me, Harry?"

"No. I'll let Colonel Ready do that. After he finishes butchering me. After he finishes with . . . Come on, sit down, have a drink."

Harry waved toward the table like a host. He boomed at Flaubert to get bread and cheese.

Philippe ran into the back to help his father.

Warily, Devereaux walked to the table and sat down across from Harry. He waited while Harry poured vodka into the glass. "We don't have any ice."

The vodka had a synthetic, warm taste on his tongue. It burned his throat.

"Who is she?" Harry said.

"Rita Macklin," Devereaux replied. He poured another drink.

"Do you have a way out of here?"

"Yes," Devereaux said.

"How?"

"A boat. In the fishing village," Devereaux lied.

"Big enough for the two of us."

"And Rita."

"They took her to the Palais Gris. To the cells." Harry winced. "You don't want to know too much about that place."

"Goddamn," Devereaux said, his hand curled into a fist.

"He had me in there last week. He wanted the notebook."

"I didn't think there was a book."

"He tortured me. Electricity. You know the way they do those things."

"I thought I could figure out what he wanted and give it to him or kill him and get away."

"You're not CIA."

"No."

"What are you?"

159

"Nothing. I'm not in the old business," Devereaux said.

"They'll kill her now. A reporter from America. Either kill her or let her tell the world about St. Michel."

"We get her and then we get away. That's all."

"All right," Harry said. "It's the only chance for me. But it won't last that long, you know. I'm dead. Dead to CIA, dead to everyone. Ready kept me alive because he plays the edges all the time."

"Why did he need you?"

"Me," Harry said. His eyes stared at nothing. "Or the book. The book proves it. I can prove it. CIA was afraid of me, you know that? Six years ago. They had a contract."

"Why?"

"I wanted out of it. I wanted quits for real."

"And you knew something."

"I know everything," Harry Francis said.

"Ready was sent here by CIA," Devereaux said.

"Yes. I was his mascot. He said he'd never let anything happen to me. Ready was supposed to flip the island. He flipped it. And then he got rid of Langley. Ready plays the edges, I told you that."

That was it, Devereaux thought. Ready was CIA until he had control of the island and then he double-crossed the Langley Firm. And Harry, whatever Harry was, was something useful to Ready. Just as Devereaux had been useful. Just as Rita Macklin was useful. A hostage or a reporter. If one thing happened, she would have been safe; another, she was in danger; another, she would have to be killed.

"You were killed," Harry said. "That's why I didn't want to kill you a second time."

"That's what they thought."

"They buried you."

"Yes."

"Flaubert has clothes. Give him your rags, he'll give you pants and a shirt."

"How do we get into the palace?"

Harry Francis grinned then. "That's never the trouble.

Getting out again is the hard part. You don't have a weapon, do you? And what about me and my knife? That's not a match for M-seventeens."

"The weapons, everything was funded by Langley."

"That's one of the embarrassing things they'd prefer not to tell the world about. That's one of the edges that keeps Ready where he is. He's like a cat on glass. If he slips, he grabs at anything. He's the original man for leverage. Games in games. You have to admire the bastard."

Traps in traps, Devereaux thought. And now there was no more time to find a safe way to spring one.

26

THE BUTCHER'S YARD

Sister Mary Columbo heard the first firing dimly.

She had been asleep on the cot in the tent in Manet's camp.

She was stronger each hour but the pain held her down. She wondered if the *New York Times* reporter had gotten her story out. It had been raining all night and all day and now it was nearly night again and the rain thudded dully against the canvas of the tent. The tent was soaked with humidity; her face was wet. She opened her eyes when she heard the little pops that were the rain-muted sound of guns.

The sound came very clearly through the clatter of rain and the thudding of wind on the tent sides.

It was the sound of battle joined. The grace of time had never let her forget those things.

The automatic weapons made lines of fire across the camp. The tracers on the bullet tips—to guide the field of fire—raced across the campyard and defined the perimeters of death.

The bullets scarcely made a sound when they thumped into a body. There were some cries of men and women in the camp but they were muted by the drumbeat of rain.

Sister Mary Columbo crawled off the cot and pulled on a rain poncho and rolled under the cot. A moment later, bullets ripped into the tent canvas where she had lain. For a long time, she lay still and listened to cries and screams. Then she crawled to the tent flap and looked out.

Flares sputtered in the rain. Flares filled the open, mourning sky above the camp. The white flares in the sky caught Manet's men in freeze frames. She remembered the deer in Pennsylvania; she had driven through the hills and the deer stood at the side of the turnpike, confused by the rows of headlights marching in the darkness.

Grenades shook the ground.

The tracer patterns danced across the ground. Burst by burst, the machine guns defined the ground. Muted by rain and the weight of the storm, the bullets sounded damp, like firecrackers set off by little boys on the Fourth of July when it is raining.

There were kerosene lanterns in the camp but the flares reduced everything in the darkness to whiteness. As the flares would die, one after the other, and fall in the night sky, the darkness would resume the ground, glowing red in the light of the lanterns.

Gautier and his first wave pushed into the center of the camp like the prow of a liner poking into a hostile sea. They shot at everything around them. Manet's men were frenzied by terror. One threw down his rifle in front of Gautier and Gautier shot his face off.

Everyone shot in madness. They shot at cases of food and at men already torn apart by grenades. They shot at the women huddled at the mouth of the empty bauxite mine.

After Collier had ordered him to trap Manet, Gautier had not waited for his second assault wave, but had moved quickly from Madeleine into the hills. He planned to kill everyone and then to move on to St. Michel tonight and finish the job. Before dawn, St. Michel would be recovered.

The M-17 in Gautier's hands shook as he drew it slowly, like a child drawing a careful line, across the field of fire, back and forth, so that the bullets did not bunch into a single target but had the effect of making the weapon seem more formidable than it was.

Gautier saw Manet, whom he had known for twenty years. He shot Manet in the belly and Manet said something to him that might have been a word or only a scream. He shot him again.

Then Gautier saw one of his men fall forward next to him. His back was pitted with bullet holes. Gautier stared at him, confused, because the man had been at the edge of the camp, and there was nothing behind him but the trees that encircled the camp. Gautier turned toward the trees and saw soldiers coming toward him.

Sister Mary Columbo, on the muddy ground at the mouth of her tent, saw the soldiers also. Neither she nor Gautier understood; the soldiers comprised the army of St. Michel.

The army surrounded the camp, Manet's rebels, and Gautier's freedom fighters. There were two hundred men wearing rain-soaked red berets. They were stationed behind every tree and rock at the camp's perimeter. When Ready gave the order the slaughter began.

The big machine guns, mounted on tripods, were set at four places around the camp. Two men operated each of them. The machine guns were fed by the loaders, and the gunners simply plowed the field of fire, defined by the tracer tip on every tenth bullet. So far to the right, so far to the left. The machine gunners did not need to see what they hit; they only needed to see the field of fire at the perimeters defined by the tracers.

Each machine gun had so many square meters of ground

to cover and everything in that area was to be destroyed. It made death simple.

It was the way theory had been taught before Vietnam changed everything and before guerrilla warfare suggested that death might become an individual business. The theory was the same followed by air force planes on pattern bombing runs. Define the bomb run north and south, then circle and turn and come east to west, making a cross of death on the ground below.

When one machine gun reached the far point of the pivot, the gunner brought the barrel slowly back on the pivot pin to the second point and then back again, always slowly, like a plow turning the earth. The bullets cut down the stalks of men and plowed the ground.

There were nearly four hundred men and women in the middle of the camp. They ran to the edge of the woods to find escape; they screamed and were cut down. They hid behind tents and boxes and were cut down.

Sister Mary Columbo stared at the horror and waited to be killed. She wanted to be killed, she told God.

Another flare burned white above the camp and then another. Everything was burning. Behind a pile of dead bodies, other men—still alive—were shooting back in the darkness. The machine guns plowed the bodies of the dead and killed the living behind them. Splintering bone and tearing flesh, blinding and gouging, hacking at limbs already stiffened in attitudes of death.

The guns became too hot to fire and the gunners burned their fingers on the metal. Some wrapped their hands with damp cloths to keep firing.

At the end, all the firing ceased. In the lights of the fires, of the lanterns, of the flares were reflected the mad eyes of the soldiers. There was an excitement to making death that is slow to cool in some men. It never cools for many because it is a pleasure they can experience no other place. They go from war to war to go from death to death, to experience the pleasures of it all.

Colonel Ready, who stood at the edge of the camp now in the silence of after battle, was one of them.

He said, in a clear, soft voice: "Cease fire."

But when some of the men kept shooting into the camp, into the bodies of the dead, he said nothing.

His grin was quite fantastic now in the red glow of the kerosene lanterns and the flares and in the red glow of the burning tents. It was raining as before but the explosions of the night had deafened all to the sound of the rain. He did not feel the warm rain on his face. His face was as open as the door of a furnace. His scar was white as molten metal.

The lust was on him. It had warmed him from the moment he had received the signal from Anthony Calabrese that the invasion force was timed for noon. Although Teddy Weisman thought he was using him, Calabrese worked for Ready. Just as Frank Collier and CIA thought they were setting him up. Just as Celezon thought he had his secret police. Just as Devereaux thought he would trap him. Just as they all used him and ended up being used by him.

Now everything would be made clear. Colonel Ready smiled and looked up at the rain and opened his mouth and let the rain fall down his throat. He felt sated by the stillness of the camp in death and uplifted by the smell of blood on the breath of the suffocating rain. The lust had filled him all morning and into the afternoon, anticipating all this killing.

The lust had been on him when he raped Rita Macklin and the pleasure of it was beyond description.

27

A CHILDREN'S GAME

Harry Francis said, "When I was with Papa in Cuba, he organized games. They were mock wars. He took some of the children along with some of us who hung around with him and he made armies. He led the children across the estates and threw stink bombs to ruin the patio parties of all the rich people because that is what it was like in Cuba in those days. He gave the kids firecrackers. Everyone had a good time."

"That sounds silly," Devereaux said.

They stood in the darkness at the perimeter outside the Palais Gris, on the edge of Rue Sans Souci. The street ran down the gentle hill to the darkened city. The rain fell in blackness. They were both soaked. Devereaux had a weapon from Flaubert. It was a little knife with a hook at the end of the blade that was used to scrape the guts out of fish.

"It wasn't any more childish than this. Than real wars. Except nobody gets hurt."

"Everybody gets hurt all the time."

"That notebook was my life and you don't even understand that."

"Tell me when we get out of here."

"It doesn't matter, the notebook will still be here. He might use it a little but he could use it a lot more with me. And it guaranteed my life."

"Shut up, Harry, there's one of them coming."

The *gendarme noire* came to the edge of the fence and looked down at the town. He was tall and thin in his large shirt and he carried his submachine gun strapped to his shoulder. He looked sad in the rain because rain dripped from the edge of his nose, as though he had a cold. Devereaux reached for his forehead in the darkness in one movement and pulled his head back and cut the young man's throat as he fell on his back. He did not make a sound. Devereaux slipped the sling of the submachine gun off the thin shoulder of the dead guard and checked the action.

"One down, fifty to go."

"They won't all be here."

"Where are they?"

"Killing people in the hills." Devereaux understood everything, even understood how his plan might have worked, but he did not understand about the notebook. Hemingway's notebook. It was all tied in to Harry and Harry kept making it more mysterious, as though he was slipping in and out of a lie. Was Harry the author of the notebook? Was that the reason he had called it Hemingway's book? But the pages were old; he had had the book for a long time. Harry wouldn't have kept his memoirs written down for so long, kept them so close to him so that they might have been discovered.

"You're going to tell me about the book when we get out of here," Devereaux said.

"Is that the price?"

"Yes. That's the price, Harry. And you'll pay."

"Ready couldn't get me in six years."

"But Ready has the notebook now. And I'm not him."

"You look like him. Vaguely."

"No," said Devereaux. "You're not Hemingway and I'm not Ready and there aren't any charades played anymore. Not anywhere. You will tell me everything and I'll help you get off this island, and then you can live and that's all you get in the bargain."

They spoke and then ran across the dark ground to the edge of the palace. Devereaux carried the M-17 in his right hand, his fingers and palm around the stock in front of the trigger guard where there was balance in the piece.

Harry ran his fingers along the wall and found the place where the cable ran down from the generator outside the gate. He nodded to Devereaux and cut the negative ground on the electrical line and held it in his bare hand in the darkness and stared at the luminous dial of his old Seiko and waited.

They had fifty seconds.

Devereaux sprinted into the shadows along the palace wall to the door to the cells. The submachine gun was on automatic fire and was cocked. He waited, he had no watch, everything had been stripped from him when the guerrillas dumped him in the grave. He watched the lights of the windows above the courtyard.

Fifty seconds.

Harry crossed the negative lead to the generator and touched it and the lights of the Palais Gris blew out with a pop that shattered some bulbs in the chandeliers.

Devereaux kicked open the unlocked door to the cells and fired into the darkness. He followed the shots into the room and pushed his back against the damp wall and waited for the reverberations to cease. He could see nothing. He heard cries in the darkness and other sounds coming from the back where Harry said the cells were located.

Then Harry Francis was beside him in the doorway, illuminated by a stroke of lightning. They saw each other at the same time they saw the *gendarmes noires* in the interior door. Devereaux fired six quick shots and the bodies of the policemen were jammed in the door.

Harry breathed hard next to him.

"Get their pieces."

In the next room a policeman lit a kerosene lantern and bathed himself in the soft yellow light. Harry threw the knife. It thudded into the chest of the policeman and he fell across the threshold to a third room. The light still flickered.

"There," said Harry and he nodded to the door of the third room, a room Harry knew had a tile floor and walls.

Devereaux pushed the door open. It frightened him that it was unlocked. Harry had said they did not need locks in the cells of St. Michel. There was no escape from the cells except by dying.

She was on the floor, huddled in a blanket, staring at the

door with dull, dead eyes. The cell was damp. Her hair lay wet on her head. Her eyes were dead.

And then he saw how she had been beaten and that her green eyes were blackened and her cheeks were bruised and her mouth was swollen and cut. There were marks on her arms and purple blotches on her body.

"Rita," he said, as though he were breaking a beautiful fragile dish in a large, silent room.

She stared at him and did not move.

"Come on, Rita."

"No," she said. "You died. You're too late. You're dead."

"Rita."

"No," she said. She once had dreamed of her brother in Vietnam and spoken to him like this. Just as she spoke to this dream.

He took her hands and pulled her to her feet.

"He said you were dead," she said. "I told you. I told you to kill him."

"I should have killed him."

"I told you." She was crying suddenly, as though she had found tears. Her voice changed in that moment. "I told you to kill him and you let him live."

28

THE SERPENT

Celezon thought he saw them in a flash of lightning running across the darkened courtyard of the palace. There was the woman Colonel Ready had taken. There was Harry Francis. He smiled at the comical figure of Harry Francis running so heavily in the rain, in the darkness.

And there was a third man he thought he had seen before. In cold Europe. So. He had come. Colonel Ready was certain he would come, was certain he would use him. As he had used Celezon. Colonel Ready was like Fate. He knew everything that would happen, even as those who thought they were free of Ready made it happen the way that the colonel wanted it.

There was another stroke of lightning splitting the raindrops, parting them as a beaded curtain in one of the cafés in Madeleine. But they were gone.

Celezon stood heavily at the tall window, in his uniform, his back to the darkened room. All the lights were gone, there had been shots fired in the cellars.

And in the hills above Madeleine, Colonel Ready's army was destroying the world.

"Escape," said the soft voice behind him.

Celezon turned and he was still smiling.

Yvette came next to him. She was clothed in a white garment, her skin was very white, very soft, and damp with the heat of the evening in the torrent.

"Escape," Yvette Pascon said to him and she clung to him.

"There is no escape, dear one." Every intimacy had been between them, in words and touch.

"No. You must not. We must escape him and if not us, you must. You have the people."

"I have nothing, dear one."

No one would believe Celezon spoke so softly.

But she was his sister. She was his sibling in the voodoo he had shown her as a neglected child. It was true what they said of her in the hills: she slept with her brother. But not Claude-Eduard who was impotent, who was a fool, who was propped by Yvette and Celezon until the day the Americans had come with money and power and placed Colonel Ready in charge of the army of St. Michel. Money corrupted his corrupt brain and corrupted the simple of St. Michel until they did not understand that Ready was a demon who had to be exorcised by fire, by blood on fire, by water on blood on fire. He had slept with her, loved her as a husband would love

170

his wife, but she was his sister. She was of the voodoo, she understood, even imperfectly because her blood was the blood of the whites. But she tried to understand and it was enough for Celezon.

The nuns had been very bad for the people in the hills.

The nuns were holy people but they did not dress as priestesses. They did not believe in the voodoo. Worse, they did not respect it. They made magic from syringes and crippled the faith of those in the hills.

The archbishop respected the voodoo.

He understood there was a religion for the people of the lower world in the town and the stronger religion for the people of the upper world. The archbishop was a wise man to respect the voodoo. He ate well in a strange land and had no enemies.

If the nuns were killed, Celezon had thought that day when he had ordered the killing, it would cause harm to Colonel Ready who was the enemy of the religion of the hills. And Yvette Pascon's enemy.

And Celezon's enemy.

"What will you do then?" She hissed like the serpent. She stood behind him and removed her gown and was naked. She smelled of the ripe odors of love. He had only left her a little while ago.

"If I go, they may kill me in the hills. I am the commander of the *gendarmes noires*."

"You are a priest."

"And what is Colonel Ready?" asked Celezon thoughtfully, staring at her nakedness.

She held him then, pressing her naked body against him.

"Death," she said.

29

ANTHONY CALABRESE

"Ready killed the nuns. Killed my cousin. He's killing every-one now."

Calabrese tried to make the words sound calm but the desperation came in his syntax. He held the pistol to the head of the operator in the St. Michel Exchange. It was the only line open to the outside.

Anthony Calabrese pressed his ear to the telephone. He waited for some voice at the other end and for a long time, there was only static on the line.

He was sweating and his gold chain was glued by sweat to his chest. Everyone was terribly afraid: the operator who saw the pistol in his hand, the security guard who was face down on the floor with his hands behind his neck, Anthony Calabrese. They had left him out too long.

"What about Rita Macklin?"

"Dead, I think."

There was another pause.

"Christ, I got to get out. Everything is blown. Ready is mad."

"Yes," said Hanley. His voice was cool over the lines. "Mad, I suppose. It's a dramatic term but it might be right."

"He killed the nuns."

"As you said."

"My cousin."

"And the American agent."

"Whatever his name is. Dead. In the hills. Manet killed him."

"All right." Another pause. The line crackled. The sky was filled with lightning. "Come out."

"Come out? Come out?" His voice was rising. "Come in and get me, copper. I can't get out. How the hell do I get out? I'm trapped in here. He doesn't need me, doesn't need Weisman, doesn't need anyone. End game. He beat everyone."

"Come out," said Hanley in a quiet voice. "You must have thought of ways of escape."

"I didn't think of this happening. I thought . . . something . . . was supposed to be pulled back."

"We never interfered with Langley's plan," said Hanley.

"You dirty bastard, you fucking whore," said Anthony Calabrese. "You're fucking around with Langley, you get me so screwed up in your own mind about it, you end up fucking me. I'm your fucking agent. I'm in the cold. I want to come in."

"We can't help you. I'm sorry, Anthony."

"You're fucking sorry? You sorry son-of-a-bitch." He waited a moment. He tried to let his voice come back to him. He waited, but he knew his old voice, before the events of the day, would not come back.

"I was a fucking snitch, I was working on Weisman, I thought you were going to take care of me—"

"I'm sorry, Anthony. Are you certain you can't get out?"

"Yes. What the fuck am I going to do?" He felt heat rising, he thought his head would explode. "You were going to send in a helicopter, a plane . . ."

"There's a planeload of American journalists at the airport. We can't get them out. How can we get you out?" The voice was calm, reasonable. It was easier to be reasonable sitting at a desk in an office in the bowels of the Department of Agriculture building in Washington where Hanley was. The office of the operations director of R Section.

"I did what you told me."

"But nothing happened as we expected," said Hanley. The voice wavered now because the signal was disrupted by the storm on the gulf.

"You wanted Teddy—"

"We have Weisman now where we want him—"

173

"And Colonel Ready—"

"Ready was not that much our concern. We only wanted to know what Langley would do."

"Games. Spy games. You people don't have no fucking sense of morality."

"And you, Anthony? A member of the Family. You have morality?"

"I know right from wrong."

"And you were wrong."

Pointless. Pointless and stupid and he didn't have time for this. He stared at the black face of the chief operator whose eyes were bulging with terror, whose lips were wet with sweat.

He dropped the phone. He stared at the operator, at the guard. He saw the operator in the guise of his victim. He didn't want to kill anyone.

"I won't hurt you."

He ran from the building and he ran through the rain but no one came after him. There was no escape on St. Michel. It was a large prison, a cage that imitated freedom like some of the zoos that keep animals in natural habitats. They were not free; Anthony was not free. They killed his cousin and it seemed like a sin to Anthony Calabrese. It was night and the capital was dark and quiet; there was rain; there were no soldiers. They were in the hills now, killing.

Anthony Calabrese ran down the road that skirted the harbor, away from the center of the city.

He was nearly struck by the taxi in the street.

The man smiled at him.

Daniel, the schoolteacher. That fucking fool.

"Monsieur Anthony," Daniel called cheerfully, a schoolteacher calling his happy class in from recess. Daniel waved out the side window of the cab. The dirty snitch Daniel who traced Monsieur Harry through the boy, Philippe; the informant for Colonel Ready who greeted all the guests at the airport and took them to the right hotel. The hotel that was always full unless it had been arranged to make room for someone Colonel Ready wanted to watch.

Anthony smiled, ran across the road, and put the gun into the side window, next to Daniel's head.

"Do you want to die, you fucking snitch?"

"No," said Daniel with happiness. He smiled to make Monsieur Anthony understand it was not his wish to die.

"Get out."

Daniel was sweating or perhaps it was only the rain.

Anthony Calabrese had no reason to hit him. He had not struck the guard at the telephone exchange or the operator. But Daniel was his brother, his fellow betrayer. He struck himself and knocked Daniel to the pavement instead.

There was no escape, but he pushed the car into gear and went through the narrow streets and turned south on the old coast road toward Madeleine.

30

FOOLS

Devereaux held Rita's hand as they ran. They ran along the edge of the road away from the woods that reached from the palace to the suburbs of St. Michel. Her feet were bleeding from sharp stones and fallen branches. She felt no pain.

Harry Francis ran behind them, puffing, the M-17 gripped firmly in his fleshy hand. He did not feel its weight. He felt as light as he had felt twenty-five years before, running behind the big man in Cuba, throwing firecrackers at the swells on their patios, assaulting the bastions of the rich.

She was dazed, running from instinct.

"I can carry you," he said when they were away from the town and they saw that no one was following them.

"No," she said. "I can do it alone."

It had been raining for thirteen hours. The mud was everywhere, rivulets of rain fell from the hills down to the coast road. The road was covered with water. They ran on the road for a while and the water cooled her wounded feet.

"Where?" she said once.

"The fishing village. Another mile."

"I can run another mile."

She took her hand away from him and shrugged out of her blanket. She ran naked. She was beautiful running in the rain, in the storm, naked in the middle of the blackness. He saw her in the cracks of lightning that flared over the terrain.

They ran past the Café de la Paix, darkened by the blackout or perhaps, by the storm. Philippe stood at the door. The boy made no sign to them. He did not make a sign to the boy.

"All his fault," Harry gasped.

"You're a fool, Harry," Devereaux said.

She heard none of this. She ran ahead of them. She thought she was running on the beach. She thought of the pain and the pace. Her body ached with blows given her; her bowels felt strangled. Her groin ached and she ran until her legs ached as her body ached. She ran with her head up, free in the rain that beat on her.

And then they saw the lights of the car behind them and Harry waved and they went to the side of the road and waited for the car to pass, thin lights stabbing at the rain and darkness.

The car whooshed past, splattering water on the roadside. In that moment, crouched next to her nakedness, Devereaux saw her face clearly. She was crying but her eyes were as empty as Cain's eyes had been on the boat.

In a few minutes, the village was ahead of them. The shacks were darkened. The car that had passed them was parking at an angle in front of one of the shacks.

Devereaux and Harry glanced at each other.

"Someone from the palace beat us," Harry said.

"In one car?"

"Then who the hell is it?"

They were on the beach, running across the sand. The surf was high now and the tide had pushed the water almost to the edge of the shack closest to the water. The harbor was cut naturally into the sand at this point. There were rocks on either side but the harbor was shallow, no more than an odd indentation in the perfect flow of the beach along the nine miles between St. Michel and Madeleine.

Devereaux touched the M-17. Harry looked up. His face made a protest but he handed the other man the gun.

One of the fishing boats had broken up against the rocks and its hull was splayed like broken ribs. The boat had sunk to the bottom of the harbor at the stern; the bow was pointed at a crazy angle to the sky.

Devereaux ran in a crouch to the edge of the first shack. He waited and listened. He heard a sound from inside the shack.

He pushed the submachine gun on semiautomatic and clicked the safety. The figure appeared in the doorway; it was holding a handgun.

Devereaux raised the submachine gun to fire, and a sudden burst of lightning illuminated the figure's drawn features.

"Cain," Devereaux said.

"Jesus Christ. You got out."

"Not yet."

"There's someone around here. I didn't know what to do except wait. There's a war going on down around Madeleine. Boats and shooting and soldiers shooting off their fucking rifles. Man, I tried to get in but there's nothing I can do. They're burning boats in the harbor. I figure if you were there, you're dead or part of it."

"Colonel Ready. Celebrating victory over the rebels."

"The bastard always wins," Cain said.

Devereaux said, "I've got her. And another man."

Cain turned as suddenly as a terrier hearing a secret sound.

They saw Calabrese at the same time. He had come from

177

the car; he had been between the other two shacks. He was at the edge of the surf and he carried a handgun.

Cain fired without speaking. The two rounds went wide. The man was down, firing. Rounds slammed into the wall of the shack.

One of the fishermen was at the door of the second house and he was shouting but it was impossible to understand him above the wind.

The figure between the shacks fired a third time. Then he rose, running, toward Devereaux.

Devereaux raised the rifle and tried to see clearly enough to get a good shot.

Cain fired again and the bullet was wide.

"No."

He heard Rita's voice next to him. "That's the American. The one . . ." Her voice was anxious and confused. "Anthony . . ."

"Anthony!" she yelled into the wind.

The figure stopped.

"We're Americans!"

Anthony was confused. "Who da fuck are you?"

"Anthony!"

He heard her voice and lightning revealed her nakedness. In a moment, they were crouched in darkness again, together at the edge of the shack.

He stared at her. He stared at the bruised face, the blackened eyes. "Jesus Christ, they did that—"

"Colonel Ready did this," she said to him.

And Devereaux felt his finger heavy on the trigger guard. He squeezed it because he wished to squeeze the trigger instead, to kill something.

"*Compass Rose* has two sea anchors but there's no protection, she's dragging in toward the harbor—"

"How did you get in?"

"Snorkel. Over the side. It isn't so bad underwater," Cain said. "You took the dinghy, remember?"

"I can't see it," he said.

178

"Black against black," Cain replied. "Look there and wait for the lightning."

They saw it, a ghost ship, dragging at the anchors, pulling them toward the harbor.

"I put it a quarter mile off. Less than a hundred yards now."

"How deep is it?"

"Seven, eight feet at that distance. She draws five feet."

"We can't get out there," she said. The rain slid down her body. Then Harry Francis tore off his shirt and draped it over her shoulders. It was so immense that it covered her like a loose smock. Harry was naked to his short trousers and in the flashes of light, they saw he was grinning. He was pleased with the action, with killing, with the raw feeling in his throat from running all the way from St. Michel. His heart was pounding wildly in his chest but he didn't even think about that.

Cain said, "I been thinking. They know me here. I told you." He looked at Devereaux. "I brought them some shit this time, they're all half conked out. Let's take one of their boats. One of the dinghys. *Compass Rose* is dragging and if it gets beached at low tide, I'll need a half dozen men and a winch and high tide to take her off."

They dragged a beached dinghy into the water. One of the fishermen watched from the door of the shack, warmed by alcohol and marijuana. He saw they were stealing the dinghy; he didn't care. He thought they were going to drown in the storm.

■ ■ ■

All the men were on deck. They heaved the anchors and the engine churned and the props bit the water and the *Compass Rose* protested and bucked into the storm for a hard-won half mile and the anchors were dropped again and the *Compass Rose*, on the open sea, faced the storm and bowed to the pressure of the waves and rode up and bowed and rode up and

179

bowed. It was going to be all right, Cain said and they went below, exhausted and wet.

She sat on a bunk, huddled in a rough woolen blanket, wrapped with towels. She had sat and said nothing while the men had worked on the deck to raise the anchors.

Now they were together in the cabin, exhausted, quiet. They stared at each other as the boat bucked in the waves and the rain pounded at the deck above them so that all the sea sounds were magnified. The cabin was compact, storage lockers all closed, everything made fast. Cain was a careful sailor and smuggler.

"I have a bottle of rum," Cain said but he made no effort to get it.

Even Harry Francis could not arouse himself from the lethargy of that moment.

Devereaux sat across from her. None of them sat next to her. He stared at her. After a long while, she stared back at him. They did not speak.

He got up and went to the pantry and found the rum and put it in a mug. He found sugar and a little lemon and water. There was no question of heating it. He took the mug and gave it to her.

None of them spoke again for a long time.

31

AFTER ANGEL

The sun rose in the clear sky in the morning and the breeze was fresh and smelled of the cleanness that comes to the world after a storm.

Everything was simple to explain. Every explanation fit precisely into that which was said before, into that which followed.

The journalists were taken from the airport to the palace and given breakfast and explanations. In the late morning, they were taken to the countryside where the battle had raged.

The American journalists, skeptical at first, were won over by the openness of the regime. And by the evidence.

There were the American weapons displayed and the new clothing of Gautier's "freedom fighters," who had linked with Manet's rebels and been fully overcome by the combined forces of the army of St. Michel and the regular security police.

The CIA was behind it all. There were documents on Gautier's body. And Manet's body. There was the testimony of the terrified survivors who insisted they had been trained in a secret CIA camp in Louisiana. The journalists were given free access to the prisoners who wished to speak the truth about the long night of fighting in the hills above Madeleine.

Colonel Ready's face and voice were recorded on video-tape and the videotape was airlifted to Miami by midday so that it would be on the evening news.

Colonel Ready explained about the Central Intelligence Agency plot against the regime of President Claude-Eduard. He said there had been two waves of assault troops. He showed the journalists the beached landing craft of the rebels, some of which had been broken up by the storm the night before. He even named the case officer in charge of the operation: Frank Collier.

By the middle of the afternoon, the senior adviser in the White House said that the president would investigate the charges coming from St. Michel. By 4:30 in the afternoon, a press conference was scheduled for 9 P.M. eastern time.

Frank Collier, in Room 236 of the Pier House hotel in Key West, Florida, apparently blew his brains out sometime between 2 P.M. and 6 P.M. It was a stroke of luck for CIA. They had a body and a grieving widow and three lovely children in the battle for hearts and minds of Americans, most of whom did not care about what happened on St. Michel.

The best of all came from Colonel Ready again in the middle of the afternoon. The journalists, already sated with the richness of the story, were given Sister Mary Columbo.

An American nun rescued from the rebel camp by the army of St. Michel after she had survived an ambush nearly four days before on the road to Madeleine.

■ ■ ■

Hanley spoke. His voice was somber, judicious.

"There was no way to get Calabrese out if his cover was blown," he said.

"So you let him be killed."

"I did not kill him, Mrs. Neumann."

"You didn't save him."

"Calabrese came to us through DEA two years ago. We turned him. He had been linked to several drug deals for Mr. Weisman and the branch of the Family that runs such operations on the southwest coast of Florida."

"I thought that was for the FBI."

"Not the business offshore. We were interested in Colonel Ready."

"Why? He belonged to CIA."

"That was part of our interest. The other involved the operation six years ago before Colonel Ready went to St. Michel. With CIA funding, I might add."

"What happened?"

"Four years ago, we learned he had been the CIA operative directing traffic against our own efforts in the matter of that priest in Florida."

"When November met Miss Macklin," Mrs. Neumann said. "And now you tell me. When they're dead."

"Now there is a need to know. You did not need to know then. Devereaux did not need to know."

"But he did. If he had understood that Colonel Ready had been involved in a case against him —they had tried to stop both Devereaux and Miss Macklin, to kill them—he might have been forearmed."

182

She spoke as flatly as he did and it annoyed him. He was attempting to be judicious. She was mocking him.

"Mr. Calabrese was to let us set up Colonel Ready. It would have been a coup for the Section. We don't have much influence in the Caribbean. Our Caribe desk is thin."

"Empire building."

"Yes, Mrs. Neumann. Build an empire and get the funding for it. Act only when you have the funding and you will never get it. It is the way of the government and the world."

"But Ready was controlled by Langley," she said.

"No. Langley had given him a long line and he had slipped it. He was playing a lone game. He might have been ours. At least, we might have been able to give him to the director of Central Intelligence. They would have acknowledged our strength and we would have found the resources—"

"Hanley, this is too cynical for me," Mrs. Neumann said. She got up, wrapped in her sweater. She stared down at him and almost pitied him. "You don't even understand how cynical this is."

"It is realism," Hanley said. He wanted her to sit down. He had been awake all night with the death of Devereaux and Rita Macklin and Calabrese on his conscience. They would stay on his conscience for a long time, until the next deaths took their place.

He wanted his confidante in the Section to stay, to talk to him.

"No. That's not what it is. It's a game when we win and it's just cynicism when we lose," she said. "I have work to do."

■ ■ ■

They were under way before dawn. When the sun came up in the eastern sea, they were less than two hundred miles from Key West. At first the sun was hidden by a speckled line of clouds and then the clouds broke up near the waterline and the sun, turning from blood red to orange to yellow, rose above the sails.

Her bruised face was turned to the sun. She had a clean shirt from the storage locker and a rolled-up pair of jeans, fastened to her thin waist by a length of rope. She had not thought she would be able to sleep in the crowded cabin. Harry was in one bunk, Calabrese was on the floor. She had the other bunk. Devereaux and Cain had sat in the galley and spoken of matters between them reaching all the way back to Vietnam. She had slept after a while.

There was no one on the deck but her when Devereaux came. He had a mug of coffee. She took it in both hands and dipped her lips to the scalding liquid.

"I'm hurt inside," she said.

"We should make Key West before night."

"I want to throw up all the time but I can't. Just when I think I'll throw up, it stops," she said.

He stood next to her and looked at her profile in the sunlight and did not touch her. They held the railing and watched the tranquil sea fall away from the hull. There was foam on the sea in their wake.

"What did he do?"

She told him then, softly, like a reporter reciting another person's story. It was the only way she could tell him. She told him about the arrest and the cell, the beating and the fire-hose torture. She said that after an hour or two, she had been given back her clothes and told to dress. They had watched her dress. They had brought her bag from the hotel and when she chose to put on her jeans, they gave her a dress. It was the blue dress she had worn that night to the reception in the palace, when she had stood at the window and watched Harry Francis led to the cell she was in.

She spoke of "Rita" and "her" and "she" because if she had said "I," she would not have been able to tell him at all.

"Colonel Ready came then and took her to a guesthouse that's in the back of the palace. He told her it was a caretaker's house from the days when the estates were inhabited by landowners. It's up the hill from the palace. She screamed at him—she told him that she was a reporter. He said she was nothing. That's when he told her he had the notebook. That's when he said Manet had killed Devereaux."

For a long moment, she was silent, intent upon the sea gulls following the air current in the wake of the boat. The sea smelled fresh in morning, made new by the storm that had passed in the night.

"She loved Devereaux," said Rita Macklin after the pause. And then there was another pause. "Colonel Ready showed her the ring she had given him once. He said Devereaux was buried in a grave on a hill."

"It was true."

But she did not look at him.

"He said she had passed to him, from one agent to another. The spoils of war. She hit him then and he laughed at her. They were in the little house and he said he would see how good she was. He took off his pants but he left his shirt on and she knew what he was going to do. He came at her and she hit him with a candle holder on the table and drew blood but it did not stop him. He tore her dress off and she hit him with her fist and that's when he began to beat her. Until then, he hadn't struck her. He beat her up badly. He kept hitting her even after she had stopped fighting him. He put her on the table in the front room of the cottage and he stood at the end of the table and forced her legs apart."

Devereaux took the words like blows.

"He said he had been CIA when . . . when the priest in Florida, when . . . when she had tried to find out what happened to her brother and got the old priest's diary and the CIA had tried to kill her. He said it happily. He said he would tell her a lot of stories about CIA now that it was all over, now that he didn't have to pretend. He said he always intended to kill Devereaux. He said he had brought Devereaux to the island in case his plans blew up. Then he could blame Devereaux and the Section and give CIA and whoever else was interested someone to chase. He said he always planned for an escape. Just in case."

When you are in a boat running well before the wind, when the sea is empty around you, everything is diminished, including your sense of your own life. It was easier, standing at the rail, to speak of that creature she had been only yesterday, to see that all that had happened to her did not matter a great deal.

"He said he told her everything because she was always going to be on St. Michel. She was going to be his whore now because Devereaux was dead. He asked her if she understood and when she didn't speak, he hit her again and then she said she understood. She didn't want to be beaten anymore."

When you are truly alone on the sea, all the terrors of a crowded world carry no weight. There is only you and this moment of life and the breath you take now; no one can frighten you. But the sea cannot wash away hatred. That always remains, waiting for the land again when it can be used.

"It's not enough to kill him. Not anymore," she said. "There has to be something worse than killing him."

"Yes," he said. "There has to be."

She looked at him for the first time. Her green eyes were not dead anymore. She had told the reporter's story and put it in sequence and now her eyes could see again. "This time, you have to do it. You understand that."

"Yes," Devereaux said.

32

CELEZON

Colonel Ready had planned to arrest Celezon when he returned to the capital. Ready had tolerated him when the pretense of the government had to be maintained. Celezon had been Yvette's choice, not Ready's, not the CIA's.

Celezon had rallied the *gendarmes noires* left in the capital and two of them pointed their M-17s at Celezon and said he was under arrest.

Six others of them killed the two in the square in front of the palace.

Yvette gave him francs and jewelry. Celezon and nine men were in the hills when Ready entered the capital.

Celezon, priest and brother, was welcomed into the shroud of hills as the man they had been waiting for, the people in the hills, the people of the stronger faith.

33

HEMINGWAY'S NOTEBOOK

Two days had passed.

Harry Francis sat on the balcony of the rental condo on Estero Island and read the papers. The balcony was screened and it was exactly like all the balconies on all the stucco condominiums that faced the gulf. Because he had been a spy, he had spent a lifetime reading newspapers and clipping items and making notes and guesses and passing it along to Langley as information. He was never the worst agent nor the best. But he had been in the Caribbean so long that everyone had forgotten how good he once had been.

He wore simple horn-rimmed magnifying glasses purchased from a variety store. They were too small for his full face. He had tilted them on his nose to get the right degree of magnification. The sun was behind the condominium so the balcony was in shadow and Harry squinted as he read of the abortive invasion of the island of St. Michel, an invasion, it was claimed by the St. Michel government, that had been trained and financed and supported by the Central Intelligence Agency.

So now Harry was a dead man walking, along with Colonel Ready. And Colonel Ready had Hemingway's notebook.

Harry dropped the papers on his lap suddenly like a sick man. He contemplated the emptiness he felt; perhaps it had always been there and it had been covered over by all the drinking and gambling and the girls.

He had been a writer. It was all he had wanted to be. They had recruited him because he was a writer. The agency could always use one.

He always gave the stories to the censors at Langley and they would suggest changes before he sent them to the editors. Sometimes they told him to tell more of the truth in a story and sometimes, most of the time, they told him to tell less.

He was not the only writer. Howard Hunt had been one, he had written short stories and novels. Hunt's stories had been studied by KGB to see if there was any truth or a signal in them that might apply in Moscow Center. Hunt had retired from the agency three times, which meant, of course, that he had probably not retired at all.

Harry Francis was sure he had retired when he quit six years before. They had wanted him to drift down to St. Michel in his retirement and keep an eye on things. An eye on things. Exactly the casual way they had worded it. He had gone and been caught in Colonel Ready's web from the very beginning. It took a long time for the agency to catch on, to stop asking him for reports. Nearly four years before, they had asked him to do a little writing job, a simple manual of sabotage and guerrilla operations to be used by Spanish speakers in the Caribbean. "Make it very Dick and Jane stuff," said Frank Collier at the time. He was paid five thousand dollars.

Devereaux stepped onto the indoor-outdoor green carpet of the balcony.

The gulf sparkled in the sun. The gentle surf lapped on the long beach that stretched the length of the island, from the shacks to the bars in Fort Myers Beach town on the north all the way down to Big Carlos Pass.

Harry took off his glasses and put them on the plastic-topped table. "How is she?"

Devereaux said nothing. He sat down.

"She's tough," Harry said.

"Nobody is ever as tough as they think they are," Devereaux said.

They sat across from each other for a long moment and listened to the scolding of gulls floating above the beach. On the sand, Rita Macklin was running along the shoreline, splashing into the water in bare feet, running herself through pain to exhaustion. She had slept for most of two days. She had not eaten. She had lost weight. It showed in her face, in the delicate lines of her cheekbones. When she was awake, he sat with her. He knew it had been his fault, all of it. He should have killed Ready in France that day, on the shore of Lac Leman, and he had not done it because he thought there might have been a way out of it. For him. And, as an afterthought, for her.

Harry brought two cans of Coors from the refrigerator and put them down on the transparent tabletop. Pelicans dove in the shallow tidal pool just beyond the shoreline. The tide was beginning to recede and people walked on a sandbar a quarter mile from shore and watched the sand sharks cruise in the deeper waters beyond.

"I've been reading all the accounts. The Company is in trouble again."

"And you."

"And me," said Harry. He sipped the beer.

"I wrote the goddamn manual for the guerrillas. The Famous Writers' School of Guerrilla Manuals. Do you think I could make a living that way?"

"You retired from the agency six years ago."

"Nobody retires. It says so in the contract. It's like being a priest. You can pretend you're retired but you're really a retired priest with full faculties. You don't turn in your badge at the door."

"How did you manage to live six years with Colonel Ready?"

"Carefully."

Devereaux waited.

Harry took another sip of beer and seemed to gargle it a moment and swallowed. "By doing what he told me to do. I was sent down to watch him. A retirement job. Except he was watching me. He had me almost from the beginning. So I told him about the notebook. I told him I had this wonderful notebook from Hemingway that told all about many wonderful things. To know all these things was to have power."

"What things?"

"I never told him directly. Even when he got more brutal in the last couple of years. The notebook was proof, you might say. I was a witness to the truth, but who was going to believe an ex-spook who might really still be a spook? I was just another guy with a story to sell to *Penthouse* magazine or something and it wasn't worth telling if I couldn't back it up. Hardly any sex to it. Unless you count the girl in Santo Domingo when we went in there." Harry blinked. "Anyway, she was a long time ago."

"What about Hemingway?"

"You saw the fucking book."

"Yes."

"Code. It was a code. I taught him a code."

"Tell me about Hemingway."

"No." He paused again. "But let me tell you about the good colonel. He dealt with anyone who wanted to play cards with him. An equal-opportunity whore. A soldier of fortune."

"I know about Colonel Ready."

"Teddy Weisman worked a deal with him and then turned around and worked a deal with CIA to screw Colonel Ready. But that wasn't all of it. Teddy really was going to double-cross CIA. He told Ready all about it. He wanted to get back at CIA for Cuba, for what they did to Teddy Weisman in Cuba."

Devereaux said, "How do you know all this?"

Harry said, "I'm a fucking spook, ain't I?" Then, calmer: "Because Colonel Ready let me know. He was always sucking me in. He told me things I couldn't do anything about."

"You could have warned CIA."

"They thought I was working for Ready by that time. They wouldn't have believed me. And if they had believed me, what was in it for me? I don't give a damn about the colonel or about the agency."

"What did CIA do to the crime syndicate in Cuba?"

"Not the syndicate. Just Teddy Weisman. Teddy Weisman wanted revenge for a long time. The Italians say that revenge is a dish that's best eaten cold. He waited."

"You know all about Cuba."

"I was there. Before and after. I was there in the Caribbean anyplace you wanted to name in the last twenty-five years. I was the agency man in the Caribbean."

Neither man spoke for a moment. They listened to the sound of sea birds and the sea.

"Ready took over St. Michel as a CIA contractor. CIA didn't want to be burned by going in directly so they used Ready and got burned anyway. Ready had been free lance by then, he had worked on some business in Florida for them about that old priest . . . remember the story . . . about some old priest who came out of Asia and knew where some missiles were or something like that."

"Yes. I know the story."

"Ready got burned but he was still valuable goods to them and they put him up in St. Michel and he seduced the whole fucking government in less than eighteen months. And then he started to play games with CIA. He fucked them and they cut off their support, but by then they couldn't do anything about it."

"That's when Ready started dealing with Weisman."

"Little deals. Everyone has always used St. Michel as a staging area for dope smuggling. The island has two things going for it. Nobody really gives a shit about it, and you can buy the government for thirty pieces of silver. You'd be surprised how difficult countries like that are to find even in the Caribbean. All the big powers have interests and there's a lot of media pressure and if there isn't, you can usually get someone like Castro to make a stink about it loud enough to be heard in Miami. What I'm saying is that when you look at St. Michel, you may not see anything at first and that's the beauty of the place. You can have anything you want there. Anything. Any kind of scenario."

"I don't understand about Manet."

"Manet is a true believer. Was a true believer. And Ready found a way to use him, to get him guns and butter. Manet thought he was taking handouts from Ready and would turn on Ready when the time came and Ready all the time knew he could knock off Manet anytime he wanted. He wanted Manet as a genuine Communist threat to entice a CIA invasion of St. Michel."

"Why? That doesn't make any sense."

Harry finished his beer and picked up Devereaux's unopened can and opened it and began to drink. "It makes all the sense in the world from Ready's point of view. You have to understand that I think Ready is a little bit crazy."

Devereaux said nothing. He had not moved in all this time. He sat with his hands resting on his knees. His lazy gray eyes did not leave Harry's flushed face.

"I did that free-lance manual four years ago for CIA. The comic book the president talked about. What do you think that was all about?"

Devereaux waited.

"I'm a great writer, I told you that. But they didn't pick me for the job just for that reason. They were warning Ready through me. I wrote the manual in Spanish. And they said they were going to make another contract with me. I had to tell Ready, I had to tell him about the second manual, the one I wasn't going to write for them, the one they told me would be coming up in a few months."

Devereaux guessed: "A manual in French. A manual of

sabotage uniquely suited to the people of St. Michel. Written by someone who knew the island and knew its weaknesses."

"Yes."

"So Ready knew the CIA was coming against him from somewhere at some time. He wanted an ally, so he promised Teddy Weisman he could own the island. And he used you, Harry. But how did he use you?"

"Jesus Christ."

"Now we come down to it, Harry. You were in and you were out."

"R Section sent down a man named Cohn more than a month ago to feel me out. They knew I was feeding information back to Langley again. They wanted to know what was going on. And it made the agency nervous to know that R Section was snooping around."

"What information, Harry?"

"Jesus Mary and Joseph," said Harry Francis.

Devereaux did not move and Harry did not speak. Not for a long time.

"He told me what to say," Harry said.

"He told you to set up the invasion."

"Yes."

"He told you to tell them where to land Gautier and his men."

"Yes."

"And you betrayed Langley."

"Yes."

"And now you don't have anywhere to go."

They said nothing again for a long moment.

"Harry."

The old man looked up.

"Why is the book important?"

"Which one?"

"There are two books."

"Yes. One that is written. And one that is not written."

"Tell me."

"Castro wants some leverage."

"Why?"

"He wants to be friends with Uncle again. On his own terms. He wants to come in from the cold, you might say."

"How do you know this?"

"He told Colonel Ready."

"Why would the book help?"

"Part of it is proof. An embarrassment to the agency of something that happened twenty-five years ago. How we screwed up a beautiful friendship, betrayed a great man and a great writer, how we lied to presidents and the country. It all happened twenty-five years ago and you might think nobody cares now, but they do. Nicaragua might be a lie too, one in the making. And maybe there were other lies. Washington has no intention of compromising with Castro or Cuba, but they might have to bend if Castro could use the notebook."

Devereaux got up and went to the screen of the balcony and looked down on the sand. The red tint in his hair was fading and the gray was sprouting again. A strip of bandage gauze covered part of his scalp where the bullet had furrowed a crease.

"Nobody cares what happened twenty-five years ago."

"You don't understand history. Or the Caribbean. It is happening now. What was St. Michel except the same goddamn fantasy played out by CIA?"

And Devereaux understood then and turned and his eyes were cold and his voice surged flat and broken like ice in an arctic sea.

"You. The storymaker."

And Harry Francis smiled. "I told you you were good. I told you that."

"You set up the invasion in Cuba."

"I was the inside man."

"It was bound to fail."

"Yes."

"You set it up to fail."

"No. I just knew that Castro knew. There was nothing I could do about it. I came in clean and I used that beautiful man and I came out dirty and that's all. I did all the dirty jobs all around the Caribe for them for twenty-five years. I made my life very dirty. And when it all came down to it again, I was in the same position in St. Michel."

"CIA never knew."

"No. And neither did Ready. The only one who knew what I did in Cuba was Papa. He knew. He wrote the note-book and told me he knew. He had it all right and he wasn't so much mad about it as bitter. And he was a sick man and he killed himself three months after the Bay of Pigs."

Bay of Pigs. In 1961, the new president, John F. Kennedy, took the blame for an aborted invasion of Castro's Cuba. The invasion was planned and executed by CIA. The invasion foundered in the Bay of Pigs on the Isle of Pines in Cuba. The invasion force consisted of Cuban patriots. They were slaughtered in the hundreds. And Harry Francis, who had been the CIA inside man in Cuba, had known that it would fail before it began because he had known that Castro's intelligence agency had expected the invasion in that place, at that time. And he had not warned his own agency.

"But why would the book be good now."

"Because nothing has changed in twenty-five years. It puts everything the agency did under a cloud. The agency has not changed and if you don't think that will back the administration into a corner in places like Nicaragua and in Costa Rica and even on relations with Cuba, you don't understand your politics."

"Because the book was proof and it would back up your own memoirs. Your memoirs is the second book. The second Hemingway notebook—because you're Hemingway as well, aren't you, Harry?"

Harry smiled and it was a very sad smile. "Yes. In my own scenario, that's my role. My own little role."

"But you didn't write it. You told Philippe about the second book. You pointed to your head."

"Yes, damn it. I never wrote it."

195

"You're a traitor to your country twice, Harry. You don't even have a place to go to ground, do you?"

"No," Harry said.

"But if you had the notebook—"

"It was my bona fide. It could have been useful."

Devereaux put the notebook on the table.

Harry stared at it and he felt a pain in his chest and he breathed very deeply for a long moment.

"You had it."

"Yes. Cain dropped me off at the fishing village and he waited for me there. I came back when I found the book and I wanted to go to Madeleine, I had to find out about Manet. I didn't trust Ready's deal with me. Cain had an unused log-book, I made up a code and put it in the book. I hid the notebook on the *Compass Rose*."

"But *Compass Rose* didn't wait for you at Madeleine."

"No. Cain had no guts for it. But I wasn't worried about the book. He wouldn't find it and I would always be able to find the *Compass Rose* if I got off the island again. I had to go into Madeleine. I had to find another way off. I had to take Rita off the island. I figured if the worst came, if Ready got me, I could tell him about the book and send Rita to get it for him and let myself be the hostage. It was just a precaution."

"You've got the book."

"Yes."

"It's genuine, you know."

"Yes. When we landed with Cain in Key West, I found someone at the Hemingway house there who knew about his writing. He studied the book and he said the numbers were all written by Hemingway—there's a lot about numbers in Hemingway's correspondence, particularly the way he slanted his letters and the way he did the number seven. Hemingway wrote a lot about money."

"I know everything about him," Harry Francis said and he touched the book as though it was holy.

"What about Hemingway?"

"He loved intelligence, it fascinated him. I was in Havana in 1958. He was working then and it was going good, about the days in Paris when he was young. Batista was running Cuba, everyone knew he was finished. Castro was in the hills and he was giving interviews to Americans there. Like me. I was a writer. My vocation and my cover in the agency."

"And you became Hemingway's friend."

"Not his friend. The trouble was, he couldn't have any friends anymore, he was too important for that. He could have pals. I hung around with him. He invited me to the farm south of Havana."

"What's the key to the code?"

"I taught him the code for fun. He was fascinated by intelligence work. He picked it up. The key was a page in *The Sun Also Rises*."

"When did he write it?"

"When he was getting ready to kill himself. He was in the Mayo Clinic in early 1961. After the Bay of Pigs. He knew I had known about the invasion, he knew what I was, he had his own sources."

"No. You told him. You wanted him to forgive you."

Harry was silent again and he stared at the book in his hands. "Yes. I wanted him to understand me."

"That you were a liar and a coward and that you betrayed him and betrayed everyone else."

There was only silence left after that and the sound of the gulls beyond the building was part of it. Devereaux looked over the sand beneath the balcony and saw Rita running on the sandbar in the water. She might have been running on the water because the illusion was good enough to make it seem there was no sandbar beyond the line of the shore. The pelicans dove into the receding waters of the tidal pool and then rose again like lumbering seaplanes struggling from the glue of the water's surface.

"What was the invasion of St. Michel?" Devereaux said.

"Rehearsal." He could scarcely be heard above the silence.

"For a second go at Castro."

"Yes."

"And Castro knows."

"Yes. He's afraid. And he dealt with Ready. Arms and everything. He wanted the CIA to fail."

"And you kept your silence."

"Ready wanted to finish off the CIA once and for all. He also wanted to use you, make you a scapegoat, tie a can to your tail. When the invasion failed, CIA would be after your ass as well as Ready's. You were the R Section man come back to life in St. Michel."

R Section. Set up by Kennedy after the Bay of Pigs invasion because Kennedy had known that CIA had betrayed him. A rival intelligence agency to check on CIA, a spy to spy upon the spies.

"If St. Michel worked, it would work against Cuba. The money would come for it, CIA would get a green light," said Harry Francis. "Hemingway's notebook was a proof it had been done once. Hemingway named me in the book, told how he had been used by me, told about the secret negotiations between Castro and President Eisenhower in 1960 to set up normal relations. Langley sabotaged those talks. Hemingway knew about it, hated it, was afraid of it, of what was going to happen to him, to the farm in Cuba. He loved Cuba. He loved the United States."

"And who did you love, Harry?"

"Hemingway. He was everything I wanted to be, everything I saw in myself."

"The book would tell about you and Cuba and then you were there to back up the book. Why didn't you give it to Ready? You gave him everything else."

"I was afraid. Once he had the book, he didn't need me that badly."

"You stink, Harry."

Harry sighed. He opened the pages. "Hemingway killed me in the book, he killed me in code the way he could do. It was the last thing he could do to me because he was going to have to kill himself because things were very bad for him and he was depressed."

Devereaux said nothing. He stared at Rita Macklin running in the surf of the gentle gulf.

And Harry began to speak, to recite the first page of the notebook, a man who had learned hard words by heart.

Harry Francis liked to play games. Once we went down to Havana together and we played at being spies because everyone knew the government was going to fall. The difference between playing spy and being a real spy is in the stakes of the game, because the game is always the same. Harry was a real spy as well as one who played at it; but he never wanted to play for the high stakes. The stakes make the game serious and that is how you tell whether the game is worth playing.

Harry played football in college and he was built well. He had big hands and sandy hair and the women liked him. He told me he was doing some writing and that he wanted to be a writer. I told him what I knew about it and he showed me some of his things and this was while we were down at the farm. That's when I knew he would not make it because he thought that writing was a kind of trick. He wasn't willing to play the game for the big stakes and I suppose that is what was wrong with him. He broke his nose playing football in college and he said it had hurt like hell. He had paid for an expensive operation to get it straightened out and he never played football again. Harry said he hated the pain and I believed him. He talked a lot about pain. He talked about writing a lot when he got drunk at the harbor in the afternoons, when I was not writing and I went down to see the fishermen and have a glass of good wine with them.

But Harry was fun once and he taught me this code. He was fun to be with the time we went down to Havana to spy on Batista. I didn't take Harry seriously before we began to play the big game together. After that, I took him more seriously but I hated him enough to kill him if I had not been ill.

Devereaux turned after a long moment and stared at Harry. "I can save your life," he said.

"I don't want to live," said Harry.

"Yes, you do. You don't have the guts to die," said Devereaux. "But you'll live under sentence—you'll have terms and they'll all be observed, all the rules. You understand?"

And Harry nodded.

And Devereaux began to tell him the way he was going to be used.

34
STRONGER IN THE BROKEN PLACES

She was in pajamas, lying on the bed beneath the coverlet. She had bought pajamas when they came back and they had said nothing about it. He slept in the living room of the condominium, on the couch, and they said nothing about that arrangement either. Devereaux entered the bedroom and thought she was sleeping. It was late afternoon and the rooms were full of golden light. Harry Francis had told him everything that was written in Hemingway's notebook.

He sat in a chair near the double bed and looked at her for a long time.

Her breathing was regular, her cheek was against the sheet at the corner of the pillow. Her eyes were closed very tight so that there were wrinkles at the corners of her eyes. Her right hand was near her mouth and it was balled into a fist. Her body pressed flat against the sheets. She slept very hard, he thought.

She opened her eyes and it was still afternoon.

She did not start or make a sound. She turned on her side and looked at him.

"Did he tell you?"

Her voice was soft and flat.

"Yes."

"Is it worth it?"

"Yes," he said.

"Can we use it?"

"Yes."

"What about Harry?"

"Harry did something bad. A long time ago. And more recently. I don't know about Harry but I have to use him."

"But he doesn't know that. He doesn't know that you're not sure of him. Of what you're going to do with him."

"He knows now. He has to know."

"Are there any secrets?"

She meant from her; he understood she meant that. "No. I'll tell you everything about it."

"How can you use it?"

"I'm not sure of all the parts of it, but I can use it. And Harry. I can use him. And Anthony. Anthony will be very useful."

"I'm as cold-blooded as you are," she said. "I don't care about any of them. I really don't care."

"No, Rita." He wanted her very badly. He wondered if she would ever heal. She had been broken and it had been his fault and she did not accuse him. If she had accused him, it would have been easier.

He had no feeling about Harry Francis until the last moment on that long afternoon as Harry told him about the secrets of the notebook.

Harry had become very emotional. He had wept and he had gotten a little drunk in telling the story. But at the last moment, he had said that Rita would be all right. He had said that because he said he knew that Rita was what had mattered to Devereaux. He said that sometimes a broken limb heals and it is stronger in the broken places. He said Hemingway had written that.

It was such a clumsy, intrusive thing to say. To that moment, Devereaux had not decided about Harry Francis because Harry had done a bad thing a long time ago and carried a bad secret with him for twenty-five years and made it worse all along the way.

But they had all done bad things.

"I wanted to save my life," Devereaux began.

"No. I don't need any words," she said.

"When he appeared on that street in Lausanne, I wanted to kill him and then, later, when I thought he had so much against me, I wanted you to be his hostage because I wanted time to find a way to get around him. I did it for myself."

"And me."

"No. That's not true. I would have died for you. But I wouldn't run anymore. I didn't want to die on someone else's terms. I didn't think he would do this to you. I didn't think of that."

"I did," she said. "What are you going to do?"

He had thought about it all afternoon as the sun warmed the screened balcony, as Harry wept and got drunk and told him about what had happened in Cuba a long time ago, about how the island had been lost, about how Hemingway had become ill and killed himself and how Harry thought it was because of everything that had heppened on that island.

He had thought about Colonel Ready and what he would tell Rita. In the end, he decided he would tell her everything.

"Ready always had a way out. Even in Nam. He always had two or three roads that no one else knew about. He knew that if everything turned bad, he could still retreat."

"And you know what the roads are now," she said. She sat up in bed and pulled her arms around her knees and watched him.

"Yes. I think I know them all. The first thing we do is cut off all the roads. Blow them up and fill them in. That's the first thing."

■　■　■

She ate for the first time. She even smiled at him as he fed her. He made her eggs and bacon and toast and coffee. He sat across from her and watched her eat. She wore her pajamas and a robe. Her hair was clean and bright again and her cheeks began to fill with color as she ate. It was sundown and they sat on the screened balcony. He watched the bloody sun frame her features in amber colors.

"I feel like the time we were in Vevey and found that place," she said. "Steak *haché*."

He smiled. She spoke for the first time of the long summer in Switzerland.

"I was so hungry all of a sudden. I missed home. I missed hamburgers and fat french fries and baked potatoes."

"You asked her if the chopped steak was well done," he said, still smiling. It was getting better. She smiled at him and kept eating.

It was a little neighborhood café in the old Swiss town and there were six tables and the daughter served them and the old woman brought them beer from the bar. Chopped steak smothered in onions and gravy and she had eaten it all and taken part of his portion and kept complaining about how hungry she was. She told him that her mother cooked like that, chopped steak in gravy and onions, and she felt like a little girl at home again in Eau Claire, Wisconsin, on a summer night in the big country kitchen with the windows open to the last of the afternoon breeze. The breeze always blew through the white curtains and the flow of the curtains had been like themes of unheard music, keeping time.

When she finished, he took the plates to the kitchen. It was like Lausanne when they would cook for each other as though they were giving gifts.

When he came back to her, they sat at the table and they did not speak for a long time. Until the sun was down in the sea and the warm night was filled with starlight and the moon was new.

"What did Harry tell you?"

"About Hemingway and Cuba. And how Hemingway was the middleman in secret talks between Eisenhower and Castro to work out an accommodation. How the CIA poisoned the talks. How they set up the Cuban invasion. And how Harry knew about it, knew it would fail, and let it happen anyway. Harry can't be trusted at all, but he's useful to us."

"What about the notebook?"

"The notebook proves part of Harry's story and he needs some proof because it is pretty fantastic. Except it all makes sense. Cuba is afraid of another invasion and they wanted to get the book to expose the truth about what happened twenty-five years ago. St. Michel was the rehearsal for another invasion. Cuba gave Ready arms and aid to help repel the invasion. Harry knows all this. He knows everything about everything and I have to find a way to use him. I made my trail lead to Ready because I wanted to turn him into me, into November. But he was playing a more complex game and I didn't understand it at all. I found the book and it wasn't enough to find it. I had to find a way off the island for us, I had to find Manet, I had to find some leverage—but the whole island was like a piece of glass, and you couldn't get a handhold anywhere."

"It's a fantastic story."

"We invaded Grenada and that got everyone's spirits up. We're in Costa Rica now training the police there and we have agents with the contras in Nicaragua. Not so fantastic."

"Nothing changed in twenty-five years."

"Yes. That's exactly it. That's what Harry can prove along with the notebook. Except I don't see how we can use it if we want to get away. You and me."

"So what do we do?"

"There's the problem of Colonel Ready. That's revenge. There's the problem of CIA. I think we can put the problems together but I'm going to have to come awake."

"Awake?"

"Section slang. I'm sleeping. I came awake with November, I started using the code name again, I was going to pin the tail on the donkey with Ready. Now I'm going to have to really come awake for a little while and expose myself with Hanley and the Section to make the thing stick."

"What about Weisman? And Anthony Calabrese? And the others? Ready's screwed everyone."

"In the end, that's the way I want it to look," said Devereaux. "And I want Harry right where I can find him. He's going to fulfill himself."

She stared at him and didn't speak.

"He's going to become a writer again. Fiction. Good adventure fiction with a ring of truth to it. He's going to write the first book about Cuba in the old days, about Hemingway and about other things and when the novel is finished, we'll find a publisher for him. The Section will find a publisher for him. And everyone will know that someone is writing novels about things that might be true."

She stared at him for a long time without speaking because she did not understand everything. He was thinking, he was seeing things, and his gray eyes were focused beyond her. After a while, she went to bed. He came into the room after her and he lay down next to her and he held her. She had wanted to be held by him. When she fell asleep at last, it was past midnight. He was still awake and he did not think he would sleep at all.

35

NIGHTS OF OLD MEN

"Debbi?"

Her voice on the house phone sounded sleepy.

"Come on down. In the library. I want some company."

"What time is it?"

"What am I, a watch? Fuck the time. I want company.

Get your ass down here," Theodore Weisman growled into the house phone. He put down the receiver.

Debbi heard the click. Asshole. She replaced the receiver. He treated her like meat. She worked Vegas before she met him, she could work there again.

Still, there was Dee. What had happened to Dee a couple of days ago. It never hurt to be too careful. Dee was there one minute and then she was in a black car and Dee didn't look so good being driven away.

She put on her robe. She opened the door of her bedroom which was on the second floor of the big house in Captiva Island. You could smell the sea from her open window.

Teddy had been worried the last couple of days. It was probably because of Dee, having to get rid of her. Debbi didn't like to ask him any questions because they always made him mad. Later, he would calm down and pat her behind and give her a feel—he didn't have much but he liked to use it a lot, he said—and tell her to buy herself something pretty and tell one of the guys to give her some money. Not Tone. Tone was gone too. Tone had left about the time Dee left. Nobody asked about Tone.

She stepped into the corridor and felt the hand on her shoulder.

"Jesus," she said.

It was Anthony. Anthony was supposed to be in St. Michel. "You scared me, coming up on me like that." She vaguely knew Anthony did errands for Teddy but that was all she knew.

"Be quiet, Debbi. Go on back in your room."

"Teddy just called me on the house phone."

"I know. He told me. He changed his mind. Go back in your room."

His voice was quiet and it frightened her. She went back into her bedroom and picked up the phone to call Teddy and the line was dead.

Anthony Calabrese walked down the stairs and crossed into the library and closed the door behind him. It was a nice

206

room with soft lights from the banker's lamps illuminating the cherrywood bookcases on the wall. All the best sellers were on the shelves. They were removed twice a year, read or unread, and given to the old people's home.

Teddy Weisman was sitting at the desk looking right at Anthony. Devereaux sat next to the old man with the muzzle of the pistol braced on the antique desk.

It was interesting, Anthony thought. His old eyes were filled with contempt.

"You gonna roust me, Anthony?"

"Naw, Teddy."

"Now it's 'Teddy.'"

"Shut the fuck up, please."

"Who's this one?"

"He works for Ready."

"I thought Ready and I had a deal. I thought you worked for me, Anthony."

"That was before," said Anthony. "I made a deal with Ready. It seemed like a good idea."

"You worked for R Section," said the old man. "I already talked to Ready."

"Yeah. I worked for them and flipped them. I flipped you. See, Ready figures he's got you in his pocket one way or another so he sends us up here to tell you the way it's going to be."

"You're gonna tell me that, huh?"

"We take fifty off the top. That's in front. And maintenance. We gotta have some juice on the rest of it," Anthony said.

"Why don't I just give you the casino, huh? Just make it a gift."

"You double-crossed Uncle, Uncle has got your tit in a wringer. That's number one. That's what Ready got when I went to work for him. I been on your case for two years."

"You're dead, Anthony." The old man crossed his throat with his finger. "You walk around but you're dead."

Anthony stared at the old man and did not flinch. "No,

Teddy. *You're* dead because you fucked Uncle and Ready can prove it and he wants to sell you out to keep Uncle off his back. He doesn't have to deal with you. There's a lot of people would like to open up St. Michel. Drugs, gambling, everything. He doesn't need you."

"You worked for me and you were a fucking government agent," the old man said. "Now you work for Ready. He'll get rid of you, Anthony, when he don't need you."

"Uncle is bigger than you are, Teddy. Uncle is even bigger than the whole fucking Family. Ready wants you to be nice to him. He told me to tell you that."

"You tell him he's walking around dead," Teddy Weisman said. "I don't make no deals with him no more. No more deals. You tell him to keep looking over his shoulder."

Devereaux said, "This is bullshit, you know that, Anthony?"

"Hey, I want to talk to him reasonable," said Anthony.

"Fuck bot' of you. Bot' of yous are dead."

Devereaux got up and walked around the desk and hit the old man in the face with the barrel of the gun. He hit him a second time so that he could make certain the old man's nose was bleeding. When there was blood, Devereaux stopped. The old man could taste the warm blood on his lips.

"I'll tear your balls off and stuff them in your mouth," Teddy Weisman said.

"He doesn't get it, does he?" Devereaux said.

"No, he doesn't listen. Everything I had I gave to Colonel Ready, Mr. Weisman. Everything. I want you to understand that."

"The G is after you then, Anthony. The G'll get you before I get you. You fuck the G, you fuck your own life," said Teddy Weisman.

"Teddy, lemme explain to you once more. I worked for you. I got picked up by the G and I turned. I worked for the G and I worked for you. I was screwing you for two years. Now, you turn around and you fuck up the G yourself, you pretend to make a deal with Langley to knock off Colonel

208

Ready but you and I know that it is all bullshit. The important thing is that I know that. I know the inside of the deal because I was inside the deal. I never told them that. If I told them that, they would have known Ready was going to double-cross them. They wouldn't have activated the operation. That makes sense, doesn't it?" He was lying but it was very good because Teddy Weisman kept thinking it was all the same government and that R Section and CIA would cooperate with each other on information and he would not have guessed that Anthony's information to R Section was never acted upon. Weisman was a believer in the logic of his government.

"So you work for Ready," Teddy said at last.

"Now you get it. And now you know what Ready wants to deal. And now he wants you to go through the traces for him. He wants to see money very soon, just like you arranged. He wants to see that you are going to honor the new deal."

"Yeah, I see that," said Teddy Weisman.

"So we made it clear? Because if he don't see some action soon, he's gonna get a new partner and he's going to hand you over to the G. You see what I mean?"

"I see what you mean," said Teddy Weisman.

■ ■ ■

After they were gone, Teddy Weisman sat for a long time alone in the library. His handkerchief, crumpled in a ball, was on the desk, stiff with dried blood. He sat for a long time and thought about Colonel Ready and then decided what he would do.

He picked up the telephone and made a long-distance call to Chicago. He talked to a man. He said he had a very big contract to let out and he wanted all the men necessary.

"It might run you," said the man in Chicago.

"It might run me what?"

"It might run you forty, fifty dimes," said the man in Chicago.

"I can handle the action," said Teddy. "I can handle all of it."

"Is this personal?"

"Very."

"This is not about business."

"No, it's personal."

"Okay. Does the guy ever leave? I mean, that island?"

"I don't think he's going to. He's made enemies."

"Ready. Colonel Ready. Was that the guy in the papers the other day?"

"Yeah."

"I think I still got a paper, I can take the picture out of it."

"I can get you pictures."

"You got any time limit?"

"I got no time limit. As soon as you can. I don't care who you get but I got no time limit. This month, next month, tomorrow or next year. I don't care what happens, how much it costs me as long as you tell me what you're doing, why it's going to cost me."

"We'll get it done," said the man in Chicago.

■ ■ ■

Hanley sat in the empty bar of the Holiday Inn outside Washington in Bethesda, not far from Old Georgetown Road. He had a martini in front of him. The room was dark and the musical group that usually played during the week was off for the night. A salesman had talked to him about the imminent World Series and Hanley had not followed the somewhat incoherent conversation. The salesman had finished his monologue and his drink and had long since gone to his room.

Anthony Calabrese had told him nothing except to meet at this place at 11 P.M.

"You're playing at spies," Hanley had protested.

"Yes," Anthony replied on the phone. "Only playing."

Anthony had escaped after all. It surprised Hanley but he did not think about it too much. Anthony would want guarantees, a new identity, a new contract in exchange for

210

testimony and information. Hanley was not interested in Mr. Weisman. Hanley was interested in how CIA had stubbed its toe in St. Michel and what Colonel Ready would do about it. Maybe Anthony knew some of those things.

Anthony entered the room, stood at the doorway, and walked across the red carpet to the barstool where Hanley sat. The woman behind the bar came down and threw a napkin at his place and said, "What's your pleasure?" without any inflection of real interest.

"Bullet with a twist," Anthony said and turned to Hanley and smiled a big smile. "Surprised to see me?"

"Yes," said Hanley.

"Good. Thought you'd be surprised. I got out but it wasn't so easy. I didn't think you were gonna let me stand there when the shit went down."

"I told you. We weren't interested in interfering with the operation. We wanted information."

"That's why you sent down Cohn," said Anthony.

Hanley stared at him steadily but Anthony saw he had scored. He smiled when the woman behind the bar brought the drink. "Just put it on his check."

"He paid for his drink," said the bartender.

"Good, then take it out of his change. Right, Mr. H?"

Hanley nodded and the woman shrugged and walked back to the cash register and made a check.

"Salut," said Anthony. "America. Best martinis in the world. That's what this country stands for, you know?"

"What do you want?"

"No. The question is: What do *you* want? You sent down Cohn and he bought it. You know who killed him?"

"No."

"Colonel Ready. Or his agent, Celezon. Colonel Ready knew all about Cohn, knew all about everything. What he never had was the notebook. The real thing. Like Coca-Cola, right?"

"What are you babbling about?"

Anthony sipped the martini again. "Mr. D figures you

211

want the notebook because you want leverage on CIA. You want a Caribe operation. You want to remind the administration that they need R Section to keep CIA in check. You know what would happen if Castro got that notebook?"

"What would happen?"

"Every fucking liberal in the country would be pounding on the door to let Castro back into the family of man," said Anthony. "Mr. D said the book is the proof, in Hemingway's own hand, and that with Harry Francis—"

"Where is Harry Francis?"

"Hey, what am I, Information Please? Let's say I know all about what's going on and I'm trying to fill you in."

"I'm not interested," Hanley said.

"Hey, Mr. H. Get interested. You fucked me down in St. Michel. I'm between a rock and a hard place. I gotta go with Ready or alone, I got no other option. You cut me off and Mr. Weisman, Mr. Weisman knows."

"I told you I wasn't interested in Weisman."

"All right. Mr. D—"

"Who the hell are you talking about?" Hanley raised his voice and he swore and both actions were unusual.

"Oh. I forgot you wouldn't know." Anthony smiled but he had forgotten nothing; not his instructions, not the signal. The whole thing was a little show. Hanley had to understand how important it was for him, for the Section, to do what he had to do. Anthony raised his hand and extended one finger as though signaling for the bartender.

She came down.

"Vodka on the rocks for the gentleman coming in the room," said Anthony Calabrese and Hanley gaped.

Devereaux sat down. In the dim light, he looked smaller than when Hanley saw him last, nearly fifteen months before. His hair was cut close, it was gray with little mixes of color still in it. His gray eyes were without threat, without promise. But his eyes were not empty, Hanley thought. He did not look as he had looked in the old business. Before the Section arranged his death.

212

"He pays," said Anthony to the bartender and she took the bill again back to the register and rang a charge.

"Hello, Hanley."

"I thought you were killed. On St. Michel. And Rita."

"Rita isn't dead. She wrote a story. I want you to read it. She's going to give it to a magazine in the morning and it concerns you."

Hanley took the paper in the dim light. There were twenty typewritten pages. He could barely see the words.

"I can't read in this light," said Hanley dumbly. "Why does this concern me? We got your messages. You were going into St. Michel. You left a trail."

"A red-haired man," said Devereaux. "And a scar. And he was all over the place. He was in Switzerland and Paris and London and he chartered a boat in Florida and he was in St. Michel. He was an agent named November."

"You."

"No," said Devereaux in a very soft voice, so soft that Hanley could barely hear him. He leaned forward across the corner of the bar.

"I'm not in the old business. It wasn't me."

"Who?"

"First, what are you going to do for Anthony Calabrese?"

"What does Anthony want?" said Hanley as though the man between them was not there.

"Anthony wants a new face and money and a new life. That's not so difficult, is it?"

"What's he going to do for us?"

"He's not going to tell the truth about R Section. He's not going to tell about the Section letting Ready set up CIA and use a crime-syndicate figure, all because of a little bureaucratic rivalry."

"That's blackmail. You don't blackmail the government."

"Hanley," Devereaux said and the voice was very low and flat and cold as Hanley always remembered it. He stared in the dim light and saw the arctic man and was transfixed by him.

"You forgot, Hanley." The words surged like ice floes. "R Section. It was set up after the Bay of Pigs. You forgot that."

Hanley blinked.

"'Who will watch the watchers? Who will spy on the spies?' Kennedy. He set up R Section because he didn't trust Langley anymore after the Bay of Pigs. One side had to keep the other side honest. Except you forgot that."

"We had nothing to do with St. Michel."

"You had agents all over the place," Devereaux said. "You had Cohn and Cohn was killed. You had Anthony in place, you even broke up a DEA operation with Anthony because you claimed a higher priority. Anthony is cut loose by everyone and you're going to take care of him because you have to. The way you have to take care of me."

"That's still blackmail. The government won't be black-mailed."

"You're not the government," Devereaux said. "You forgot that once. Anthony wants a new face and some money and a different name. You can fix it."

"I wanna new nose and different chin—this time I don't want to look so Mediterranean, you know? Swedish. I wanna be Swedish."

"You have the accent for it," Hanley said.

Calabrese smiled at that, struck a pose, lifted his chin, and laughed.

Hanley was silent but his lips chewed furiously on un-spoken words. When he spoke, his precise voice was shaken. "I kept the bargain," he said to Devereaux, "between me and you. And Rita."

"That I was dead? Yes. There's no way to go back on that now for you. But there's the matter of November."

Hanley did not speak.

"But November isn't necessarily inactive, is he?"

"What do you want?"

"November is the name of an agent, and the names are never used again, are they?"

214

"No."

"All the files save one speak of the agent by the code name," Devereaux said.

Hanley stared at him.

"There was an agent named November. He worked for R Section. He was used by the Section. He went to cover after a while and everyone thought he was dead. His identity was assigned to a dead agent in Zurich. But November was really an agent on St. Michel whose name was Colonel Ready and R Section alerted him to the invasion operation by CIA and he aborted the invasion. This agent—this agent named November—was the man who raped Rita Macklin on the island of St. Michel."

Hanley gaped. "He raped her?"

"Yes." The voice was as distant as thunder on a sunny afternoon in July. "It doesn't really matter who told Ready about the coming invasion. It doesn't matter that it was really Cuba because Cuba knew CIA was setting up a dress rehearsal for another invasion of Cuba. It doesn't matter who told Ready because we are going to get out our version of the truth first. Aren't we?"

Hanley only stared and did not move. Anthony Calabrese stared as well.

"I don't want to kill Colonel Ready, but I want to hang a label on him," Devereaux said. "He is November, once and for all. I was setting that up all the way to the island. I used a passport in that name in London and in Miami. I used my old code when I got information from Economic Review. I am not November; November is an agent of the R Section who double-crossed Castro in Cuba and the CIA and Teddy Weisman and who told Harry Francis everything about everything. And now R Section is going to finance the publishing career of a new writer who will set a series of thrillers in the Caribbean. A book a year. Books about the first invasion of Cuba. Books about the invasion of St. Michel. About CIA treachery in Honduras and about what really happened in El Salvador. All of them clever pieces of fiction with lots of facts and local color. Best sellers. All starring a fictional CIA operative named Harry Francis."

Hanley did not speak for a long time. He stared at his hands. As usual, they held no answers. He opened his hands and there was nothing.

He looked at Devereaux.

"I wouldn't want you to hate *me*," said Hanley.

"No. You wouldn't," Devereaux said.

"What else?" Hanley said at last, accepting everything.

"You start with this." He dropped a Credit Suisse bankbook on the bar. The book that Colonel Ready had given him in Lausanne. The bankbook was canceled; the money had been withdrawn. Devereaux kept the money.

"Colonel Ready gave it to me. He has to have his other accounts in that bank. There are ways between governments, between official agencies, to hold back funds. To put a stop on their withdrawal. Once November needs the money."

"I see," said Hanley. "But I need a real report. Something that isn't fiction. For the files."

"Harry is a quick writer. You will have it in time. But there isn't time right now. You agree?"

"I agree," said Hanley.

They did not speak. The bartender came down to them. "Want another round?"

Hanley blinked. He looked like a ghost.

"Yes," he said at last. "Yes. The three of us. All around. And put it on my check again."

36

THE NEW REGIME

The embarrassment of the Central Intelligence Agency in the matter of St. Michel and the aborted invasion there did not end for weeks after the story ceased to fascinate the general public.

There were congressional committee hearings scheduled and the president was asked questions at his press conference that he did not wish to answer. The CIA leaked various stories that blamed everyone from the Soviet Union to Fidel Castro to the Sandinistas. The bloody shirt of the Communist menace was waved again.

Fidel Castro, in a typical two-hour harangue, said he had proof positive that the United States had intended the invasion of St. Michel to be a dress rehearsal for a second invasion of Cuba. He talked the story to death and the public lost interest very quickly. *The New York Times* had planned a magazine cover story on St. Michel and the twenty-fifth anniversary of the Bay of Pigs invasion of Cuba. At the last moment, it was decided the story was not that important.

CIA disinformation specialists constructed a Colonel Ready who was an American recruited as an agent of KGB. The model was accepted as authentic in a few quarters. The KGB disinformation specialists invented a Colonel Ready who had fascist leanings and that the invasion of St. Michel had not really happened at all. Rather, it was an elaborate hoax constructed by the CIA to give Ready credibility. The story was accepted as authentic as well, in other quarters.

But at the level where it counted—among the information stolen and traded and gossiped about by the world's intelligence agencies—a third story began to emerge and no one knew where it came from. The story was mostly true and that is what confused everyone above a certain level.

There had been an intelligence agent in Vietnam who was probably Colonel Ready, though he had operated under a different name. He had been with American counterinsurgency operative intelligence in the middle 1960s and he had worked a flourishing sideline in the dope trade from China. He had planned both ends against the middle, making money and giving his employers enough real information to make himself valuable.

He disappeared from time to time in the 1970s, reportedly resigned from American intelligence agencies. He worked once for DIA, it was alleged, and another time

217

emerged in the Nixon Administration as an operative in the Justice Department, concerned with investigations of American radical subversives. He was reported to have been in Ireland, working against the IRA, in 1979, on behalf of the British intelligence operations arm, SAS.

The story gained currency because it was so elusive, so changeable. The story was formless but seamless. The story never stood still; it changed with each telling; it caught sunlight like a prism, and changed again. And the story would change one more time.

■ ■ ■

In St. Michel, in October, there were more storms, more than many people recall ever seeing at that time of the year. The island was battered by rain days on end.

Everything had changed in St. Michel; and nothing.

Claude-Eduard Pascon was still president though he was rarely seen outside the Palais Gris. In fact, there were rumors that he was confined to his own rooms on the third floor of the palace. And other rumors that he was mad.

Yvette Pascon had disappeared.

Many people had disappeared in the weeks following what was commemorated as "The Night of Storms." But she was the most prominent of them. She was in the cells, but even her fellow prisoners might not have recognized her. She had been tortured a long time. Although the *gendarmes noires* of Celezon had been disbanded, the army now performed all police functions, including the imprisonment of criminals and the torture of prisoners.

She had been quite willing to confess. She had told them how she had permitted Celezon to escape to the hills at the moment Colonel Ready was winning his glorious battle on The Night of Storms. She had confessed that she had been Celezon's lover and that she had plotted against the government of St. Michel. She confessed she was in the employ of the CIA. Later, she confessed she was also a Soviet agent. She confessed all her crimes against the republic over and over. And it was never enough.

She would have done anything they told her to do; but they asked nothing of her but answers to questions that never ended.

She would plead with the man who operated the electric shock machine to let her see Colonel Ready, to plead with him; to see her brother; to see anyone who would listen to her and would understand that she did not want to hide anything, that she was willing to confess to anything.

The man who knew the machine would tell her that her brother did not want to see her. That Colonel Ready was not available. And then he would turn on the current and watch her.

There was anxiety on the island of St. Michel because of the people who disappeared. But it was suppressed.

The whores of Madeleine and St. Michel disappeared in great numbers and it was rumored that some fled to the hills to join the rebels under Celezon and that others, unlucky, were taken to the army barracks and used by the soldiers and killed. But these were only rumors, like the rumors that the army brought truckloads of the dead out into the town in the dead of night and buried them in the great excavation pit that would one day be the foundation for the Museum of National Culture.

The government of France announced a massive aid program to its former colony and a first shipment of spare parts for Renault cars on the island was made. After that, nothing more was heard from Paris.

The Soviet Union sent emissaries to the island and for a time, in St. Michel, there were seen many white men in ill-fitting heavy suits, drinking in the cafés. But after a while, they left as well and some of the cafés closed because there was no business. It was rumored in some cities—among the diplomatic elite who gathered for their dull parties now in the ballroom of the shuttered American consulate building—that Colonel Ready had offended the Havana government with some bit of trickery and that the Soviets had withdrawn offers of aid to St. Michel.

Colonel Ready said the whores of St. Michel had been

arrested because they had been agents of the CIA. He explained this to a reporter from the *Miami Herald*. In time, cartoons appeared in newspapers in the United States and in Mexico that depicted the Central Intelligence Agency as a pimp.

And after a while, Colonel Ready did not speak to the press.

The archbishop of St. Michel, Simon Bouvier, said he was pleased by the morality of the regime since the attempted invasion of St. Michel. He said religion was tolerated and encouraged in St. Michel. He sent that message to the Vatican where it was analyzed and, in time, some money was channeled into the island.

But money was the problem and the problem deepened day by day.

Colonel Ready announced through the government newspaper that the *gendarmes noires* had been disbanded, that the reign of terror was over, that fifty-three members of the *gendarmes noires* would be executed the following morning in the square before the cathedral.

Fifty-three men in uniforms of the dreaded black police were led into the square in the morning. In groups of five—save for the last three—they were shot to death in front of the cathedral and the crowd—a very large crowd—cheered the killings, for the black police had always been very unpopular.

That evening, as he returned to the caretaker's house where he still lived, Colonel Ready was accosted by three snipers. He received a grazing wound on his left arm and fell. He returned the fire and his sentries, alerted by the shots coming from the edge of the woods behind the house, came to Ready's aid.

The only survivor confessed, after particularly savage torture that night, that he had been contracted to assassinate Ready by a man in Chicago on behalf of a very highly placed man in the crime syndicate whose name he did not know. Ready killed the assassin with his own pistol. He sent the killer's index finger by special delivery to Theodore Weisman at Captiva Island in Florida.

Theodore Weisman sent one hundred thousand dollars to a man in New York City who said he would succeed where the man in Chicago had failed. Teddy Weisman explained to Debbi—who was paid to listen to him—that he was an old man and he didn't give a damn if it cost him a million dollars and that this was a matter of honor and that the government— his own government—had screwed him three times now and that this was the last straw and that he had never spent a night in prison and never would and that Anthony Calabrese was walking around dead and that if Debbi didn't watch herself, she'd be turning street tricks in Detroit with Dee because Dee didn't know when she had it good, same as Tone who was taking up space in a junkyard on the Jersey side of New York harbor and that Colonel Ready was going to have to look over his shoulder for the rest of his life because nobody, even the U.S. fucking government, screwed Theodore Weisman and got away with it.

■ ■ ■

Two days later, Celezon and six men entered the cells in the basement of the Palais Gris at 4 A.M. and killed all four army guards and released twenty-three prisoners crowded into six cells. The cell doors had no locks on them because there was no escape from St. Michel. Celezon found a blanket and covered Yvette Pascon with it and took her with him into the hills, where the sister of the voodoo was made welcome by the people who had gathered around the priest called Celezon.

Colonel Ready, his arm bandaged, inspected the cells after the escape. He told the army lieutenant that locks were to be placed on all the cells that day and that locks were to be placed on all the doors of the palace.

The lieutenant nervously agreed and could not explain to Colonel Ready there were not so many locks to be found on the whole island. Colonel Ready would not have been willing to listen to that.

221

37

WOMEN

"Sister," Rita Macklin said.

Mary Columbo nodded, tried a quick smile, sat down in the reception room of the old convent. She had been examined in New York City by doctors who decided it was the best thing not to operate to remove the second bullet, that the second bullet was so close to the spine that there was danger of paralysis if there was a mistake. Sister Columbo said she could live with the bullet in her always threatening paralysis or death; she had lived with death a long time.

At the Aerodrome St. Michel, as they lifted her onto the stretcher to put her aboard the plane, she had turned back, like Lot's wife. Colonel Ready was smiling at her with such sincerity and good wishes in his face that the look froze her and she could not trust a smile again. She felt isolated from the other nuns, from her own family in Queens, from everyone who wanted to help her. She had withdrawn in silence and prayer because she thought she had lost her faith at last, after all the madness of the world she had seen, after betrayals, deceits, and smiles of perfect insincerity and promises made of lies. Colonel Ready had said that all the killing was necessary to rescue her. She had said that killing was never necessary, that she had not been threatened by Manet, that she had spoken to a New York reporter. . . .

Colonel Ready had explained to her as she lay in the tent, in the middle of that camp of death, the sounds of dying still in her ears. The man she had spoken to was an American spy and he had been part of the network that had supported Manet. His name was Devereaux, said Colonel Ready, and he was dead and when the colonel so easily showed her how foolish she had been, she had pretended to believe him. She had thought if she did not believe him, he might have killed her and thrown her body among the dead strewn in that butcher's yard in the hills of St. Michel.

She wanted to live that much. She felt ashamed. She was lifted into the airplane on that afternoon and looked back on St. Michel and knew she would never see the world the same again. She had repeated history for the press in St. Michel as Colonel Ready had told her.

She had wanted to live that much.

Rita Macklin, pale and thinner than she had been three weeks before, said, "I appreciate your seeing me."

"You said you had been on St. Michel, but I remember all the American reporters. I mean—"

"I was there before. When you were ambushed—"

Sister Mary Columbo stared at her. "You said in your telephone call you knew my cousin. I didn't know Anthony had been on St. Michel, I didn't know any of this."

"Sister," said Rita Macklin. It was difficult. She had to be used and it was difficult for Rita because she saw the logic of what Devereaux told her but when she saw the woman, her white face and the pain wrinkles around her eyes, she almost could not continue with it.

"What you told the reporters at the airport. It wasn't true. I think you know it wasn't true."

The nun stared at her a long time without speaking. Then she got up and folded her hands into her habit. She wore the oldest uniform of the order now, the heavy robes that fell in woolen folds to the floor, the starched bib, the heavy veil. She sought to diminish herself, in robe and silence, to retreat to a dark corner of herself and wait for faith to return.

"I have to leave now," she said.

"Anthony," Rita said quickly and her voice was harder now. She was pushing and the instinct was natural to the part of her that was a reporter. "Anthony Calabrese wanted to come to see you and he would have told you to tell me the truth. But he can't."

"Why?"

"Because they're watching this place. They want to kill him."

She stared at Rita Macklin's green eyes and red hair cut severely short, at the pale skin and thin cheeks. "Who are you?"

"I started to tell you," Rita said.

"Let's walk in the garden."

It was October and Rhode Island was closed for the winter. The grass around the convent outside of Providence was dead and brown. The trees were bare. The oaks scrawled crooked branches against the puffy white sky crowded with too many clouds.

They walked down brick paths that wound through bushes that looked like piles of stick kindling.

"What about Anthony? I didn't know about any of this."

"Anthony Calabrese was a government agent," Rita Macklin began. She would not tell her about Anthony's involvement in the Mafia before that.

"He was on St. Michel, he knew that you were there. He told me you were the only story worth writing about on St. Michel. We met the day you went to Madeleine. The day you said you were ambushed."

"Yes."

"Who ambushed you in the Jeep?"

The nun stared ahead of her, seeing not the path but the bareness of nature all around her. "I don't know. It happened so quickly. And slowly at the same time, I remember that I thought I was all right, I kept saying that I was all right, and I saw Agnes next to me, her head . . ."

"But did Manet—"

"No. He didn't do it. I don't believe he did it."

"There," said Rita Macklin.

The nun stopped, stared. She saw the same man beyond the iron fence, standing in an alcove of a building. She realized she had seen the man before in different places around the convent but never paid attention to him.

"Why does he want to kill Anthony? Why can't the government protect him?"

"He's from Colonel Ready," Rita said, dropping her words like stones into a silent lake of lies. They made ripples on the smooth water and the ripples touched each other. "Colonel Ready has men here. He wants to kill Anthony. That's why I came to see you. Anthony is waiting."

"I don't believe you."

"I can prove it. He's waiting on Broad Street. Around the corner. In the McDonald's."

"Who are you?"

"I escaped from St. Michel. I was a reporter. I was his prisoner. I saw what had happened there."

"What did you see?"

"Everything. You have to speak up. To me. The church is being blinded by the archbishop of St. Michel. He tells them all is well. He paints a picture for Rome that's not true."

"And I should tell the truth?" The nun smiled then.

"I was on St. Michel and when he made me a prisoner, he beat me. Had me beaten. In the cells. He raped me."

Sister Mary Columbo put her fist to her mouth then and bit her knuckle and stared at the thin woman and believed her. "Why should I tell?"

"Because Colonel Ready is taking the church funds going into St. Michel."

"Is that true?"

"What happened in Ethiopia? The food and money came in and the government used it to wipe out its enemies. He's doing the same thing. He ambushed you, his men did, and you know that."

"I don't know."

"At least you know it was not Manet."

"It doesn't matter for Manet. He's dead."

"But those people in the hills aren't dead." Rita stared at her with bright burning eyes. "He is evil. That's important to you still, isn't it? Colonel Ready is evil and all the evil in St. Michel is tied to him like a bell on a cat."

"I didn't tell the story because it was a condition to get out alive. Colonel Ready has a long reach. As you said, the man across the street."

"Who wants to kill Anthony. Or kill you."

"And you think this will carry weight. What I have to say? With the church?" She smiled at Rita. "You're not a Catholic."

"I am," Rita said. "I know what you mean."

"Archbishop Bouvier tolerated us in St. Michel. Radical nuns. Giving out rosaries and penicillin. As long as we didn't bother him or interrupt his meals, he didn't care."

"I want you to tell me the truth. And I will write the story."

"And we'll both be threatened," said Sister Mary Columbo. "By Colonel Ready."

"Yes."

"It won't make any difference. In Rome, I mean. Nuns do not have a voice loud enough to stand against a bishop's whisper."

Rita smiled. "You're a poet."

"A realist," said Sister Mary Columbo. "I'll go with you to see Anthony. It's chilly, isn't it? Can I get my shawl?"

"Yes."

Sister Mary Columbo touched her arm. "Are you married, Rita?"

"I have someone."

"That's good. He knows about . . ."

"Yes."

"You told me and that is such a terrible thing to tell—"

Rita stared at the face of the woman and saw her clearly and saw that she had been a nurse in war as Anthony had said and that she had survived all of life's horrors and that she was still not so scarred that she could not be hurt or that she could not comfort another person. Rita smiled at her, sadly.

"It's all right then," said Sister Mary Columbo. "I suppose I can be brave as well."

■ ■ ■

They were inside the McDonald's on Broad Street in the southern part of the city. They were talking animatedly. They had been inside for nearly an hour.

226

The man with the nine millimeter Beretta automatic shoved in the pocket of his coat waited impassively across the street for them. His name was Costello; he had followed the nun and the other woman to the McDonald's. Bingo. Anthony Calabrese was inside.

He could have walked in and finished them but it might have been dirty. He had a compunction about shooting nuns. Women, for that matter.

He waited in the doorway of a jewelry store.

He didn't see the police car until it was at the curb in front of him and then he didn't know what it meant. The two men in blue uniforms got out of the car in a funny way.

As though they were being careful.

Costello stared at them as though he were looking right through them.

"Hey," said the second one. He had the police-car door open and seemed to be using it as a shield. His holster was unsnapped and the gunmetal gleamed in the bright overcast light. "You want to come over here a minute."

Costello stared at him and then shrugged. He walked across the sidewalk to the policeman and stood five feet away.

The first one put a pistol in his hand and laid his hand on the hood of the squad car.

"You want to tell us your name?"

"I'm waiting for someone."

"We got a report of a man with a gun in the entrance of the jewelry store."

"We got a call that someone was casing a jewelry store."

"You got a gun," said the first one.

"I got no gun."

"Pat him down, Frank."

Costello took a step back.

The first one raised his pistol in one motion. "That's it. Hands against the car."

"Jesus, you guys are getting excited—" said Costello in a rising voice. He looked across the street. The three of them, they were getting up, they were moving toward the door. . . .

"He's got a piece, he's got a piece," said the second one

when he felt it and the first one put the pistol right next to Costello's head and held it there. And Costello saw them walking out of the restaurant across the street and the nun was turning to go away and Anthony was looking right at him with the woman.

Anthony was smiling right at him.

38

A PUBLISHING EVENT

The Central Intelligence Agency—through its headquarters, its case officers in the field, stringers in foreign countries who submit quarterly expense accounts—subscribes to nearly every magazine sold in the world.

But not every article in every magazine is read. The gathering of intelligence through intelligent reading is still a haphazard business. Machines cannot read and cannot analyze what they read.

Which is why the item that appeared on page 51 of that week's *Publishers Weekly* magazine might not have been noted.

The item was a paid advertisement by a publishing company that the Langley Firm knew well. The item had puzzled the reader who had passed it up through the ranks of the bureaucracy until it was finally analyzed at the fourth level and flagged and bucked to the Committee of Nineteen at the second level.

"But what on earth does it mean?" said the sixth assistant director of intelligence, who was chairing the meeting on that October afternoon.

"It means there's a spy novel to be published in the spring," said the assistant traffic manager, who had routed the advertisement through computer analysis, records, and interagency security before presenting it to his boss who, in turn, presented it up the ladder of the organization chart. The assistant traffic manager liked to state the obvious at first, to get everyone's agreement so that what he said next would not sound as bizarre.

The sixth assistant director waited and made a tent of his fingers in an attitude of prayer. He closed his eyes.

The other people in meeting room L stared at the speaker.

"David Zeno is a nonstarter," the speaker continued. "But the name of the hero of the new series is Harry Francis. Harry Francis is an agent. Was an agent."

"Harry Francis," said the sixth assistant director. "But what is this all about?"

"Harry Francis retired six years ago. He's living in St. Michel in the Caribbean. We've kept tabs on him, of course, all the retired agents. But he's alive and well at last report. He used to write books for us. Commercial. Spy novels. And he wrote the guerrilla manual that was published last year. You know the one."

Everyone knew the one. The one that had embarrassed the president during the campaign.

"Free lance. He did free lance for us. But he didn't work for us anymore," said the traffic manager.

"Did he submit this book?"

"Sir, you don't understand. He's not writing this book. A man named David Zeno is writing the book."

"What's the book about?"

"Fiction, sir. A spy novel. A new series, it said, set in the Caribbean involving a 'hard-drinking, hard-hitting CIA agent' who—"

"But that was Harry Francis, wasn't it?"

"Sir?"

"I mean, that describes Harry Francis, doesn't it?"

"Sir, his two-o-one file indicates Francis had an alcohol-related problem in—"

"Damn it, I don't care about that, I want to know what this book is about."

"We made inquiries. The publisher wasn't very cooperative. They've handled sensitive material before."

"From us?"

"And others. The agent was Henry Kaufberger."

"And what does that mean?"

"We've used Henry. From time to time. Over the past twenty years. Harry would have known about him. He said he received the proposal from David Zeno in St. Michel. He told us he never met him. We tried to explain this might be sensitive—"

"Don't even breathe near St. Michel," said the sixth assistant. "Don't light a cigarette and don't make sparks. St. Michel is explosive."

"Sir, the book is fiction and the advance paid was one hundred thousand dollars."

"That's absurd," said the sixth assistant who made $31,983.14 a year.

"Yes, sir," said the traffic manager, who was waiting to continue.

"Go ahead."

"The book is called *The Hemingway Assignment*."

"My God," said the sixth assistant director, who had read the files on Harry Francis before the meeting. Including the file labeled ULTRA. "My God."

"The novel, according to the agent, is set in Cuba at the time Castro took over and it's about Ernest Hemingway and —Hemingway was a writer, sir, in that time—and this Hemingway—actually, Hemingway actually existed but this is a novel—and . . ."

39

PREPARATIONS

Harry Francis was standing in shallow water on the gulf side of the sandbar, watching a shark cruise amiably back and forth in the waters twenty-five feet from where he stood. He held his sandals in his hand. His eyes crinkled in the sunlight; he looked as though he might be smiling.

"Aren't you afraid of the shark?" Rita asked.

He turned, startled from his revery. He did smile now, deliberately. "Sand shark."

"They bite, don't they?"

"Everything in nature bites," he said.

"And you're the old man of the sea," Rita said with an edge to her voice. She had pitied him the night she saw him dragged across the courtyard by the two *gendarmes*. She had grown to despise him, even after he had helped Devereaux rescue her. There was something so distant and judgmental about him. She had said to Devereaux: He doesn't like me. He doesn't like women.

"Why do you hate me?" he asked her.

"Because I can see what you are."

"All right." He paused. "What do you want?"

"I want him. Two days from now, when the operation is over, I want to see him getting off that boat. If I don't see him getting off that boat, I'll kill you."

He started to smile.

"Don't smile or laugh at me," Rita said. "I won't kill you the first day or even the second. I'll figure it out, how to do it, and when I've got it figured out, I'll do it so that you know I did it. You'll see it coming and you won't be able to get out of the way. If he dies on the island, then you ought to kill yourself because it'll be easier to take it from yourself than from me."

"'Stronger in the broken places.'"

She waited.

"Hemingway. I know you hate that, but he said sometimes broken bones heal and become stronger because they've been broken."

"No," said Rita Macklin. "You and Hemingway got it wrong again. You never heal completely. You just learn to live with hurt. You can walk around it, you make it as easy on yourself as you can, but it's always there. The broken arm never heals. The joints ache on rainy days. You don't get stronger, you just learn to be tougher because the pain is always with you." She stared so hard at him that he took a step back into the shallow warm waters.

"I hate you, Harry, I hate you as much as I hate Ready. Dev made his deal with you because he had to and that's why I walk around you. I hate you because you were on the island from the beginning, because you were Ready's puppet, because you kept that absurd book about something that happened a long time ago. That stupid goddamn book that Ready wanted bad enough to bring Devereaux into this. To bring me into it. You're not even a good traitor, you know that? You sold out your great friend Hemingway and you ended up selling out your country to a two-bit dictator like Ready. I'd kill you without a thought, without looking back. You remember that when you go back to St. Michel with Devereaux. You remember that I want to see him alive and that if he's dead, it's your fault. That's what you've got to know."

■ ■ ■

And when Devereaux saw her, it was nearly midnight. He and Cain had been preparing the *Compass Rose* for the return to St. Michel. Rita was in a chair by the balcony and she was waiting for him.

"It was your fault. Everything that happened to me," she said.

"Yes."

"No excuses."

"No."

"You let it happen."

"Yes."

"Why? Didn't you love me?"

"Yes. But I let it happen. You're right."

"You wanted to be safe," she said.

"Yes. I wanted to be safe. I wanted to be left alone. I wanted a lot of things and I was willing to take a chance. I was willing to have you take a chance."

"I know. I know everything. I wanted to see if you knew everything. I want to tell you something. Before you go to St. Michel."

"You don't have to," he said.

"Do you know? I love you. I hated you on the island and I will keep remembering that I hated you for what you let happen. I won't lie to you. I won't forget that."

"No."

"Dev." She stared at him. "I don't want you to kill yourself."

"I won't."

"I mean, I don't want anything so badly that you have to die for it."

"I won't die."

"I told Harry. I told him that if you died, I'd kill him."

"I won't die."

40

THE MAN WHO WAS NOVEMBER

Colonel Ready got ready for bed just past midnight in the caretaker's house. There had been more fighting in the hills during the day. Thirteen soldiers had been killed and three more had deserted to Celezon. He would sleep exactly three hours and be up again.

The Cuban emissary had kept him from sleep, had threatened and bullied about the notebook, had demanded the money back that the Cuban government had paid for the book. It was tiring but in the end he had accepted Colonel Ready's refusals.

St. Michel had worked well for a long time but now it wasn't working and there was nothing more to take out of St. Michel. In a little while, Colonel Ready would go to Switzerland and find his money and live a life of retirement. It was the last way of escape if all other ways were closed.

He unlocked his front door, nodded to the two security guards, and locked the door behind him.

The security personnel at the Aerodrome St. Michel had picked up another American that morning. He was smuggling an Uzi submachine-gun pistol into the country. He had broken easily. His name was Lemont and he had been hired by someone in New York to assassinate the man called Colonel Ready. It was all he knew. He'd been killed in the cells while Ready slept.

He dropped his pistol and holster on the table and began to unbutton his tunic. He went to the refrigerator and took out a bottle of Kronenbourg and opened it. He drank the cold liquid, the first of the long day.

Devereaux said, "You made me wait a long time."

The red-haired man turned in the little kitchen and stared at the man in the darkened doorway that led to the living room. The other man had a pistol, a Colt Python with an extremely long black barrel.

Colonel Ready flushed. His white scar brightened against the blush in his cheek.

"You shouldn't have come back," he said.

"Your two guards are dead," said Devereaux. "I didn't come alone. I brought a friend of yours. Harry Francis."

"I still have papers on you. I can still send them to CIA. Remember?"

Devereaux's voice was low, very soft. "It doesn't matter. You can't do anything with them. There's no way to escape

234

this time, Ready. It's not like Nam. It's not like any other time. Everything is cut off."

"Can I sit down?"

"You can take all your clothes off," said Devereaux.

"Pardon?"

"Strip," said Devereaux.

Colonel Ready put down the bottle of Kronenbourg and stared at Devereaux and then, smiling, finished unbuttoning his tunic. He removed the shirt. He wore no undershirt. He took off his shoes and socks. He unbuckled his belt and let his trousers fall. He stepped out of his trousers. He stood still.

"Strip," said Devereaux.

"Want a gander at my cock? Is that it?"

"Strip," Devereaux said again in the same cold, uninflected voice that was almost a whisper.

The smile faded.

He pulled down his boxer shorts and stepped out of them. He stood naked in the bright light of the kitchen. His face and arms were weathered by sun but his belly and genitals were strangely pale, as though the parts of the body did not fit together or belonged to different people.

"Are you going to kill me?"

"I've thought about it," Devereaux said.

"I have enough money to—"

"To bribe me."

And Ready smiled. "You impotent bastard, I fucked your whore for you with this." He held his penis. "Shoved it good in her and I had a good time. I beat the living shit out of her and fucked her good and I had a good time with her. She liked it. I knew she liked it. When it was over, I asked her if she liked it and she said she did."

"Get on the floor. On your belly," Devereaux said and there was no change in the note in his voice.

"You cowardly bastard, you fucking coward. I would have given it to you in the belly at least. Face to face."

"Get on the floor."

"When I die, the stuff goes to Langley. Just like that. The stuff about November."

"You know everything about November," Devereaux said.

"Damn right."

"Harry Francis is writing a book. He's nearly finished. About Hemingway in Cuba and the way he was used by the CIA. It's a good book; I've read parts of the manuscript. Langley is upset."

"Damn right they'd be."

"Langley thinks Harry lives here. On the island. That's where the manuscript was mailed from. Yesterday. It's in Miami by now and New York by the end of the week. With the colorful stamp of St. Michel on the envelope. And the postmark."

"Damn it. Harry isn't here."

"Tell Langley that," said Devereaux. "Get on the floor."

"You bastard." He was thinking very fast now. Devereaux was about six feet away from him. There was a trick that involved the feet—

"I wish you would," Devereaux said. "I'd like to hurt you."

"You are an impotent sadist."

"And you're dead," said Devereaux. "I gave you the wrong notebook but there really was a notebook. I fixed you with Mr. Weisman. Anthony and I. He wants to kill you. Has he tried yet? I know he has. He'll do anything to kill you. And until he stops trying, he'll be safe. From prosecution, I mean, for his other crimes. And Anthony is safe now. And Rita."

For the first time, the voice caught and Ready began to smile again.

"Rita wrote an article and it's about Sister Mary Columbo and what happened in St. Michel and what you threatened her with. She has some courage. The Vatican has sent an inquiry officer to Miami to speak with Simon Bouvier. The funds—the funds for medicine, for building—are being held up. Everyone is asking questions now."

"That's temporary."

"There's always more. Celezon only needs time and he's going to win. You gave Havana the wrong book and they bought it. CIA thinks you're behind Harry's novel. And you just don't have any credibility any more. With anyone. So get down on the floor because I told you to do it."

"Rita Macklin," Ready said.

"Yes," Devereaux said. "That's what you have to pay for. If it wasn't for that, I might not have to hurt you at all."

He got down on the stone floor and put his hands behind his neck as Devereaux had demanded. He lay there a moment.

"You queer bastard. Are you going to fuck me?"

"I want to give you some advice. Because we were in the old business together. When you start running, you have to be very good or there's no point in running at all. You have to be as good as I was. They might be just a step or two behind you and you won't know it. You need luck. I had some luck. And if your luck runs out, there's nothing you can do about it."

"I'm not running."

"Yes. You have to. The Soviets especially, now that they know November is still alive."

"I'm not November."

"The name in the record never changes. The Soviets know our system. You're November because our files say that you are November."

"You're crazy."

"When you start running, you'll have more problems than I did. There were just the Soviets when I was running. But there are other problems. You have Mr. Weisman. And CIA. Don't forget Langley. You screwed them and they never forget. I wouldn't be surprised if they have a contract on you as well. Everyone is against you. Even the Cubans who really wanted to be your friends."

"All I have to do—"

"Is tell them the truth?" The voice was harsher now. "You're so wrapped in lies the truth couldn't penetrate. The Soviets know about you already. There's someone in St. Michel now from KGB. Did you know that?"

"You're lying."

"Perhaps," said Devereaux.

"They were after you."

"KGB doesn't make mistakes."

Devereaux stood behind Ready's naked body stretched on the floor.

"There was an agent named November who had harmed KGB. He was involved in turning a Soviet agent named Denisov in Florida. That was you, wasn't it, colonel? You were November then. You were always November. And when an R Section agent died in Zurich in a fire, the Section tried to make it seem as though he had been November so that the wet contract would be called off. I was asleep, Ready, and you woke me."

"I—I was wrong, perhaps, there are ways to—"

"No. No ways anymore."

"The papers on you. In my desk."

"I know. I took them."

"We're even. Quits."

Devereaux said nothing.

"Man, I've got money in banks and—"

"I know. You gave me some of it once. I was telling you about the man who was November. He really wasn't dead. He was really Colonel Ready. So Colonel Ready went to London three weeks ago. He gave in his passport at customs. He was seen in all the right intelligence circles. A man with red hair and a scar and he used the account number of November to buy information from Economic Review. He was very bold and open. He left a trail from Switzerland to London to Miami and down to St. Michel. He used November's American Express card, the one that was supposed to be inactive, the one that is billed to R Section. You can't make it too easy for KGB, they'll suspect a trap. But I think it was just hard enough. You wanted me to work for you in St. Michel because you wanted to use me for everything that went wrong. And it turned out it was the easiest and surest way to make November really dead. He became you."

"This is madness, this—"

"Harry Francis has a notebook he gave to the Section. It was written in code by Ernest Hemingway. There's no doubt about it. It was all about the CIA and how it double-crossed its own government to get Castro and how CIA was going to try again on St. Michel, a dress rehearsal for another Cuban invasion. It involved a man named November who took Cuban money and arms and then double-crossed the Cubans with a phony book and double-crossed CIA and double-crossed the crime syndicate, a man who could not be trusted, a man on everyone's death list. That is who November is now. You are November."

"You can't get away with it because you can't kill me, it would be too easy to kill November again, nobody would believe this twice—"

"Unless they had the body. Unless they had the bona fides, you might say," Devereaux said. "Harry is writing fiction under an assumed name. They are true novels. They really happened but, of course, they're only fiction. CIA knows that Harry was working for you. You were R section all the time, a mole inside our sister service. November was a very clever agent, don't you think?"

"I can give you a million Swiss francs."

"No. It's not enough." He paused and listened to the echo of his words and heard Rita's voice. It was not enough to kill him.

"Devereaux. I know why you want to do this. I didn't do it. I didn't rape her, no matter what she said, she went crazy, there was a soldier, he raped her in the cells, I came in,

239

I had him shot, I can show you the grave, you have to listen to me."

Devereaux took out the knife that Flaubert had given him. It was sharp and curved and the blade was so thin that it would be dulled after one use.

Devereaux knelt on one knee between Ready's naked legs and pressed the pistol between Ready's cheeks until the mouth of the barrel rested on his anus.

"Jesus," said Ready.

"Don't move."

Ready felt the weight of the pistol against him.

"A man should leave footprints. I left your footprints in Europe. Through London, through Miami. It was a little but not enough. You have to leave footprints now."

"What do you mean?"

"For the hunters who will follow the trail."

And he cut across the Achilles tendon that was stretched behind Ready's right ankle. He cut very hard and very deep. The tendon fought the blade for a moment and then it was through and Devereaux's knuckles were white with the strain of cutting through flesh and sinew.

For a moment, Ready only felt the pistol and then it was withdrawn and he wondered what had happened.

And then he screamed.

He screamed and crawled across the floor and the blood oozed from his ankle and trailed behind him. He pulled himself to where Devereaux had stood. But he was gone.

Harry and Devereaux were down in the hillside already, screened by the woods behind the house, and they were running and they could hear the screams following them.

41

WAYS OF ESCAPE

Harry Francis had waited in the darkness. He had killed the Cuban emissary. He had cut his head off, and had put it on the gate of the Palais Gris and then gone to the caretaker's house where Devereaux had been waiting for Colonel Ready.

There was no escape for Colonel Ready. It was what everything had been about, the preparations, the meeting with Hanley. The publisher told the agent he thought the book about Hemingway might do well; it didn't matter to Harry. He had written the truth for a change and it had freed him and he did not care.

The black boat waited a half mile off the shore. Their motorized dinghy was a hundred yards offshore, in three feet of water. They ran down to the beach and crossed it to the water.

Devereaux stopped and turned and looked at the boy standing by the Café de la Paix.

Philippe stared at him a moment and then began to run. He ran across the midnight road to the beach and stopped a little apart from him.

Harry was in the water. Harry turned and scowled. His trousers were bloody.

"Come on," he said.

"Your father," Devereaux said in careful French.

"He is disappeared. He is dead. All of them disappeared."

"Your mother then."

"None. It's all right then?"

"Yes," Devereaux said.

"Jesus Christ, stay there, Philippe," Harry shouted to the child. "Jesus, we can't take him. What about Flaubert?"

Devereaux said, "Come on."

The boy and the man ran into the shallow water and the boy cut his feet on a piece of coral but did not feel the cut.

They waded out to the dinghy and Harry shouted in a hoarse voice, "He's lying, he's got people here, he just wants to get away from St. Michel."

"Like you, Harry," said Devereaux.

"Damn it, what are you gonna do with a half-black orphan with blue eyes?"

"He loved you, Harry," Devereaux said. "He wanted to protect you. He worried about you when they took you to jail."

"I don't mean that," Harry said. He looked at the boy and the boy stared at him as though he understood all the English words. "You can't save the world. Give him some money and tell him to go back."

"Shut up, Harry," Devereaux said. He lifted Philippe up into the dinghy and he climbed in and Harry started the motor and the dinghy bucked in the shallow waters toward the *Compass Rose*. There were no storms this evening. The sky was clear. The moon was full and the island of St. Michel looked quite lovely from the water, the way such islands always appear in the expensive brochures given to people who wish to vacation in a warm climate in the middle of a warm sea.

42

THE LAST OF NOVEMBER

"This is a very colorful family," Rita Macklin said.

Devereaux smiled. They were on the ferry from Evian to Ouchy across Lac Leman which is also called Lake Geneva. They were on the ferry because it was Sunday and Philippe did not attend private school. It was cold but the ferry to Evian ran across the lake all winter. They had gone to Evian to eat and to look in the shops.

Philippe, who wished to be a sailor, stood on the open deck in his pea coat with his face square to the cold, wet wind. His blue eyes were full of tears because of the wind. He looked very exotic with his dark face and blue eyes and the burghers of Lausanne would stop and examine this strange *famille* as they walked through the narrow streets near the cathedral: a man with weathered face and gray hair and a woman with green eyes and red hair and a smile and a strange black child with skin like burnished wood.

KGB had let out the wet contract again. On November. On the man who was November, who always had been November. Two Turkish killers, hired by the Bulgarian Secret Police, were in Western Europe now, on the trail of November, a man with red hair and a white scar on his face. A man who walked with a cane and a limp, very stiffly and very painfully.

He will leave footprints now.

Anthony Calabrese, who testified wearing a hood as a government agent and informer against Theodore Weisman, was pleased with his new appearance, though he thought he still looked too Sicilian and not Swedish enough.

Sister Mary Columbo had left the order and she was back in St. Michel now, in the hills, a nurse among poor people and she wondered if she was doing any good at all. She had all her doubts and all her prayers and she had taken both burdens with her.

The hell of St. Michel remained.

Celezon had entered the capital after a fierce battle. He had killed many of his enemies, in battle and in execution after. He and Yvette Pascon ruled, there was no doubt of that, and no doubt that the new and ruthless regime would be as bad as all the other regimes had been. Claude-Eduard was executed. A number of soldiers were marched into the square in front of the cathedral and a large crowd gathered to watch the *gendarmes noires* kill them, five at a time.

There was a promise of aid from Cuba as well as from the U.S. Department of State.

■ ■ ■

When they made love now, it was different than it had been before, because the rape had changed everything. But it was still all right between them. Perhaps it was better than it had been before. She had no reserve from him now and he had none from her. They had been together in this thing and they shared more than secrets now or their bodies or their words for each other. She never bought him a ring again and he never gave her a ring. They didn't want to have anything that would remind the other of loss. A ring is only a reminder of everything that can be lost.

■ ■ ■

Rita stepped from the ferry at Ouchy and the boy came after with Devereaux. They showed their American passports and the man at the control, who knew them, nodded and smiled and said the boy looked more and more like a sailor. It was patronizing in the way of old men speaking of young boys and it was meant kindly.

They passed through the controls and into the building and out of it again onto the dock.

Rita stood still and when Devereaux came next to her, they saw him.

"Did you think this would happen?"

"Yes," he said.

"Why didn't you tell me."

"It was the last way of escape. I closed it the night I talked to Hanley. Governments can do things. He talked to the Swiss and they froze the accounts. The money will be recovered for the Section in time. In any case, there's no money left for him."

Behind them, on the smoking waters of the long cold lake, the ferry signaled once in the clear, November air. The horn blast was loud and bleak and long. The ferry began to churn the waters again and pull away from the dock.

"You made him come to us."

"Yes."

"You hate him more than I did."

"Yes."

She stared at the gray face, at the patient, waiting eyes. "I'll take Philippe," she said.

"Yes. Take the metro. I'll be along in a little while, back at the apartment."

"Sir—"

"Take Rita to the metro, Philippe. Go ahead. He doesn't mean anything anymore. He won't hurt anyone anymore."

"Kill him," said Philippe.

Devereaux looked at him. "No. There's no one left to kill."

"He killed my father," said Philippe.

"He's nothing, Philippe. Only a ghost. In a little while, even the ghost will be gone."

And Philippe and Rita walked across the plaza to the park where the grass was frozen and brown. They hurried past the castle and past the Italian restaurant next to the metro entrance. They paid inside the entrance and took the funicular which rises five stations to the place on the Avenue de la Gare where there is an American hamburger stand. Where Colonel Ready had waited for Devereaux nearly three months before.

Devereaux stared at the ghost before him.

Colonel Ready limped across the square in front of the chateau. He looked very pale and his red hair was streaked with gray now. There were wrinkles of pain at the corners of his cold blue eyes and they were deepened with each step he took. He did not smile; he never smiled now; there was too much pain.

He removed the Credit Suisse passbook from his pocket and waved it.

"All the money. I can't get my money."

"Yes."

"You robbed me."

"It's all there, Ready. You just can't get it."

"How could you do all this?"

"I had the time to think about it."

"I don't have any money."

"Yes. That's right."

"I'm going to kill you then and kill your whore and the nigger kid."

"No," said Devereaux. "The Swiss would put you in one of their prisons. They are tolerant but very tough and they would put you in prison for the rest of your life. A kid in Zurich, I think it was, he got two years in prison for spraying graffiti on buildings. The prisons aren't very pleasant."

"I could kill you. I can run."

"You are running, November," said Devereaux. "There are two Turks right now who have been hanging around the café over there for a week. You were seen in Geneva. They thought you might be coming up here. They were probably told about a man with a white scar and red hair who tried to take money out of an account in the Credit Suisse."

"You son-of-a-bitch."

"I think those are the Turks. Over there. Having coffee in the window. Watching us. Watching you. The Bulgarians do the dirty work for KGB. They tried to get you in Paris, didn't they?"

"Damn it, man."

"They won't kill you in Switzerland unless they have to. I think you should take the metro up, get on a train, get out of the country. Go down to Italy. It's warmer there."

"I don't have anything."

"We were just in France." He reached into his pocket and took out a hundred-franc note from the wad and looked at it. He extended it. "The franc isn't worth what it used to be but it might be enough for a meal."

Colonel Ready reached into his pocket and Devereaux had the small PPK in his large hand. Devereaux stared at him.

"Shoot me," Ready said.

"Go away. Go kill yourself if you have the guts for it but I'm not going to do it. Go away, colonel. And don't come back to Lausanne. There's no money left for you and they know you're here. Look, they're getting up from the table now."

He turned and saw it was true.

"Bastard," said Colonel Ready and he was limping away, half running, across the square to the metro station, looking behind him and fishing for a coin in his pocket.

The two men who resembled Turks went out of the restaurant. One stared at Devereaux for a moment and then shrugged to the other. They got in the rental car and drove around the chauteau and saw Ready limp into the entrance. The one in the passenger seat got out. He ran across the street and got on the train before the doors of the funicular closed and the gates were shut.

■ ■ ■

That night, Rita said to him, "It will be all right now. Everything." But it was really a question.

He had climbed into the soft bed next to her. The night was full of silence. The windows were open slightly and the cool mountain air shivered into the room but they slept naked beneath the down covers.

"Yes," he said. "It's all done now."

"Will they kill him?"

"I think they'll get him this winter. He's good, but it's a very open trail."

"We killed him."

"Yes," he said.

"I never thought I could hate that well."

"Yes," he said because he did not want to talk to her about it.

"November," she said.

"It's the thirtieth," he said.

"The last of November. 'Thirty days hath September, April, June, and November.'"

His eyes were open and he stared at the ceiling in the darkness and smelled the clear gentle breeze that came into the room from the mountains. "Yes. That's all of it," he said.

"You're sure," she said.

It was still a question.

He didn't want to answer. He closed his eyes.

"You're sure."

He felt the curve of her lean thigh against his. He felt her hairless thigh against his leg and felt the warmth of her body coming next to him.

"Maybe I should close the window," he said.

"No. I can warm you," she said.

It was going to be all right. But they did not make love as they had intended. They held each other like exhausted survivors and they fell asleep in each other's arms and they slept, matching breath for breath, their bodies warming each other beneath the thick, light down.

A clock tolled exactly at twelve because all the clocks in Switzerland are very precise. And that was the last of November.

Lausanne—Fort Myers—Chicago